THE DEAD FILE

VINCENT MURANO and RICHARD HAMMER

St. Martin's Paperbacks

THE DEAD FILE

ISBN: 0-312-95692-4

Printed in the United States of America

St. Martin's Paperbacks edition/January 1996

10 9 8 7 6 5 4 3 2 1

It was just a little story buried deep inside the *Los Angeles Times*, on a page full of ads for retailers selling everything at low-low prices. If Ben Rogers hadn't been on the red-eye, winging his way across the country through an endless night sky, he never would have seen it. He'd bought the paper at the airport, and since he could never sleep on a plane, he read everything in it but the thick classified section.

The story never would have made the papers back east, and even now, he didn't do more than skim it with half-seeing eyes until he came on a name in the final paragraph.

In one of those small villages a little south of the Monterey Peninsula, where the locals and the vacationers maintained an uneasy truce, a thirty-five-year-old woman named Francine McCauley had taken a gun and killed first her fifteen-year-old daughter and then herself in the early hours of the morning. Only the day before, Francine McCauley had been released from a mental hospital, where she had spent most of the years since her daughter's birth.

According to the story, Francine, who had never married, and her mother, Constance, had arrived in the town about twenty years ago, Constance opening a shop selling natural foods just as the health food market was beginning to boom. The McCauleys had been in the town about five years when Francine had her baby. She never named the father, nor was anybody ever able even to make a guess. Soon after the birth of her daughter, Jennifer, Francine suffered what was described as a nervous collapse and was hospitalized. From then until the end of her life, she was in and out of institutions. Constance McCauley told her few confidantes that she was certain the real cause of the breakdown was that Francine had never recovered from the sudden death of her adored older brother, Justin. He, Constance McCauley said, had been a New York City policeman who was killed in the line of duty.

The story ended there. No more details. Not why the mother had killed her daughter and herself. Nothing more about her brother. Rogers searched his memory. It must have been before the time he joined the department when this Justin McCauley was killed. Even so, the death of a cop, especially one killed in the line of duty, was engraved on the brain and memory of every cop. Yet Rogers could not recall the name McCauley. He leaned back in the seat and began to recite silently the names of the cops, Jones and Piagentina, Foster and Laurie, and a lot more who had been killed during those early years, just before and since he'd signed on. The name Justin McCauley was not one of them. Maybe he had forgotten, though that was unlikely. It was intriguing. Maybe, if he had time, he'd look into it.

It gave him pause. Things have a way of coming around, Rogers thought. Maybe nothing is ever finished.

He closed the paper, put it on the empty seat beside him, shut off the overhead light and tried to sleep the rest of the way back to New York, tried to think about his girl, Melissa Redburn. They'd had a week together in California, after being apart for three months while he did the things John Morrison, New York's reform mayor, asked, and she did whatever movie actresses do when they're just at the beginning of a career and have been thrown a part that if not huge was one that was going to advance a new career. The distance between them was spreading now, and he was feeling emptier and lonelier with every mile.

2

He caught a cab in from JFK. The cabby fought his way through the early morning rush hour traffic, which didn't improve Rogers' mood. The cab's air conditioner seemed to be working more like a heater, and the inside was like a steam bath on this late July day. Despite the no smoking sign on the Plexiglas shield, there were butts overflowing the ashtrays and litter all over the floor. The cab smelled, looked, and felt like it hadn't been cleaned since it had come out of the showroom.

Twenty-five bucks later, the cab dropped him off at City Hall. He went down the stairs to his small office, hardly even a cubicle, in the basement. The phone was ringing as he unlocked and opened the door. He ignored it, dropped his suitcase just inside and crossed to the ancient air conditioner in the window. Switching it on, he heard the creaking groans and felt the shuddering as the compressor debated whether to catch or not, and finally he stood in the sudden rush of air that gradually got colder. He felt the sweat begin to dry on his forehead and across the back of his shirt. The L.A. papers had said New York was suffering a blistering heat wave, a Bermuda high having descended on the city with no signs of lifting. The L.A. papers were right. They didn't know how right they were.

The phone stopped ringing, the ring replaced by the sound of his own voice on the answering machine, telling the caller to leave a message and he'd get back whenever he got in. The caller began to leave a message. Harry Gondolian, an old reporter from one of the tabloids who'd been around City Hall since before memory. Would Rogers please give him a call? It was important. It always was. And he always said please. More often than not, Gondolian had something Rogers could use. The only thing was, he usually wanted a fair exchange. But then the stuff Gondolian had and was willing to share was usually worth the price.

Rogers sighed. When he'd been working in Internal Affairs out of that rat-and-roach infested headquarters in Brooklyn, reporters never called. Hell, they didn't even know who he was. He liked it better that way. He walked over to the machine, pressed a button, listened to the whine as the tape rewound, and then played back the week's messages. The tape was nearly filled. It didn't matter. He'd picked up most of the messages on the remote while he was away, answered some, ignored or filed away the rest. He fast forwarded until he reached the latest ones, from over the weekend. Half a dozen people had called since Friday. Gondolian twice. Two from an informant named Max who still kept the lines open even though Rogers wasn't strictly working on police business these days. One from a guy he knew in homicide, Carlos Rodriguez, just social, just give a call when you've got a minute and let's have lunch or something. One from Thomas X. Scanlon, an old-time pol, a power broker, member of the City Council, demanding an immediate response. Rogers had a pretty good idea what Scanlon wanted.

He sat in his old, creaking wooden chair, rubbing the grit out of his eyes. The office, the floors, the overflowing wastebasket, even the desk were just as he had left them; the cleaners had never passed through the door. On the desk there was even an old paper coffee container, the bottom thick with dregs and something growing that probably could have cured anything you might contract. He should have gone home to sleep instead of coming to the office. He picked up the phone and called Scanlon. When he identified himself, he was put right through.

"It's about time," Scanlon said. "I've been trying to reach you all week. You didn't return my calls."

Rogers said nothing. He waited.

"You've been asking questions," Scanlon said, "the kind that could get you into a lot of trouble."

"People are always saying that," Rogers said.

"You got questions about me, ask me direct, not other people who don't know their asses from a hole in the wall."

"Where do you want me to begin?" Rogers said. "You want to talk about condemnations? You want to talk about off-shore bank accounts, condos in Florida, vacation retreats up in Vermont?"

"Fuck you," Scanlon said. "And you can tell Morrison to shove it." The phone went dead. He could imagine Scanlon slamming it into the cradle.

Rogers grinned. Some guys are just too transparent. Hogs at the trough who didn't know when to stop. All you had to do was look in the right barnyard and you'd find the sty, especially if you asked for the right directions from the right people, if you made them think you had a road map anyway and you weren't asking them for anything you didn't already have.

The phone rang again. "He wants to see you," the voice on the other end said. She didn't have to identify herself. Iris Ferguson, Morrison's personal and private secretary, brought along from his Wall Street law firm when he moved into City Hall, guardian of the mayor's inner chamber. "Now," she said. "I wouldn't keep him waiting. He's in a foul mood."

"When not?" Rogers said.

He got up, went out the door, along the corridor, up the stairs into the rotunda, up another flight, turned left, went past the portraits of the hundred and more mayors who had served or been well-served by the city through the centuries, back to Peter Stuyvesant, until he finally reached the outer office. There were people waiting, sitting anxiously on the edges of all the chairs, standing against the walls, all with that impatient look that said they couldn't wait, that they had important things to discuss with the mayor. He didn't have to wonder what those important things were. He knew. Albany was beckoning. The pros had been at the mayor since early in the year to declare himself, and now he was declared and the convention next week would be just a coronation. He had a lock on his party's nomination. And the election? The polls all said he had the look of a winner. After Albany, who knew? New York governors always had their eyes a couple of hundred miles to the south. And all those guys on the edges of those chairs and against the walls of that outer office wanted desperately to take the ride up the Hudson with him, and then another ride a few years hence. They were hitching their cabooses to the Morrison engine, and they wanted him to know it. Whatever he wanted from them, they would give, gladly. It was what they had said so long ago about Franklin Roosevelt. He was like the Staten Island ferry, churning its way across the harbor and pulling all the garbage into port in its wake. You got the ferry, you got the garbage. It was the price you paid.

The receptionist looked up, nodded, made a gesture and he went past the queue, ignoring the looks and the expressions that asked, now who the hell is he? He passed through the door into the mayor's office.

Mayor John Morrison, just plain Jack to the people out there despite his patrician background, was behind his desk in shirt sleeves, cuffs turned up twice, striped club tie pulled down, collar of the white button-down shirt open. His hair had turned grayer since he'd abandoned lucrative Wall Street law for City Hall, and there were new lines in that handsome face. He was the image of a man of probity to whom you'd have no hesitation entrusting the keys to the family vault.

"You took your own sweet time," Morrison said.

Rogers shrugged. "I came as soon as Iris called."

"That's not what I mean, and you know it. Just where the hell have you been?"

"On the coast. You knew that. I told you before I left that I was going, and that I'd be gone a week."

"I must have had something else on my mind. I needed you here."

"You always need me here. And I needed to be there. You could do without me for a week."

Morrison glared, the glare turning into a grin, and he

gave a brief accepting nod. "Okay. Now, what have you got for me?"

"Couple of things. One you want and one maybe you can help me about."

"What's that?"

"Fifteen, twenty years ago, you were an ADA, right?"

"Right."

"You ever hear of a guy named McCauley? Justin McCauley."

Morrison looked at the ceiling, turning back time in his mind. He shook his head. "McCauley?" he said. "That doesn't ring any bells. Why?"

"I read something in the L.A. papers on the way back last night. It seems that this guy's sister killed herself and her kid. She'd been in the loony bin for years and the minute she got out she got herself a piece and blew the two of them away. Like that. Whoever wrote the story added a note that her brother Justin had been a New York cop who had been killed in the line of duty. I couldn't place the name. I figured maybe you could."

Morrison shook his head. "Never heard of him," he said and pushed the McCauley business away. "It was a long time ago," he said. "Ancient history. It probably never came my way. What I'm interested in are current events."

Rogers sighed. This was one of the reasons Morrison had brought him into City Hall. He was an investigator, and a good one, and he was paid to forage in dark corners, private attics, and cellars to find the damning secrets that might send some people to prison and turn others from enemies into friends.

"Scanlon?" he said. "You want his votes, his and his

people, you've probably got them. You want his ass, I can give that to you, too. Your choice.''

''What's he been up to?''

''Making his millions. What else? He's been doing it for years. The surprising thing is that nobody caught wise, but I guess nobody looked in the right places, or maybe nobody wanted to look, Scanlon being Scanlon.''

''How?''

''Condemnations, among a few other choice scams. You know, somebody wants to build a high rise, the city's planning a school or something else, you name it, the only thing being that the property's already got a little something on it, like maybe a half dozen old law tenements which the landlord has no intention of selling. So you pull out eminent domain or some other statute and the property gets condemned and gets sold at bargain-basement prices to some middleman, and then the middleman, who knew the score all the time, turns around and makes a bundle selling it to the people who want it real bad and are willing to pay whatever it takes to get it. A very lucrative business, especially when you have an inside line to what's in the offing and a little clout with the right people.''

''Hard to believe,'' Morrison said. ''Too blatant. Scanlon's not that stupid.''

''You won't find his name,'' Rogers said. ''The guy's got a hundred dummies. But he's there all the same, Gepetto pulling the strings.''

''I suppose you can prove it.''

''You know me. I wouldn't say it if I couldn't. I can even tell you the holes where he's squirreled the acorns.''

Morrison turned that over, nodded, reached for the intercom on his desk. ''Iris,'' he said, ''get Tom Scanlon and tell him I'd like to see him as soon as he's free. Make it a nice polite request." He looked back at Rogers. "If he goes along, fine," he said. "Then I've got the votes I need on the council. And I can count on him this fall. At least he won't get in my way."

"And if he stonewalls, he goes away for a long vacation?"

"You said it, I didn't."

"You didn't have to."

"Don't worry," Morrison said. "He'll cave. He hasn't got the guts of a weasel."

Politics. The fine art not of compromise but of deception. The better the politician, the more adept he was at it. The best could persuade the people out there, maybe even the people inside, make them believe he wasn't really a politician at all, that he was really just an average guy defending the other average guys against the avarice of the professional politicians who were looking out for number one, who were in it for themselves and who always had their hands in the public till.

Rogers had seen it in the police department, when he'd been in Internal Affairs and watched, with his own suspension of disbelief, Chief Bill Dolan make the guys in blue believe he was one of them. The department had yet to forget or forgive Rogers for his part in stripping the mask from Dolan's face and, in the process, bringing shame and major disgrace on the department.

Now he was watching the whole process on a far broader scale, from the elbow of Mayor Jack Morrison, the Ivy League patrician who had ridden a tide of reform, of public disgust with politics as usual, into City Hall and into command of the nation's largest and most complex metropolis. For the people out there in the streets, Morrison was the nonpolitical St. George battling the corrupt political dragons. Jack Morrison, one-time Wall Street lawyer, one-time assistant attorney general in Washington, one-time prosecutor, scion of Fifth Avenue affluence who could trace his lineage back to the Revolution and before, was a man of the people, a man above politics. For the people out there, it now seemed, Jack Morrison was the man they needed in the Governor's Mansion in Albany, the man who would put the state back on the right track, as he seemed to have done with the city. And if he could put the state to rights, then that large white showplace on the Potomac might be his for the taking.

That was the public face. But like most people, he had other faces. He was no amateur, despite the pose. He was a political animal to the core, a man with a long and unforgiving memory. He knew where the bodies were buried, or if he didn't know, he was cynic enough to be sure there wasn't a man alive, especially not a professional politician, who hadn't buried a few. It was Rogers' job to find those bodies and find out why they had been buried. When Morrison had what he wanted and needed, he used it ruthlessly. And it was then that those who stood in his way discovered the choice he was prepared to give them. It wasn't much of a choice. And it didn't take much internal debate before one-time enemies became, if not precisely friends, at least yea-sayers.

Rogers had watched it happen a dozen times, maybe more, since Morrison took over the mayor's chair. It had been a thing Morrison had developed and mastered as a prosecutor in the Manhattan D.A.'s office and later as an assistant attorney general in the Justice Department's Criminal Division, and he had carried it along as essential baggage when he moved into City Hall. The first couple

of times Rogers had sat in on one of those you-do-this-
or-else sessions, Morrison disinterring the bodies Rogers
had found, and uncovering a few other corpses from the
private files he'd amassed on just about everybody he'd
ever come in contact with, there had been screams of
outrage and you-can-go-to-hells and storming-outs in
high dudgeon. Only Morrison didn't go to hell, he went
to the current prosecutors and the screamers got their
names all over the front pages and all over indictment
papers and, eventually, exchanged their names for numbers, while Morrison got the right kind of headlines. It
only took a couple of examples before a call from Morrison brought an instant visit, and when Morrison
explained what he wanted, he got it.

Rogers didn't like it. He hadn't liked it from the start
and he had never made a secret of that. "You're a damn
moralist, Ben," Morrison said. "You still believe right
is right and wrong is wrong and there are no shades of
gray. If a guy's got his hand in the cookie jar, if he strays
from the straight and narrow, you want to send him away
and that's that, no excuses, no compromises, no trade-
offs. It sounds easy. For you, it is. But I'm trying to run
this city and I need some of those guys. I need to put
them in a corner where they don't have any choice but
to go along on the important things we're trying to do.
Hell, if I did what you want, then we'd just have to start
all over with a new bunch and we'd end up the same
way, only it would take a hell of a lot longer. In politics,
you have to be pragmatic. There's an old saying—the
end justifies the means."

"We've all heard that one," Rogers said. "Only it
seems to me that the ends usually get screwed up because
of the means."

"Not if you keep your eye on the goal. If you do it right. You have to make sure you know what you're doing and why. I know what I'm doing, and I know why I'm doing it. You can bank on that."

"You didn't use to believe that. At least I didn't think so."

"That was then and this is now. Times change and you have to change with them or else you end up waiting for a train that's already left the station."

"Sure," Rogers said, "only the list of guys who want to throw you in front of the next train stretches from here to Coney Island and back."

"Maybe," Morrison said. "But there isn't a one of them who can do anything but dream. Fear, my friend, is a wonderful thing, a powerful weapon. Combine it with power and you can do just about anything. You just have to make sure you're doing the right thing."

"The right thing? I wish I knew what that was."

"The right thing," Morrison said, "is to be in a position where you can fulfill your dreams, and the dreams of the people who count on you."

Not a politician? "You want to be governor that bad?" Rogers asked.

Morrison shrugged.

"And you really believe all those guys are going to line up behind you, or at least not put any roadblocks in your way, and it's going to be a cakewalk from here to Albany?"

"You said it. I didn't."

"No. But you believe it."

The intercom on the desk emitted its sound. Iris said that Tom Scanlon had arrived.

The next hour was not a pleasant one. No matter how

many times Rogers sat there during scenes like this, he couldn't rid himself of the sour taste. Politics had never been high on his dream list, and the more he learned and the more he got involved the lower it sank, until now it was almost out of sight. Scanlon appeared all belligerence. The belligerence didn't last. He started to crumble when Rogers, at Morrison's nod, spread out in a monotone all the little things Scanlon had been doing to make himself a very rich man.

By the time Rogers finished, he was sure that Scanlon was in the mayor's pocket. But it wasn't quite that simple. Scanlon looked around, puffed himself up, his face growing redder, the veins on his neck hardening and standing out like steel cords, and he began the go-to-hell routine again, and the you've-got-stuff-on-me-I've-got-twice-as-much-on-you, and the let's-just-see-who-comes-out-on-top. Scanlon would go to the papers, and even if the things he said didn't stick, let's just see what they did to Morrison's chances of moving onward and upward.

Morrison studied him for a moment. "You really are a blowhard, Tom," he said. He sighed. "I didn't want to do this, but you've forced my hand." He opened a drawer in his desk, pulled out a file folder, and retrieved a tape cassette. He held it for a moment. Rogers watched him carefully, a foul taste beginning to fill his mouth. He didn't know what Morrison had on that cassette, he'd just as soon not know, but he was stuck in that room now and he'd have to listen.

"I've had this for a while," the mayor said. "Just one of those things that came up when we were looking into something else, and there you were. Big as life. And dirty as a slime pit. I didn't believe it at first. But it's you, Tommy, no doubt about that." He reached for a tape recorder on the credenza behind him. He put the cassette in the recorder, pressed the play button and then leaned back.

Scanlon's voice and that of another man suddenly filled the room. The two were dealing. The other man was selling and Scanlon was buying. What he was buying might not have been a crime in the strictest legal sense, but it was the kind of thing that would probably destroy Scanlon if it ever came out. They were talking about movies, only not the kind that play in the first run theatres, not even in the third run. They were the kind that play in the sleaze bags that used to line Forty-second Street, especially in the peep show emporiums, before the good citizens began a campaign of purification and gentrification and pushed the porno business into a score of small pockets scattered around the city. By the time the tape ran itself out, Scanlon looked sick.

"Little boys and little girls, Tommy," Morrison said, his voice without emotion, not condemning, not revealing anything. But then the tape had been revealing enough. "Little girls and little boys," he said again, reversing the order. "What is it with you? You just like to watch, or is it more?"

Scanlon said nothing. What could he say?

"You've been a bad boy, Tom," Morrison said mildly. "If I were of a mind, you could go away for a very long time, maybe not on this but certainly on what Ben dug up. You wouldn't like that. And you wouldn't like the world to know about the secret life of Thomas X. Scanlon, either. Can you imagine the public disgrace? Can you imagine what your family would think, especially that very nice wife of yours? By the time you breathed fresh air again you wouldn't have much use for that pile, and there wouldn't be a living soul who'd have much use for you."

Scanlon was sweating, and it wasn't because of the heat wave. Scanlon raised a quivering hand. Five or ten minutes earlier he had been raging, ready to battle the mayor down to the final out. No longer. "Jesus, Jack," he muttered, the voice pleading, all the belligerence and strength dissipated, "I've done a lot of good. All through the years. You can't deny that. You can't just flush it down the toilet."

"Not me, Tom," Morrison said. "If it goes down the toilet, nobody's to blame but yourself, you and your greed, and whatever else is inside you."

"God, Jack, you wouldn't. My family. Everything. Just name it. Whatever you want."

Morrison took his time. He glanced over at Rogers and, a satisfied smile turning the corners of his mouth, nodded. He looked back at Scanlon, reached for a type-written sheet on his desk and handed it across to the councilman. Scanlon took it eagerly, scanned it, looked back at the mayor. "I read you," Scanlon said.

"I figured you would," Morrison said. "That's a list of bills that have been stalled in the council since the first of the year. You've been doing the stalling, Tom. Well, the city needs action, it needs those bills, the people need them, I need them. I want them moved and I want them passed now."

Scanlon nodded. "I'll see what I can do," he said. "You know politics. Everybody has his own agenda. You're right. It's time we got off our asses. You can count on me."

"I knew you'd see things clear and straight, Tom. It

just took a little reasoning to make you come to your senses."

"You know it."

"Oh, one more thing," Morrison said. "You know, Tom, you're not getting any younger. You look a little tired, worn down, so when the session's over and you get this package through, you ought to think about retiring, taking it easy from here on out. The summers in the city are just too damn hot for a man of your years, and the winters too damn cold. Ben tells me you have a nice little summer place on a lake up in New England and a nice little condo down in Florida. It occurs to me that the time has come for you to take advantage of what you've got, spend your summers up where it's cool and your winters down in the southern sun. Enjoy yourself away from the rat race, away from all the wheeling and dealing. What do you say? Agreed?"

Scanlon didn't like that. He started to argue, his face flushing again, and if he'd had a blood pressure cuff on the top number probably would have registered two hundred fifty at the very least. Morrison held out a hand. "No arguments, Tom. It's the best course for everyone. Time for the next generation to take over, anyway. So it's a done thing. Right?"

Scanlon nodded slowly. After all, he didn't really have much choice.

3

The sour taste stayed with Rogers all the way back to his cubicle in the basement. There the air conditioner had done the best it could and if it was still hot, at least it was bearable. He sat down at his desk. The filthy coffee cup with its penicillin dregs was still there. He tossed it into the trash can. He thought about going home and sacking out. There was nothing pressing, nothing that couldn't wait another twenty-four hours. The phone rang. He shook his head and picked it up.

"Ben. Harry Gondolian. I've been trying to reach you."

"You've reached me, Harry."

"Can we get together?"

"Can it wait? I just got in from the coast and I'm beat. I'm on my way home to get some sleep."

"I thought we might have lunch."

"Not today. How about tomorrow?"

"Whatever you say. I have a few things that might interest you. And I want to talk a little. The desk asked me to do a take-out on the people around Morrison, the people nobody hears about. Kitchen cabinet stuff.''

"Hell, Harry, I'm just an errand boy."

"Sure. Like I'm a file clerk. Whatever, let me buy you lunch anyway. We'll talk a little. Strictly off-the-record, like always."

"You won't get much."

"I'll take that chance. What the hell. How about tomorrow, at one, at the food bazaar by the federal court? I'll even stand you to crab cakes."

Before Rogers could answer, Gondolian hung up.

Harry Gondolian was as much a fixture around City Hall as the portraits of the mayors that lined the walls, and whose histories, public and private, he seemed to know down to the most closeted and intimate details, warts and all. Ask Gondolian, newcomers were advised, and if he's in the mood he'll tell you more than you really want to know, but precisely what you ought to know if you're going to make it at City Hall. The thing was, he had to be in the mood, and he had to like you, which wasn't always the case, which, in fact, was rarely the case. He tended to guard what he knew, what he had dug up over the years, as a private treasure trove to be spent frugally and with care. He'd arrived in the press room fresh out of City College. There were some who believed he'd set up shop there about the time the city elected its first mayor, or if not then, at least so long ago that the guy who sat in the mayor's office then was now little more than a vague memory. But Harry Gondolian, just as he guarded his memories and his sources and all the secrets he had stored up over the years to use as he saw fit, still guarded the same old battered cigarette-scarred desk in the corner with its ancient rotary phone that linked him to his paper's metropolitan desk. He still sat in the same old battered and creaking wooden arm chair that groaned audibly whenever he sat and pushed it away from the desk on its lopsided wheels. Other reporters had come and gone, passing through on their way up the newspaper chain, to Washington or London or Tokyo or some far away war, or dropping out, giving up the press and disappearing into more financially rewarding callings like flaking for the famous, for the fifteen-minute celebrities, or advertising, where the bucks were bigger and easier. The newcomers typed their stories these days on computer consoles connected by modem directly to their editors' desks. Gondolian still wrote on a typewriter, not even an electric, and then picked up the phone and read his copy to a rewrite man.

Rogers met him the day he moved into the basement office. There had been a knock at the door, the door had opened and a little unprepossessing man, a study in gray—unpressed gray suit maybe twenty years out of fashion, white shirt washed so many times it had turned gray and frayed at the collar, gray tie pulled down just below the open collar button, gray fringe around a balding head, gray complexion as though the sun or even the outdoors had never touched the skin, thick glasses magnifying watery gray eyes—had walked in and stood in the doorway, looking around.

"Name's Harry Gondolian," he introduced himself. "I work City Hall. I like to get to know the people who pass though. You're Ben Rogers. I know about you. I know about everybody, everything there is to know." It was not a boast. It was simply a matter-of-fact statement.

"I've heard your name," Rogers said. "I've read your stuff."

''Naturally,'' Gondolian said. He glanced around some more. ''They haven't fixed this dump up for you. Not even a fresh coat of paint. It looks about the same as it used to. The last guy who sat behind that desk was a bag man.''

''Not my thing,'' Rogers said.

''I wouldn't say that,'' Gondolian said. ''Bag men collect. You're a collector, from what I hear. You just collect things besides bread. Like information.''

''There's a difference.''

''You could say that. I'm sure you believe it.''

''You got something special in mind?''

''Not at the moment,'' Gondolian said. ''I just wanted to get a look at you, up close. We're going to see a lot of each other, if you stick around.''

''I doubt that.''

''Which? That we'll see a lot of each other or that you'll stick around?''

Roger grinned. There was something about this little guy that drew him.

''We've got a lot in common,'' Gondolian said. ''We're both collectors. One of these days, maybe, in fact, more than one of these days, you may want some of what I've collected, and I may want some of what you've collected. We could both make a nice profit.''

''Not likely.''

''Don't bet on it,'' Gondolian said. ''You'd lose.'' He nodded, turned, and walked out, closing the door behind him.

He had been right. Gondolian knew, maybe through some sixth sense or the kind of intuition that's the mark of the investigator, which he certainly was, whenever Rogers was off on one of the mayor's little errands, and a file folder or just a short note would appear on Rogers' desk, pointing him in the right directions, pointing out the dead ends. It happened often enough so that when Gondolian asked for a little favor in return, usually just a lead or an insight into Morrison's intentions, or something else that was going in Rogers' domain, just so long as it didn't hurt Morrison or break confidences that had to be kept, Rogers obliged.

And so, in this strange way, they had been drawn to each other and had become friends.

The next afternoon at one, renewed by a night's sleep, Rogers left his office, locked the door, walked out of City Hall and across the plaza toward the federal courthouse and the food stalls that ran along the south wall. The lines in front of the booths that purveyed everything from hot dogs and hamburgers to pasta and pizza snaked sinuously out into the paved al fresco eating area, where tables with their striped parasols offering a small sanctuary from the scorching heat and blinding sun were packed with lawyers, judges, defendants, cops, passersby taking a lunch break from the courts and office buildings in the area. More people wandered fitfully about carrying loaded cardboard trays looking for a vacant chair somewhere, anywhere. Rogers stood for a moment looking about. He spotted Gondolian. The reporter had taken possession of a small table to one side, his briefcase on one empty chair, his jacket on another. In front of him was a tray with a sandwich, pastrami on rye with a pickle, and a paper coffee container. The perpetual cigarette dangled from his lips, the smoke curling up around his glasses. In front of one of the empty chairs was another tray with a plate heaped with crab cakes. Gondolian's eyes scanned the plaza. He saw Rogers, and beckoned toward the empty chair. Rogers walked toward him.

"Sit down. Lunch awaits," Gondolian said, sweeping the briefcase from the chair onto the pavement.

Rogers stood over him for a moment, then sat. Gondolian didn't look well. He looked grayer than ever, tired to the bone, like all the energy had drained out of him. Sweat coated his forehead and stained the back and underarms of his gray shirt. It was hot, sure, but the sweat on Gondolian didn't look like what comes with heat and humidity. "What's up, Harry?" Rogers said.

"Eat first, before everything gets cold," Gondolian said. "We can talk while we eat." He dropped the cigarette to the pavement, letting it smolder and burn itself out. He picked up his sandwich, looked at it, put it back down, took another cigarette and lit it, then, the butt dangling precariously from his lips, picked up the coffee and took a sip.

Rogers took a forkful of the crab, enjoying the taste. When he swallowed, he said, "I owe you one, Harry. You opened the door on Scanlon."

"Just a crack," Gondolian said. "The rest you did yourself. Besides, who's counting? It was a payback, anyway. One hand washes the other, like they say."

"You've given more than you've received," Rogers said.

"About even, I'd say," Gondolian said. He lit another cigarette.

"More than even," Rogers said.

"What the hell," Gondolian said, "I'd have written it for the paper. The only thing is, the publisher's got the hots for the motherfucker. He won't hear a word against him. I laid it out in spades and he said it was full of crap.

Everything should be so full of crap. You know, one of these days I might take a close look at the bastard. Can you believe it? He thinks he's a newspaperman. What he's done to the paper you shouldn't do to your worst enemy." He drew deeply on the cigarette, started to cough, pulled out a handkerchief and held it over his mouth. It took a minute before the paroxysm eased. There was more sweat on his face. He looked sick. It also looked like there were red stains on the handkerchief, though Rogers couldn't be sure, Gondolian shoving it into his pocket out of sight quickly.

"Are you all right?" Rogers asked, concerned.

"Fine. Couldn't be better," Gondolian said.

"You don't look it. And you don't sound it."

Gondolian looked away. "Don't press, Ben," he said to the air. "One of these days I'll fill you in."

Rogers studied him, waiting.

"I got a couple of things. I'll tell you about them later."

"What gives, Harry? Why the flood?"

"I'm feeling generous right now," Gondolian said. "Clearing the decks, like they say."

"Okay, if you say so." Rogers looked skeptical. Gondolian must want something. In time, he'd find out what. "Now, I've got one for you."

Gondolian looked at him.

"You ever hear of a cop named Justin McCauley?"

Gondolian searched his memory and slowly shook his head. "The name means nothing."

"It doesn't mean anything to me, either, and it didn't mean anything to Morrison. I came across it on the flight back from the coast and I can't get it out of my head."

"Why?"

"A story I read in the L.A. paper."

"You believe what's in the papers?" Gondolian had his sardonic grin plastered across his face.

"When I'm sure of the facts beforehand," Rogers said. "Anyway, the story was about this guy McCauley's sister. She was a loony who killed herself and her kid. The story said her brother had been a New York cop who died in the line of duty, whatever the hell that means. It must have been something like fifteen, twenty years ago. The thing is, I don't remember it at all. Do you?"

Gondolian tilted his head back and stared up toward the sky, his eyes narrowing, watching the drifting of the smoke from his cigarette. He took his time. Then he looked back at Rogers and shook his head slowly. "No McCauley piece in the jigsaw puzzle of my mind."

"It's weird," Rogers said. "That's not the kind of thing somebody makes up. Well, what the hell, when I get the time I'm going to track it down."

"Do that," Gondolian said, "and let me know what you find. Now, tell me, you got your bags packed?"

"Haven't even unpacked yet," Rogers said.

"Not what I mean, and you know it. You looking forward to residing in the Athens of the north? Albany, you know, is the repository of culture and enlightenment. If you look hard enough you might find some." He started to laugh, and the laughter brought on another bout of coughing.

Rogers watched him carefully. "Why the hell would I want to move to Albany?" he said. "I'd rather be in Brooklyn. I'm strictly a New York guy."

"The line is you'd rather be in Philadelphia," Gondolian said. "But never mind. Whither the mayor goest, so goest thou. And Mr. Morrison is sure he's going to Albany, where the living may not be easier, but the governing sure as hell is. Morrison's another one my publisher loves. God, that man's taste."

"If it's what Morrison wants, that's what he'll get," Rogers said.

"I wouldn't take the odds," Gondolian said. "You know how many mayors wanted to be governor? All of them, every last one. You know how many made it? You couldn't name the last one, and neither could I, and I know everything there is to know about this city. Listen to me, Ben. You walk one step over the city line and you mention our dear mayor, never mind which one, Morrison or the one a couple of hundred years back, and the yokels say, 'up yours.'"

"What the hell, you read the polls. They all say he'll win, in a walk."

Gondolian shook his head and gave a snort. "Polls. Bullshit polls. You believe the polls, you believe Alf Landon moved into the White House, and so did Tom Dewey, and you believe Eddie Koch got to be governor. Don't you know everybody's favorite pastime is lying to the pollsters? There's only one poll that counts, and that's the one on election day when John Q. steps behind the closed curtain and exercises his constitutional rights. Besides, your boy's made himself a shit load of enemies. They'd give up all the graft they've stashed away to see him get his. They'll make nice-nice to his face, but behind his back, let me tell you, it's going to be the night of the long knives."

"Morrison can take care of himself."

"As long as he's got you to watch his back."

"I'm sorry I'm late." The voice was breathy, soft. It came from a small, slight young woman, hardly more than

a teenager from the look, with short dark hair stylishly cut
to frame a narrow pretty face. She was holding a tray
with a small salad, barely enough to nourish a rabbit.

"You're never late, Annie," Gondolian said. He
motioned to the vacant seat, shoving his jacket onto the
pavement to make room for her. "Sit," he said. She
sat. He introduced her to Rogers. Her name was Annie
Kendall. "Annie," Gondolian said, "is my legs, my ears,
and my nose, too, these days."

"I'm his gofer," she said.

Rogers studied her, then looked back to Gondolian.
"You robbing the cradle these days, Harry?"

Gondolian smiled a little. "Looks can be deceiving,"
he said. "She's older than she looks, which doesn't hurt."

"I'm twenty-four," she said.

"All of twenty-four," Gondolian said. "My goodness.
That's practically ancient." He looked at Rogers.
"Annie's good," he said. "Annie's very good. When they
put me out to pasture, she'll step in and it'll be like no
change."

"I believe that," Rogers said. "You bet."

"Believe it," Gondolian said, "because it happens to
be the truth."

"Bullshit. You'll never retire. They'll have to carry
you out feet first. Even then you'll come back to haunt
the place."

"No bullshit, Ben," Gondolian said, and there was no
pretense in his voice. "The day is not long hence. But
nobody will miss me. Annie will be just fine. I recruited
her. I'm training her. She catches on quick. She's got the
background and the talent. Cum laude from Princeton.
Top of the heap at Columbia journalism, though why she
did that is beyond me. Journalism. God help us. In my

day we didn't call it journalism, it was just reporting. You wanted to be a reporter, you went to college or you didn't go, what the hell, it didn't much matter. You learned history and English, and you studied a little psychology and sociology, maybe, but the main thing you did was read newspapers, and this city was full of them back then. You read the goddamn *Trib* of blessed memory, you studied Homer Bigart and that bitch Maggie Higgins, and if you wanted to be a pundit you read maybe Walter Lippmann. All of 'em, they could make you believe you were right there with them wherever they were reporting from, and they made you understand what the hell it was all about. That's how you learned to write for a paper. Jesus."

"He says things like that all the time," Annie Kendall said. "It's his passion. I think he has a love affair with the way things were in the old days, when reporters were reporters."

"And not bloody journalists," Gondolian said. He looked at Rogers. "Get to know her, Ben. She can be your buddy as long as you're here. Pretend she's me. You two can be useful to each other."

"You already said that."

"I'm getting old, that's the trouble. My mind's going. I keep repeating myself." He looked over at the girl. "I told you," he said, "Ben and the honorable would-be governor are this close." He held out his hand and laid one finger over the other.

"I know," she said. "You've told me."

Gondolian looked down at his watch. He shoved the tray with the uneaten sandwich to one side. "Got to run," he said. "The majority leader wants to talk, and who am I to say nay?" He got up slowly, stiffly, paused a moment to light another cigarette, and then moved away, toward City Hall. His pace was slow, labored, with no spring or life in it.

Annie Kendall watched until he disappeared. She turned back to Rogers. "The man's the best there is," she said, "and he's dying."

"Gondolian? He's impervious. He'll outlive us all."

She shook her head. She looked angry. "No," she said. "I mean it. He's dying. Do you think I'd be here if he wasn't? He's worked alone for fifty years. Now, all of a sudden, he's got me working with him, doing things he could do in his sleep, feeding me his files, quizzing me on them, telling me things he's never told anyone. The bastard's dying. The goddamn cigarettes. He's dying and he's still smoking them, one after the other. Oh, Jesus Christ."

"How long?" Rogers asked simply. There was no need for pretense, no need for anything else.

"Six months, maybe," she said. "At the outside. Probably less."

"They can't do anything?"

"Both lungs," she said. "Inoperable. And he won't take radiation or chemo."

A small group of men, some in blue, some in street clothes, abandoned a nearby table. They had been watching Rogers for some time, and the looks were not particularly friendly. They stood, staring for another moment, and then turned away.

Annie Kendall watched them. "I thought," she said to Rogers, "all cops were part of one big family. You know, bosom buddies through thick and thin, no matter what. They have something against you?"

"Probably," he said. "They think they do. From the

old days in Internal Affairs. I wasn't the most popular kid on the block, their block anyway, and I'm still not."

"More than that," she said. "I checked you out. You broke the code. They don't forgive and they don't forget what you did to the old chief."

"The blue wall," he said. "They protect their own. At least, that's what the twisted ones try to persuade everybody else, that cops are just one big happy family and you all either stand together or hang separately."

"No matter what? No matter how venal?"

He shrugged. "They think they ought to handle it themselves, on the inside. Outsiders don't understand. That's what they say. They think it's us against them, the 'them' being everybody but cops."

"What makes them think they're so special?" she said with belligerence. "Everyone lives inside a wall, a blue one or a white one or any color you want to name. Only lawyers understand lawyers, only doctors understand doctors, I suppose only garbage men understand garbage men."

"How about journalists?"

"We'd like to be. Everyone would. But we're not."

"Who is?"

"Nobody. Just that everybody thinks he is." She turned away, reached into her purse and pulled out a small notebook and a pen, scribbled something in it, tore off a couple of pages and handed them to him. "I have to go," she said. "I wanted to meet you. I'm glad I did. Here, take this. My number. Give me a call one of these days, like Harry said."

He took the pages and glanced casually at them. On the first page was a telephone number. Hers, he guessed. The pages beneath contained some names, a question and a suggestion in Gondolian's writing. "Rasmussen. Weinstein. Jessup. What do they have in common besides the obvious? Find out."

He had heard of all three. It would have been impossible to live in the city for more than a week without having heard those names. And he had met the three a number of times over the last several months.

The Reverend Melvin Rasmussen was a charismatic black preacher, a major and militant force in the demand for black rights. Any time there was trouble between blacks and the cops or anyone else, Rasmussen was certain to be well out front, voice and arms raised, stirring the crowd to action.

Rabbi Moishe Weinstein led a growing and militant ultra-orthodox Jewish sect. He seemed to see Hitler and anti-Semitism behind every word, every action in which Jews and anyone else came face-to-face in moments of trouble. And when those moments arose, Weinstein's was inevitably the loudest voice in the forefront shouting, "Never again!"

Harvey Jessup ran a militant gay rights group. From his office in Greenwich Village poured a flood of pamphlets, petitions, and fliers demanding more money to fight the AIDS epidemic, equality for gays in every aspect of life. Whenever there was a march or a rally, Jessup was in the front rank, and if the demonstrations started to slow down, it was his voice that spurred the crowds on.

What they all had in common was militancy, a passion for confrontation, and, if their words and actions in public could be credited, a consuming detestation of each other. Another thing they had in common was that all three had been early backers of Morrison when he ran for mayor. One of the planks in his platform then had been support for a Civilian Complaint Review Board, which they all not only wanted but demanded. As mayor, Morrison had given it to them, and so now they were already rallying support for his bid for the governorship. Those were the obvious. What, Rogers wondered, were the not so obvious?

Rogers looked up at Annie Kendall. "What gives?"

"Don't ask me," she said. "Harry said to give it to you and when you had a chance you should get in touch with him. He can tell you a few things you ought to know. Only don't wait too long."

After Annie Kendall went her way, Rogers wandered east toward the river and the waterfront, walking under the elevated FDR Drive toward the South Street Seaport. The heat was becoming more intense as the day wore on, and the tar on the roads was soft and sticky, every step like pulling feet out of a pot of glue. At the seaport on this summer afternoon, the tourists were out in force. There were a lot of middle-aged men in Bermuda shorts and black socks and shoes, cameras strung around their necks, guide books in one hand, wives and children trailing alongside. School was out and there were a lot of college kids, and some younger, probably still in high school, both the girls and the boys in tight shorts or ragged jeans, holes in the knees and seats, and t-shirts advertising some rock group or the Hard Rock Cafe. They all wandered about the cobblestone streets and along the piers, staring at the tall ships moored at the wharves, lining up to clamber aboard, examining the wares of the street vendors, moving in and out of the trendy boutiques with their overpriced fashionable goods.

A medium-sized shabby guy with stringy matted hair that looked as though it hadn't been cut within recent memory, a scraggly beard, and the torn, ill-fitting clothes of the homeless, wandered through the crowd trying to cadge handouts. Rogers watched him, then moved forward.

"Hello, Max," he said.

Max looked toward him. "Mr. Rogers," he said. "You got my message."

"I got it," Rogers said. "Both of them. Now, Max, give the lady back what you lifted from her purse."

"Me?" Max said, all innocence.

"You," Rogers said. "I thought you were above such things these days."

"Who could resist?" Max sighed. "Like taking candy from a baby."

"Give it back," Rogers said.

Max shrugged, turned and moved toward a middle-aged woman who was standing by a railing near the tall ships with her husband and three teenage kids. Her purse dangled from her arm. It was gaping open. She started at Max's approach, a mixture of alarm and terror. Max said something soothing and his hand held out a wallet to her. She looked at him, at it, down at her open purse. She took a deep relieved breath, retrieved the wallet and murmured something to Max. He shrugged and his expression said, you can always depend on New Yorkers to come to your aid in time of trouble, even the homeless can be your friends. She opened the wallet, took out a bill and handed it to him. He took it and shoved it into his pocket, smiling a thanks at her. She put her wallet into her purse and snapped it shut, tightly, then turned away, not looking at Max again. Max watched her back for a moment, then turned and headed back toward Rogers.

"What d'ya know," he said. "Honesty has its rewards."

"I've been trying to tell you that for years," Rogers said.

"What the hell," Max said, "you can't expect a leopard to change its spots overnight."

"It's been longer than overnight," Rogers said. "You left messages. You wanted to see me."

"Yeah. I don't know if you're interested, seein' as how you ain't a cop no more."

"I'm still a cop," Rogers said.

"You work for his honor these days."

"Temporarily. I'm still a cop."

"Yeah? Anyway, the thing is, I seen a guy. I thought you oughta know."

"Who?"

"Victor Santangello."

"Bullshit," Rogers said. "No way. Victor's in Atlanta, doing twenty-five to life, four times. Consecutive, not concurrent. He's there forever."

"Was," Max said. "Maybe the operative word is *was*. From the look, he ain't there no longer. I seen him the other day, big as life, bold as brass."

"Where?"

"Up on Columbus. That Cuban place where he always hung out. Back at the old table, right in the window, just like old times. He had company. He was with a guy."

"Who?"

"Somebody I recognized. Guy you maybe know."

"Who?" Rogers repeated, this time a demand.

"Cop, even if he was in civvies," Max said. "They was real cozy like. I couldn't hear what they was sayin', naturally, bein' as how I was outside, just passin' by, and they was inside."

"What cop?"

Max put on a guileless face. He shrugged.

"How much?"

"Twenty."

"That's what you got from the lady. Let's call it square."

"Mr. Rogers," Max protested.

"Max," Rogers said.

"Okay, okay. Don't hassle me. Guy was Charlie Westerman."

"Bullshit," Rogers said. "I've met him. I know people who know him. Everybody says Westerman's a straight arrow."

Max laughed. "Tell me another," he said. "When the cash is on the line, there ain't no straight arrows. Whatever, I thought you oughta know, seein' as how that used to be your kind of thing, an' seein' as how it was his honor what put Victor away back when. In the old days, Victor had a memory like an elephant and he was a certain payback guy. I don't figure Atlanta changed him much, Victor bein' Victor." He paused, examining Rogers' face. "I hear more," he said, "I'll be in touch."

He turned and strolled away into the crowd, taking up his murmured entreaties for some spare change to help the homeless. People parted ways for him, pulling away, trying to stay clear of the beggar. Rogers watched him for a while, until he faded from view.

He turned over the information Max had imparted. Victor Santangello free was bad news. He was supposed to be in Atlanta, for murder, narcotics trafficking, and assorted other felonies, the only way out in a pine box.

Victor Santangello was a Cuban who had struck it rich after he sailed away in a small boat from Castroland and beached in south Florida. He made good connections among the Cuban émigré resistance, especially when he formed a partnership with a pliant Alcohol, Tobacco, and Firearms agent and a CIA operative to supply weapons to the rebels at a nice tidy profit for all three. And pretty soon he made some other connections, this time with the Colombians, moved to New York and turned into one of the main importers and distributors of the stuff they grew, processed, and exported. The thing was that Victor was greedy, and Victor had a violent streak, both of which distressed some of his friends and some of his competitors. So they set him up for the feds. The guy who prosecuted the case for the government was John Morrison, and it was a nice jewel in the Morrison crown when he convinced the jury to send Santangello away forever, and then some. As the guards led a manacled Santangello out of the courtroom, he turned, screamed imprecations at Morrison and told him, and the world, just what he intended to do to his prosecutor, and persecutor, the day he got out—and get out he would, he promised.

And, apparently, get out he had. He must have made some kind of deal with the feds. It happened. And the feds were never very anxious to let the locals know such things, and Morrison, being New York's mayor and no longer a federal prosecutor, was now a local.

Rogers turned away from the seaport and moved slowly back uptown, to City Hall and his office. The cubicle was at least bearable, though only just. He sat at the desk and picked up the phone, dialed a number and waited.

The phone was answered after the third ring. "Homicide," the voice said, "Rodriguez."

"Carlos," Rogers said. "How are you?"

"Hot as hell," Rodriguez said. "Ben, for chrissake, I been thinkin' about you. I left a message on your machine the other day."

"I got it," Rogers said. "We'll have lunch in a couple of days, sure. But that's not why I'm calling. I want a favor."

"Ask, and if it's possible, it's yours."

"You ever hear of a guy name of Victor Santangello?"

Rodriguez's voice grew serious. "Yeah. I heard of him. More than heard of him. I got a hole in my shoulder from the bastard, back when I was just startin' out. Why?"

"I hear he's out."

"No way."

"That's what I said. But my stoolie saw him in that Cuban place up on Columbus."

"When?"

"Two, three days ago. And he was having lunch with a cop. Charlie Westerman. You know him?"

There was a long pause. "I know him," Rodriguez said slowly, without emotion.

"You got time to take a look?" Rogers asked. "I'd do it myself, but . . ."

"I know," Rodriguez said. "The mayor's off and running, and it ain't easy to keep pace. Yeah, sure, I'll get on it. I'll get back to you as soon as I have something."

4

With the convention only days away, Morrison was taking no chances that anything might get in the way of a trouble-free convention with the nomination by acclamation and a united party at the end. With Rogers and his closest aides always at his side, he raced through the state, mending fences, solidifying support, winning new friends and allies. For a couple of days and nights it was a swing across the northern tier, Albany and on up into the Adirondacks and westward skirting the Canadian border, and then a swing west across the center of the state, to Schenectady, Utica, Syracuse, Rochester, Buffalo, and points in between, then across the southern tier, to Binghamton, to the triple cities. When he wasn't touring outside the city limits, he dashed from the Bronx to Staten Island, from Queens to Brooklyn and Manhattan. It was constant movement with little rest and no pauses. It was exhausting. But it was paying off. Everywhere he was greeted and cheered by larger and larger throngs, the numbers growing at every stop.

Convention week arrived. City business was put to the

side. Headquarters were set up in a suite at the Statler Hilton on Seventh Avenue, a short walk to Madison Square Garden where the delegates were gathering. From that suite, Morrison watched every move on and off the floor over a dozen closed-circuit monitors lining the walls, constantly checking with his managers and handlers or summoning wavering delegates and political bosses to private meetings. It paid off. The sessions went smoothly, hardly a dissenting voice heard anywhere within or outside the arena. His was the only name placed before the delegates, and the platform he dictated was adopted without contention. On Thursday, after intense competition among the leaders for the privilege of making the nominating speech, Jack Morrison became his party's nominee for governor by acclamation.

He would make his acceptance speech Friday evening. The day was spent in a room off the headquarters suite with his speechwriters, rehearsing and making last minute changes. Just before seven that evening, he emerged from the room and beckoned to Rogers and a couple of other close advisors. "I want you guys to come with me," he said. "Stay close."

Without another word or glance, he turned and started out of the suite. One of the security people raised his walkie-talkie, pressed buttons, shouted into it: "He's on his way." The message went down to another member of the security team in the lobby, who passed it along to others outside the hotel, along the proposed path to the Garden, inside the Garden itself. The alert was out. Take no chances now. The candidate would momentarily be on public view, out in the streets, surrounded by mobs, vulnerable, and with all the nuts that populated not just the city but the world these days, who could be sure there wasn't one waiting to write his name into history standing somewhere outside?

Morrison strode along the corridor toward the elevator, ringed by those closest to him, and those whose job it was to protect him. He paid little attention. One of the security team rang for the elevator. When it arrived, he held Morrison back for a moment while he checked the interior, glancing up first at the mirror that reflected the empty car, glancing around to make sure it was empty. Satisfied, he nodded, and the group entered, the elevator moving down toward the lobby floor. There, more security. Guys in plainclothes, holding walkie-talkies, were waiting, ringing the elevator entrance, their eyes moving steadily around the lobby, checking constantly. As Morrison stepped out of the elevator, some moved in front of him, some trailed a few feet behind, others moved along on either side. Morrison ignored the protection, striding through the lobby and out onto the avenue.

There, a small regiment of city cops and state troopers was waiting, to clear the way, and scattered were less obtrusive security people—from the city, the state, and even the federal Secret Service—eyes constantly on the move, scanning the crowds, scanning the surrounding buildings. Morrison could have gone through a side entrance and taken a limo the short distance to a private entrance to the Garden, which the security teams had tried to convince him was the wisest course. He couldn't be convinced. He wanted to bask in the public adulation, and so he announced he would walk the few blocks across the avenue up to Thirty-fourth Street and to the Garden. Several thousand people who had been waiting for hours for his appearance let up a roar as he stepped through the hotel doors onto the street. The crowd had been growing steadily, filling the avenue, which had been closed off to traffic by a score of police barricades. The shouts and the cheers became a steady rising chant, ''Morrison, Morrison, Morrison.'' He was loving every minute of it. He forced himself away from the troopers and cops, plowed into the crowd, which closed in around him, pressed the flesh, smiled, waved, rode the crest. The security guards were shouting into their walkie-talkies. Eyes were scanning every face. But Morrison, diving into the crowd, was separating himself by inches, by feet, by yards from his entourage. It was impossible for Rogers or any of the other aides to keep up with him. That was all right with Morrison. He was at the center, which was where he wanted to be.

He stepped back and the cops made a path for him toward the Garden. A man broke through the ranks and tried to reach him. The cops held him back. He shouted something, loud enough to reach Morrison. The mayor paused, looked toward the voice. Harry Gondolian. Morrison made a gesture, and the human barricade parted and Gondolian approached, stepped to Morrison's side, leaned toward him and started to say something. It was impossible to make out words over the deafening roar that enveloped them from all sides. Morrison leaned closer to Gondolian. Gondolian said something again. Morrison stopped and stared at the reporter.

From a distance of ten or twenty feet, Rogers saw it, though he did not hear the shots; no one could have heard them over the din. Morrison's head exploded into a mass of blood and bone fragments; he reeled back and then fell to the pavement. An instant later, Gondolian's head erupted, blood and bone spraying out, and he fell beside Morrison.

There were screams, panic, as people in the crowd tried to flee, shoving, pushing, doing anything to escape. Others were staring upward, not at anything in particular, for there seemed to be nothing to see, but just up at the hotel windows, at the surrounding buildings, pointing in every direction. The cops and the troopers had their guns out, but there was nothing to target. Nobody could figure out where the shots had come from.

Rogers forced his way forward, shouting, until finally he reached Morrison. He knelt down beside the mayor. There was nothing he or anyone could do then. Jack Morrison was dead. He took a quick look at Gondolian. The old newspaperman was dead, too, sprawled lifeless on the pavement. Maybe he was supposed to die soon, but not this way. Rogers started to curse, trying to order his mind, trying to figure out what he ought to do.

A hand touched his arm, held it. He looked up. Bending over him was a tall man in his forties, dressed in a neat summer suit, gray showing at the temples of his dark hair. "Ben," he said, his voice shaking, his face pale, "what the hell . . ."

Rogers tried to shake off the arm, tried to focus. At first, everything was vague.

"Ben," the man said again.

Gradually, Rogers made him out, recognized him. George Strickland, a government agent he had known for years, with whom he had worked on a couple of cases for Morrison down in Washington. Strickland had been close to Morrison for more than a decade, ever since Morrison's stint in the Justice Department. The friendship had continued even after Morrison left Washington and Strickland had moved from the Justice Department to the Secret Service.

Rogers looked up. "George," he said. "Jesus."

"Ben," Strickland said, "let's get the fuck out of here. There's nothing we can do here. Not now." He took Rogers' arm, lifted him from his knees beside Morrison's body. Rogers did not resist as Strickland, flashing a wallet with an official federal shield prominently displayed, led him away, back through the nervous, edgy cops who had gathered uncertainly. He steered Rogers onto the sidewalk and around the corner, into a saloon half down the block.

The bar was crowded, three deep at the counter, everyone staring up at the television screens flickering with colored images of reporters and anchormen in the foreground against a hazy background of the scene just down the block, a panorama of men racing every which way, of blue-and-white cars with their roof lights flashing, sirens shattering the gathering darkness. The sounds came from the television and through the doors of the saloon, the noise blending so it was hard to tell the origin, screen or street.

"Chickens with their heads cut off," Strickland said. "They don't know what the fuck to do." He waved at the bartender, who didn't see him, his eyes on the screen. Strickland shouted. The bartender turned reluctantly. "Scotch," Strickland said. "Twice. And doubles. On the rocks."

The bartender turned away, his eyes still held by the images on the screen, reached blindly for a bottle, glasses, ice, poured, still without looking, carried the glasses, reached across the mob and handed them to Strickland and Rogers. The screen filled then with a scene, by now familiar from constant repetition over the last hour, of a tall man, hand outstretched, moving through a cheering crowd, another smaller man approaching, then both men falling, heads disintegrating.

They drank, Rogers letting the acrid taste burn his throat. "George," he said, "what were you doing out there?"

"My job, Ben," Strickland said. "I was assigned. And it was something I wanted to do. Didn't Morrison tell you that I was going to take a leave and come aboard? Drink up now. Wash it away." He took a deep drink from his own glass.

"He had enemies," Rogers said. "We told him. He wouldn't believe it."

"That kind of enemy?" Strickland said.

Rogers shook his head. "I didn't think that kind."

"Some nut," Strickland said. "Another Oswald, another Sirhan Sirhan, another James Earl Ray. Looking for a place in the history books."

"He's got that."

"You know it. When they find him. And you can bet your ass they will. Before the night's out. Bastards always think they can get away with it. They never do."

"Or maybe they don't care," Rogers said. "Maybe all they want is that moment when they changed the world. Screw the consequences."

The reporters up on the television screen were interviewing the police commissioner, the head of the local FBI office, and the former Public Advocate, now the new mayor, who was acting as though he didn't quite believe it. They all said the same thing. They couldn't understand why anyone would want to kill Morrison. The shot had obviously come from a window in one of the buildings that lined the avenue. A search was going on right then of every room in every building that overlooked the spot. They'd find whoever did it.

"If," Strickland said, "he isn't twenty miles away by now. Which is the probable scenario."

Whatever happened to Gondolian? Rogers thought. Nobody mentioned him. Nobody even thought of him. It was as though he had vanished from the consciousness of those on the screen as thoroughly as he had vanished from life.

They stood around the bar for another half hour, watching the television, watching how the more things changed the more they stayed the same, having another drink.

"Shit," Strickland said finally, "this is a waste. Nothing's going to happen for a while. Let's get the hell out of here."

Rogers nodded.

"What now, Ben?"

Rogers shrugged. "Who knows?"

"Where are you off to?"

"Back there," Rogers said, waving vaguely toward the west, toward the avenue.

"What good can you do?" Strickland said.

"Not much," Rogers said. "But it's where I belong. He wasn't just the guy I worked for. He was my friend." He shook his head, paused, then added, "And so was Gondolian."

"Who?" Strickland said.

"The other guy. The one with him."

"I wondered," Strickland said. He watched Rogers, then, "I think I'll tag along. Maybe I can help. I'm good at that. I know a lot of people. You know that." They started out, moving toward the avenue. Strickland put his hand on Rogers' arm. "Look," he said, "if we get separated, which will probably happen down there, give me a call in the next day or so and we'll put our heads together."

Rogers looked at him. "You still in Washington?"

Strickland shook his head. "The Federal Building here," he said. "Let me give you my number." He reached into his pocket, pulled out a card and handed it to Rogers.

They made their way down the block, toward Seventh Avenue, toward the barricades and people in uniform, the bright lights illuminating the avenue as far as they could see.

5

He hung around for another hour, doing little more than watching and listening while the cops, the troopers, reinforcements from the federal government, and a lot of politicians ran in and out of all the surrounding buildings, finding nothing. But, as Strickland had said, if the shooter was smart, he'd have been long gone thirty seconds after the shots were fired.

After a while, Chief O'Bannion noticed him. "Rogers, for chrissake, go home. You look beat."

"I worked for him," Rogers said. "I thought maybe I could help."

"I've got enough fucking help as it is," O'Bannion said. "I don't need any more. In fact, I could use less. Go home. Get some sleep. I'll want to see you in a couple of days. We're going to have to have a long talk about your future. Call my secretary." The chief turned away. Rogers watched him go, then turned himself and started toward the subway.

The red light on the answering machine glowed. He pressed the button, listened to the messages. Melissa three times from the coast. He'd call her in the morning, when he could think straight. Slowly he took off his clothes and fell into bed.

The phone woke him from bad dreams. He glanced at the clock. Three in the morning. He picked up the phone, muttered something. "Ben. We got the son of a bitch." It took him a moment to orient himself, to recognize the voice. Carlos Rodriguez from Homicide.

He sat straight up in the bed. "Carlos," he said. "Where? When? Who?"

"Not now," Rodriguez said. "Just get down here if you want in."

"Where?"

"The Statler. Fifth floor. Room 547." The line went dead.

It took him less than a half hour to reach the hotel. The street outside was an undulating ocean of humanity, swarming, jostling, shoving in light brighter than day. Huge floodlights illuminated the front of the hotel and the street outside for blocks, and the scene was made even brighter by scores of television lights beaming directly at the front of the hotel. Trying to get through the doors into the interior were maybe a hundred reporters, from all the local newspapers and wire services, and from papers far away, and it looked like the television and radio newsrooms had emptied out, dispatching every available man and woman to the scene.

Using his gold shield as both identification and a magic pass, Rogers tried to squirm his way through the crowd toward the doors and then into the lobby. An army of uniforms guarded the entrance. A couple of them recognized Rogers when he came face-to-face with them. One of them gave him a sour look.

"What do you know," he said, "the mayor's little errand boy." He laughed. "But that's the past. Right? What now, Rogers? Staten Island's my bet." Rogers wasn't particularly popular with the guys in blue, and Morrison had been only a little more so. After all, he had forced a Civilian Complaint Review Board down the department's throat, and he had been trying to enforce a rule requiring cops to live inside city limits. The cop waited a moment, then shoved some of the throng back, making a passage toward the door. Rogers moved through.

He came to halt just inside. It would have been impossible to move any farther; there was not an inch of vacant space. Over the heads of those in front of and around him he saw, at the far end of the lobby, Police Commissioner Michael Sullivan and all the super chiefs: Frederick Beaman, head of the local FBI office; Bobby Simon, who, until a few hours ago had been the Public Advocate and was now the Mayor; and half a dozen others. They squinted into the television lights that blinded them. In front of them was a jungle of microphones.

A hand touched his shoulder. He turned and looked. It was Carlos Rodriguez, muscles bulging under his too-tight jacket; his thinning black hair brushed as usual, straight across his head from a low part, as though it would disguise the fact that he was getting balder by the day.

"You missed the real fun," Rodriguez said. "Up on the fifth floor."

"Yeah?" Rogers said. "Give."

Rodriguez shook his head. "Just listen," he said.

''You'll get the outline. It's like the goddamn newsies have a pipeline to the Almighty. We hardly found the shooter and they were swarming the place. How the hell they found out I'll never know. But they always do.''

Police Commissioner Sullivan had moved toward the microphones. He peered into the television lights out toward the crowd, raised his hand and waited. Gradually the noise died and the lobby grew quiet.

''We have an announcement to make,'' Sullivan said. ''From the way you people got here, I imagine you have an idea what it is. We have the person who killed Mayor Morrison.''

The shouts of who, where, how, and a lot more roared through the room, drowning out whatever Sullivan was about to add. He stepped back, raising his hand for quiet, and waited.

''Hold it,'' Sullivan said. ''If you wait, we'll give you what information we know.''

''Yeah, sure,'' Rodriguez whispered into Rogers' ear. ''He means what he wants to give.''

''Naturally,'' Rogers said.

''To take things in order,'' Sullivan said as the reporters quieted, ''the shooter is now in a room on the fifth floor of the hotel.''

''In custody?'' somebody shouted.

''In a manner of speaking,'' Sullivan said.

Rodriguez grinned broadly.

''What does that mean, Commissioner?''

''The man is dead.'' There was a roar, indecipherable voices shouting. Sullivan waited. ''We had nothing to do with his death. The medical examiner estimates that he has been dead for several hours, since right after the shooting. Apparently he killed himself.''

"How?" A dozen voices shouted that question in unison.

"He put a gun in his mouth and blew the back of his head off," Sullivan said flatly.

"A fuckin' rifle," Rodriguez said. Rogers looked at him. "Later," Rodriguez said.

"The man's name," Sullivan continued, "was Steven Gold, according to papers found in the room, and according to the registration forms he filled out when he checked in. At the present moment, we know little else about him. We're checking. When we know more, we'll tell you."

"How did you find him?" somebody shouted.

"I was about to get to that," Sullivan said. "When we initially checked the floor right after the shooting, that is the rooms facing onto the avenue, the door was locked, the room dark. The hotel manager opened the door for the officers who were searching. A quick look inside revealed nothing of interest at that moment. The officers did not make a thorough search at that time, since there was nothing that seemed suspicious about the room. After all, they were hunting for a live suspect, not a dead one. The fact that he might be dead didn't enter anyone's thinking at that point in time. They left, closing and locking the door behind them.

"A few hours ago," Sullivan continued, "a second search of the hotel was made, this time a more thorough one, by detectives from the Homicide Bureau joined by agents of the Federal Bureau of Investigation. I want to tell you this has been a cooperative enterprise, everyone working in unison."

"Sure," Rodriguez grinned at Rogers. "First time in history. Wanna bet?"

Sullivan went on. "During this more careful, room-by-room search, the door to the room was opened and the lights turned on. At first nothing seemed out of the ordinary. But when the second group of officers entered and began to examine the room, they discovered the body of Mr. Gold together with the weapon."

"Anything else?"

"We're not prepared to say at this time what else was in the room."

"Who is this Steven Gold?"

"According to the registration form and his papers, he's from Los Angeles. We're checking on that now."

"What else?"

"When we know more, we'll tell you."

"Why did he kill Morrison?"

"We're looking into that. At this time we have no answer to that question. We don't speculate."

For another half hour, between the "no comments" and other evasions, Sullivan, Beaman and the others sketched in, with very few details, what they said was the general scenario.

According to the version they played for the press and the public, the shooter, Steven Gold, had checked into the hotel at the beginning of the week. He had a confirmed reservation. They either didn't know or wouldn't say what he had done during the time until the shooting. It appeared, they said, that he was fully aware of Morrison's schedule for the last day of the convention, and apparently also knew enough about the dead mayor to figure out how he would go from the hotel to the Garden. He had obviously posted himself at his window and waited. When Morrison appeared, and when he had a clear shot, he had aimed and fired. He fired twice, in rapid succession. One shot hit Morrison in the head and the second hit Harry Gondolian. He then turned the gun on himself.

"That, ladies and gentlemen," Sullivan said, "is the sum total of what we know at this time. When we know more, you'll be the first to be told. Now, thank you and good night."

He and the others turned away, ignoring the discordant roar of shouted questions hurled by the reporters. They marched away from the microphones, away from the lights, and disappeared into the hotel manager's office.

Rodriguez looked at Rogers. "Okay," he said, "you got what they want to give. Let's go someplace and have some coffee."

As they turned away and started toward the exit, Rogers spotted George Strickland. The federal agent was off to one side of the lobby, leaning against a wall, taking it all in. He looked around then and saw Rogers. He waved a hand, the gesture saying "wait," and then he moved toward them.

"You got a special pipeline?" Strickland said. "I thought you were going home to bed, and now you turn up here."

"Carlos called me," Rogers said. He introduced the two men.

"Where are you off to?" Strickland asked.

"Coffee," Rogers said.

"Mind if I join you?"

"Come ahead."

The three men passed out of the hotel, shoved their way through the crowd, walking south several blocks until they came to an all-night coffee shop. They went inside, took a booth toward the back, as far as they could get from two couples, high school kids maybe, not much older, at a front booth, pouring down black coffee, obviously trying to sober up some before heading home or wherever they were going. Nobody was supposed to serve booze to kids under twenty-one. Rogers knew it. Rodriguez knew it. Strickland knew it. Everybody knew it. It was the law. But it was obvious that somebody didn't give a damn about the law. Maybe the kids had phony ID, but one quick look at the four of them should have told whoever they weren't far from the cradle and he was breaking the law. But then it was a law more on the books than in practice. All you had to do was walk into one of these all-night coffee joints any night of the week, especially on weekends or during the summer, to know that.

A bored guy in a stained white apron stepped around from behind the counter, walked toward them, and paused a couple of feet away as though he wasn't really interested. Rogers and Strickland ordered coffee. Rodriguez ordered herb tea. He was a health food nut. The guy looked at him, shrugged, went back behind the counter, poured two cups from the big metal tureen, poured steaming water into a third and dropped a tea bag into it. Balancing the cups one on top of the other, he carried them to the table, plunked them down and went back to his tabloid.

When they had taken a couple of sips, Rodriguez said, "Did you believe all that garbage?"

Rogers looked at him.

"Shot himself. With a fuckin' rifle. C'mon."

"It's possible," Strickland said.

"Maybe he had arms like a gorilla," Rogers said.

"Yeah. Sure. Only his arms weren't no longer than yours."

"Okay. I'll buy that. What do you know?"

"Enough. I'll tell you," Rodriguez said. "Because I was one of the guys that found him. You know what it looked like? I'll lay it out for you. First he takes a goddamn glass cutter and slices out the window. Then, like he's a sharpshooter, bang-bang, he gets off two shots, kills two guys. Then he sits down, and all nice and easy, he takes off his shoe, puts the fuckin' barrel in his mouth, fires the goddamn trigger, maybe with his toe, for chrissake, and it's good-bye, Charlie, or whatever the fuck his name is. A guy maybe fifty. Middle age anyway. Expensive clothes in the closet and drawers. Tailor-made. A fuckin' movie producer, if you believe the crap he had on him. Rich son of a bitch. Sure, it's possible. Anything's possible. Little green men in flying saucers, that's possible, too."

"You don't buy it?" Strickland said.

"They're buyin' it, that's for sure," Rodriguez said. "They want to wrap this thing up fast, all nice and tidy like a Christmas present."

"But you think the wrapping doesn't fit."

"I want to think about it some more. That's why I'm sittin' here with you guys, to kind of spew it out and see where it lands."

"Something about this whole thing stinks," Rogers said. "Take the damn scenario they laid out for the world."

"What about it?"

"They said he fired twice. He hit Morrison with the first shot and poor Harry Gondolian with the second. It was like he wanted to make sure, so he fired at Morrison the second time, only Morrison was already down so Gondolian was in the line of fire and got it."

"Something wrong with that?" Strickland asked.

"Yeah," Rogers answered, "something's wrong, very wrong. I was maybe four or five feet away. I had a ringside seat. I saw Morrison get it and, maybe a second later, Gondolian. But even at the time, something bothered me, something about the trajectory. I think the shooter changed his aim, not by much, just enough, and if I'm right, he wasn't just trying to blow Morrison away, he was after Gondolian, too."

Rodriguez and Strickland stared at him. "You sure?" Strickland said.

"I'm sure," Rogers said. "You get a chance, take a look at the videotapes. I'm positive they'll show it that way."

"Why?"

"Who knows? Maybe somebody fed them the wrong lines. Maybe nobody took a look at the tapes. Maybe they figured that's the way it should have happened, so that's the way it happened. Whatever, it's something I'm going to find out."

"Count me in," Strickland said.

"Make it three," Rodriguez echoed. "You think maybe he wanted both of 'em?" he asked then.

"That's the way it looks to me," Rogers said. "Maybe I'm wrong, maybe it's the way they said, that he fired twice at Morrison and got Gondolian by mistake with the second. I don't know. I just don't like the way it smells."

Rodriguez thought about that, and slowly nodded. "It's something to look into," he said. Then, "Ben, on that other thing you called about."

It took Rogers a moment to remember. Then he nodded. "Santangello?"

"Right. I been lookin' around. Nothin' definite yet, but I got a couple of leads. Just so you know."

6

The sun was just lightening the summer sky when Rogers turned into his block and headed for his old brownstone. There was somebody sitting on the stoop, slumped over with fatigue, maybe even asleep. As he reached the stoop, she woke and looked up.

"I've been waiting for you," Annie Kendall said.

"All night?"

"A few hours."

"I'm sorry," he said. "There were things to do."

"There always are, especially at times like this," she said. "Why did he have to kill Harry, too?"

Rogers didn't answer. "Come on upstairs," he said. "I'll make you some coffee."

She followed him through the door, up the flight of stairs to the second floor apartment, waited while he unlocked the door, then followed him inside. She stood and watched while he measured out coffee and water and turned on the automatic maker. Her eyes moved about the apartment, examining, taking everything in.

"You don't live here alone," she said when he turned toward her.

"At the moment, yes," he said. "Most of the time, no."

"That figures," she said. "The place is too nice. No man has this kind of taste."

"That's a sexist remark if I ever heard one," he said.

She shrugged. "It's true, nevertheless."

"You just know the wrong kind of guys," he said.

She ignored that, waited a moment, then, "Did you get to talk to him?"

He knew whom she meant. "No," he said. "The last week, things just piled up. There wasn't enough time. I planned to get to him as soon as the convention was over."

"There's never enough time," she said. "Now there's no more time." Her shoulders shook. She straightened, held herself and regained her composure. "Why did they shoot him, too?"

He shook his head.

"I mean," she said, "it was like they weren't just after Morrison. It was like they wanted to get Harry as well. Maybe they wanted to get Harry and got Morrison instead, and then they got Harry."

"Maybe," he said. "And maybe not. Right now, who the hell knows anything? The whole thing doesn't make sense."

"What are you going to do now?"

"Have some coffee," he said, and went back into the kitchen, poured two cups and carried them back to her. They sat on a sofa, put the cups on the marble table in front it, and sipped in silence for a while.

"Why did you come to see me?" he asked. "Why now?"

"I don't know," she said slowly. "I didn't know what to do. Harry liked you. He confided in you. I thought maybe you had some answers."

"None," he said.

"Are you satisfied?"

"No."

"Well, what are you going to do about it?"

He shrugged.

"If you're not going to do anything," she said, "I will."

"Sure," he said.

"You don't think I can?"

"Harry said you were good," he said.

"He was right. I am."

"You'll be asking for trouble."

"You think I care?"

He studied her. "The stuff Harry had," he said after a silence that dragged on, "the things he wanted me to look into. He must have had files, notes, that kind of thing."

"He did."

"You know where they are?"

"Yes. I've been going over them all night."

"Are you going to share?"

She didn't answer immediately. Then, "I'll think about it. It depends."

"On what?"

"On what you intend to do with them."

"It depends on what's in them."

"Enough," she said. "A start anyway."

"Then I want to see them."

"Let me think about that," she said.

"You've already thought," he said. "That's what brought you here now."

"Maybe," she said. "That, and other things."

"What?"

"I wanted to take a good look at you."

"You're looking. What do you see?"

"I'll let you know in a day or so."

"Meanwhile?"

She looked away, then back at him. Her expression was unreadable. Suddenly she got up. "Thanks for the coffee," she said. "It's time for me to go home." She started toward the door.

"You'll be in touch?" he said, watching her.

She paused, her hand on the doorknob, her eyes holding on his face. "I'll be in touch," she said, and then was gone.

It had been a lousy day and a lousier night, and it didn't get any better. The sky was turning from night black to predawn gray by the time Rogers tossed his clothes into a heap in the corner of the bedroom and flopped across the bed. He was exhausted, both muscles and mind like lead and about as responsive, but sleep didn't come. He'd drunk too much of what they called coffee but tasted more like ten-times reheated dishwater laced with caffeine at that all-night diner. His mind wouldn't stop replaying, in real time and slow motion, those blood-drenched seconds when the heads of first Morrison and then Gondolian shattered and filled the street with brains and bone and blood. He played the images back, looking for something, for anything that he might have done to stop it, any clue that he'd missed along the way, and found nothing. Sometime in the middle of a replay, sleep came.

The phone woke him a couple of hours later, bringing him back to a sun-drenched morning and a world that had changed beyond recognition. He turned in the bed, stared at the phone, and let it ring a couple of times, his eyes going toward the bedside clock radio. Nine o'clock. He reached for the phone and mumbled his name through the foul morning aftertaste that coated the inside of his mouth.

The day got a little better then. He heard his name and he heard Melissa's voice from three thousand miles away asking with concern, "Are you all right?" It was six in L.A. "I've been trying to call you all night."

All right? It was a dumb question, if you thought about it. The whole damn world, the world as it had been twenty-four hours before, had changed so drastically that it was no longer recognizable. Morrison was dead and so was Gondolian, and so was that guy Steven Gold who they said was the shooter, and maybe he was and then again maybe he wasn't, but he was dead, too, and where the hell did that leave the city and the state, and, in particular, where the hell did that leave Rogers? So was he okay? Without thinking, he said, "Sure."

"Really?" she said.

He'd never lied to her, and he didn't want to begin now. He said, "No, not really."

"I can't believe it," she said.

"Who can?"

"Do they know who?"

He guessed the news hadn't reached the west coast yet, or more likely, she hadn't turned on the radio or the television or picked up the papers, so she hadn't heard. "They think so," he said, keeping the doubts out of his voice.

"Good," she said. "At least there's that. And you, what are you going to do?"

"Who the hell knows," he said. "Too soon to think about that."

"I'm coming to be with you," she said. "I'm taking the noon plane out of here."

"I think I like that," he said. Then, "You can do it?"

"It's the weekend," she said. "They don't need me until Monday."

"What airline?"

She told him.

"I'll be there," he said. "With bells on."

There was no question about trying to go back to sleep after they'd both hung up. Even if he wanted to, it would have been impossible. He went into the bathroom, shaved, showered, and dressed, then went into the kitchen and made coffee. He picked up the papers from the mat outside the door and scanned them quickly while he waited for the coffee. The headlines were screamers, big, black, and bordered, but the stories underneath contained nothing he didn't already know. He knew they wouldn't. There just hadn't been time either to collect any late news or to print anything that had been discovered in the last couple of hours.

He poured coffee, then switched on the radio while he sipped and began to learn a little more. The radio and TV people had obviously been out through the early hours, camping on people's doorsteps, ringing bells— phone and door—waking people from sound sleep and asking all those questions no sensitive person, or at least nobody not jaded by or impervious to disasters could bring himself to pose, and searching every record available in those small hours. How much of what they had learned was true and how much was only speculation, half-truths, distortions, or just plain lies would only emerge later. Meanwhile, it was being spread across the airwaves, and if it turned out to be not so, it would make no difference, it would become the accepted truth and the real truth would never supplant it.

Rogers had been through it often enough to listen now with a skeptical ear. Still, he listened, and if what he heard didn't totally add up and didn't completely come together to form a logical picture, he filed the pieces away, figuring that later he would take them out and in a cold light try to find a meaning in them.

Steven Gold was not exactly a nonentity. It was still early, of course, so there were plenty of gaps. But the correspondents had put together enough over the last hours to sketch at least an outline of the man now labeled an assassin. Rogers listened to the reports, made notes and, when the commentators were starting to repeat themselves, tried to sort it all out and make some sense of what he had heard.

He had a problem. It didn't add up. Gold just didn't fit the classic profile of an assassin. A lot more would emerge over the next few hours and days, naturally, so maybe the missing elements would be there. But at this moment, they weren't.

Gold was, in fact, the antithesis of the classic assassin. He was a man who had risen from a background of poverty in the Bronx to carve out a place for himself and make his mark in the world where entertaining people was a major business. He had graduated with honors from one of the city's prestigious special high schools and gone to Columbia on scholarship. In the first years after his graduation he had been some kind of assistant to an assistant on a couple of Broadway shows, one of those names that appears in insignificant and barely readable type at the back of *Playbill*. About twenty-five years ago, he had packed up and gone west to seek fame and fortune, it seemed, in the movies, not as an actor but as a producer. His career on the west coast had been a study in onward and upward. He was recognized as a success in his profession by his peers. He had won praise for the quality of his films and awards, including two Oscars, and was generally admired. He was rich, very rich, Hollywood rich, with a mansion in Bel Air, a weekend place in Malibu, a retreat in Aspen. And like so many of the Hollywood rich, he was an outspoken advocate of noble causes, putting his money where his mouth was. He was, these first reports said, married to a one-time starlet, an apparently successful marriage that had lasted about twenty years, and from which had issued a couple of kids, a boy and a girl, both teenagers.

As interesting as anything in the reports, perhaps most interesting, was what one his friends, who came awake long enough in the middle of the night to talk to a reporter, said. According to him, Gold was an admirer of Morrison, and had actually anted up the legal limit for the Morrison campaign. He had gone to New York, the friend said, to be in on the mayor's triumph and offer his help in the campaign to come.

As far as Rogers could see, there was nothing there that would mark Gold a potential danger to anyone. Maybe something would come out later. But at this moment, some very large questions leaped out. If Gold was the assassin, why? If not, had he been set up, and if so, why?

It was early afternoon by the time he left the apartment and set out for City Hall. He wasn't sure exactly why he was going there, but he wasn't sure then what else to do, where else to go. The world might have changed around him, but he needed a sense of order, a sense of routine, of doing things as he normally did them just to keep his sanity. Maybe it was Saturday, but he was used to working seven days a week, and he wanted to keep to that, especially this day.

There was a pall over City Hall when he came out of the subway into the park that fronted the low classic building. The flags were at half-staff. But it was more than that. There was that sense of the world coming to a halt, and not just because it was a summer weekend and a lot of people were probably out on the sands in the Hamptons or Coney Island or Jones Beach or somewhere. Though maybe they weren't, not this weekend, not after what had happened.

There were clusters of people standing around, looking as though they weren't sure why they were there, or what they ought to be doing. They were just standing, looking up at the flags, at City Hall, at nothing. A long line of silent people moved steadily up the stairs and into the building, their faces, their body language expressing shock and disorientation. A second line moved unsteadily through the arches, heading down the stairs, some of the people crying, the tears staining their cheeks. The silence was eerie, as though somebody had dropped a muffler across the face of the city.

Rogers watched for a moment, then turned away and went into the building by a side entrance and down to his office in the basement. It was as he had left it, nothing disturbed. He switched on the air conditioner, then walked across and sat behind his desk, staring blankly at the walls. He looked up. There was a steady shuffling sound on the floor above. He glanced at the answering machine. The light glowed. He switched it on. A message from Carlos Rodriguez, at mid-morning. Just the name and a please call when you can. A message from Strickland, a half hour earlier. Strickland had tried the apartment, he said, and left a message there. He figured maybe Rogers had decided to go in, so he was leaving another message in the office. Either way, when Rogers got the message, he should call so they could get together and begin to sort things out. Strickland had picked up some stuff that was of interest. Anyway, he wanted to share it.

Rogers switched off the machine, sat back, staring at the ceiling, listening to the shuffling, trying to focus on what had happened over the last twenty-four hours, trying to come to an understanding of the uncertain future. There were no answers. He shook his head, rose and went out the door and up the stairs into the rotunda. In the center, flanked by an honor guard of cops, state troopers, and National Guard, and behind velvet ropes, was a closed coffin draped in the flags of the city, the state, and the nation. The endless parade shuffled past, pausing a moment to stare down at the coffin, some people genuflecting, crossing themselves, murmuring silent prayers, crying softly. For all his faults and ambitions, Morrison had reached these people, and they had come to mourn him, not knowing what else to do. Rogers stood and watched them, thinking that it must have been like this back in the 1960s when the nation had mourned Kennedy in much the same way.

He turned away and went out of the building, nodding to a couple of people he knew, but saying nothing. He wandered, his feet taking him north, up Mulberry Street. The narrow street was crowded as usual for a hot summer afternoon, but there was a difference. People wandered about, but there was a strange silence. The crowds might pause to look in the shop windows, which was normal, but when you looked closer, you saw they really weren't seeing the wares laid out for their inspection, they looked like they had lost their sense of direction and were just going through old motions, trying to hold onto the familiar with a kind of desperation, as though anchoring themselves to what still existed. In a dozen store windows he noticed old, fading pictures of Jack Kennedy, and now, adjacent, hurriedly framed and draped with black ribbons, pictures of Jack Morrison. Even here, where Morrison's popularity had been a sometime thing, there was the same shock, the same sense of loss that had spread like a storm of tears across the entire city.

It had not been his intention to walk this way, but then he had not meant to walk any way, had merely wandered without thought and without direction, letting his feet take him where they would while his mind grappled with the new world. But now he found himself standing before a nondescript building just off Mulberry Street, staring at the small bronze plaque announcing the office of Parnassus Associates, real estate. There was nothing for him here now, nothing that the powerful man in the office upstairs could do for him. He started to turn away.

The door suddenly opened. Generoso Ruggieri stepped through into the afternoon sun. For half a century, Ruggieri had inevitably been surrounded by a covey of hard-eyed guys in tight-fitting suits, their eyes as steely and alert, and as expressionless, as their faces. Not this time. Today there was just a single man one step behind, hardly a bodyguard, only a guy in his middle years and a little soft, a little paunchy, dressed not in a suit but in a polo shirt with a fashionable insignia, a pair of light-colored summer trousers, and new running shoes. He looked like a retainer, not someone who could move fast, not someone who was packing a piece and was ready to use it.

As always, Ruggieri was in an expensive suit, summer weight for the weather, a neat solid maroon silk tie at the neck of his white shirt, black shoes so highly polished they reflected the images of the mid-afternoon street. He had aged in the time since Rogers had last seen him, more than might be expected. He was probably eighty, maybe even older. He used to look twenty years younger. Now he looked his age, and he looked tired, his normally ruddy complexion sallow.

Ruggieri saw him and halted. The look they exchanged said the last time would not be mentioned, would be buried in the back of the mind, deep enough to pretend that day had not happened.

Ruggieri smiled, a warm smile, even his usually cold eyes warming with the greeting. "Mr. Rogers," he said. "A surprise, and a pleasure. Much time has passed. You have come to see an old man?"

Rogers shook his head. "Just an accidental meeting," he said. "I just happened to be walking by."

"Of course," Ruggieri said. "But, still, you will walk with me a little?"

Rogers nodded. "Why not? Where?"

"Just about the neighborhood. My doctor tells me if I would live a little longer I must exercise. And watch my diet, of course. So every afternoon I walk for thirty minutes. I will tell you in all honesty, I would prefer a little pasta, a little wine. But the doctor says now those things must be only a memory. Though, what should I do with a few more years, a man of my age? Still, the doctor orders, and a doctor's orders must be obeyed. Why else would one pay a doctor?" He reached out and put one hand on Rogers' arm, and together they moved along the street at a slow pace. The retainer moved with them, a step behind.

"You have been well?" Ruggieri asked.

"Yes," Rogers said. "And you?"

"For a man of my years, as well as can be expected. Your grandmother, she continues in good health?"

"For a woman her age," Rogers echoed, "as well as can be expected."

"That woman," Ruggieri said, "she will outlive us all. And your young lady, the so beautiful Melissa. All is well with her, and between you?"

"Yes," he said. "She's in Hollywood right now, making a movie."

"Yes," Ruggieri said. "I have heard that her career flourishes. For that, I am happy. When you see her, you must extend my regards. She is a remarkable young lady, wiser than her years."

They walked a block in silence, Ruggieri nodding now and then to people in the street, the people bowing to him with respect, the neighborhood people anyway. Strangers just stared. If they didn't know who he was, they immediately recognized that he must be someone important.

"It was a terrible thing that happened yesterday," Ruggieri said.

"It was," Rogers said. "But I thought you didn't have much use for Morrison. He'd been out to get you for years."

"He failed in that," Ruggieri said. "But you are right, I did not like him. I thought he was a man with two faces who spoke from all sides of his mouth. He spoke what his listeners wished to hear. It was never possible to know if he truly believed the words he spoke. Even so, it is a terrible thing to kill a man of stature, a man of authority, not because of the man himself but because of what he represents and because of the uncertainty that follows. To kill a man of importance, a mayor, a governor, a

president, is to show all men that they too are mortal and
vulnerable, and that is a thing men do not want to accept.
So the world must strike out blindly in all directions, and
many will suffer. The murder of this man Morrison will
affect many men in many worlds. Nothing good can come
of it. I hear they know the man who killed him, and that
he has killed himself.''

"That's what they say," Rogers said without emotion.

Ruggieri halted, turned, and looked at him searchingly.
"You do not believe it?"

"I had a friend," Rogers said, "who used to say that
before you believed the simple answer, you'd better take
a look at all the alternatives."

"A wise man," Ruggieri said. "I would like to meet
him."

"His name was Felix Palmieri, and he's dead."

"Ah yes, I remember. He was your partner. It was a sad
thing. A murder that, like all murders, had consequences
beyond expectations. How can I help you?" Ruggieri
said. "I will do what I can if you would like my assistance,
but I must tell you I no longer have the resources. I
have retired. At my age, one should put aside matters of
business. That is for younger, more ambitious men. At
my age, it is enough merely to live each day."

Rogers had heard the rumors over recent months that
Ruggieri had withdrawn from the empire he had created
as much as inherited from those who had gone before.
He had not completely believed them. Very few men of
his power had ever left any way but feet first. Maybe
Frank Costello and one or two others, but not many. In
a ruthless world, the ambitious remove every obstacle on
their climb to power. Ruggieri had done that so many
years before, and it would have been natural if it had

been done to him. Still, times change and the prisons, as much as the graveyards, were filling with the bosses and the under bosses and the ordinary soldiers, new and more ruthless rivals, from Latin America, Asia, and elsewhere were moving in on what had once been private preserves at the same time that the natural inheritors were finding their own way into a more legitimate world where the rewards were, if not as great, still great, and the risks far less dangerous.

It is a wise man who recognizes when his time has passed and the available rewards are no longer worth the risks. If there was one thing about Generoso Ruggieri it was that he was not stupid. His eyes had always seen a longer distance down the road than most of his contemporaries and rivals, which was one reason he had lasted in power so long, and been so impervious to those who had tried to unseat him. Now, perhaps seeing the future clearly, he had made the necessary decisions and been allowed to make them, and so, perhaps, the rumors were true after all.

Ruggieri saw the initial skepticism in Rogers. He smiled a little. "Believe it," he said. "It is true. Still, if you need something that is within my power, there are people who owe me favors, and I will do what I can."

Rogers thought about that. This man was, after all, his grandfather, though neither of them would acknowledge it, certainly not in public. Ruggieri had known it before Rogers did, which was probably why Ruggieri had never asked a favor of him, never sought to compromise him, had in the past offered and given his help without seeking a fair exchange, or any exchange at all. He decided to take a shot. "Have you heard," he asked, "that Victor Santangello is on the streets?"

Ruggieri looked at him, then nodded slowly. "I have heard. People tell me they have seen him. I can only assume he made some arrangement with the federal people, some fair exchange. I would not put it above him."

"He hated Morrison."

"That is common knowledge." Ruggieri thought a moment. "You think perhaps he had a hand in the events of yesterday?"

"I don't know. Anything's possible."

"You would like to know his movements, his interests?"

"I wouldn't mind."

"I will ask. I cannot promise anything. But I will ask."

"I can't ask for anything more."

"You have others looking into this, too."

"Of course."

"Good. Now, what will you do?"

Rogers understood that Ruggieri was onto another subject. He shrugged. "It's not up to me."

"You are not popular with the people in power in your department. You no longer have a protector in high places. These could be very difficult times for you."

"I'll get by."

"I am sure you will."

They had come full circle in the half hour, were back now in front of Ruggieri's building. The older man stopped, released Rogers' arm and turned toward the door. He looked back over his shoulder. "Come and see me again. I have much time and I am at your command. If I learn anything, I will get a message to you. Meanwhile, stay well and protect yourself." He disappeared then through the door. The retainer, memorizing Rogers' face first, followed.

8

Dusk was settling over the city as he turned from the parkway into Kennedy Airport, the distant skyline of Manhattan flickering through the haze. He parked and headed for the terminal, passed inside and down the concourse, flashing his shield at the guards to get access to the arrival area. The plane from the coast reached the ramp and began to unload, the passengers hurrying along the red carpet into the terminal. He spotted Melissa the moment she appeared and moved toward her. She saw him and reached out, their arms going around each other and holding on.

"God, I missed you," she said.

"Likewise," he said. He held her off for a moment, fixing on her face. She looked troubled, even a little angry. "What's up?" he asked.

"Later," she said. "In the car."

"Whatever you say. How long can you stay?"

"I have to make the plane back tomorrow night. They need me on Monday."

"You can't stay longer?"

"Not this time. Pretty soon we'll be done and I'll be back."

"Until the next time."

She gave him a look. "If they want me," she said.

"They want you." He took the small overnight case from her hand. "Well, let's make the most of the time we've got."

They turned and moved together through the terminal and out to the parking lot where they retrieved the car. She sat silently in the passenger seat, staring through the window while he paid the parking fee and drove out onto the access road, heading for Manhattan. Then she turned and looked at him. He caught the look from the corner of his eye.

"Okay. What is it?" he asked.

"He didn't do it, you know," she said, the tone matter-of-fact, as though the statement was a given.

"Who didn't do what?"

"The papers this morning, the radio, the TV, they're all saying Steve Gold killed Morrison and that reporter, and then he killed himself. Steve Gold never killed anybody. And he had no reason to kill himself."

"I'm listening."

"Anybody who knows him knows he isn't capable of killing anyone. Or anything. Just ask."

"You know him?"

"Of course. And so do you, if you think back. At least you've met him."

He thought. The memory didn't come.

"The first time you came out to the coast, right after I got there," she said. "He produced that first film I did. We went to a thing at his house. There must have been a zillion people, but he came over and introduced himself."

He found a vague memory then of a guy with thick glasses, a tanned face and, in the non-Hollywood style of the moment, a dark suit with a white button-down shirt and striped tie knotted at the neck, and gleaming black shoes. He had no memory of the conversation, and he probably couldn't pick the guy out of a lineup of ten stock brokers or bankers, or even lawyers, with glasses and dressed that way. But if Melissa said Gold was the guy he'd met that night, then it had to be Gold.

"How well do you know him?" he asked.

"Very well," she said. "He and his wife, Abigail, have kind of looked out for me. They found me my house. They've introduced me to a lot of people. Abby and I see a lot of each other. I know him well enough to know he isn't capable of doing something like that."

"People can always surprise you," he said mildly.

"Not him," she said flatly, as though there wasn't a possibility of anyone contradicting her.

"That's what his friends were saying on the radio this morning," he said.

"They're right, of course."

"You're all so sure?"

"Yes, damn sure," she said. "With good reason." She looked straight at him, and he caught that look, too. "I want you to clear his memory," she said. "I don't want Abby and the kids to have to live with this for the rest of their lives. I want you to do something. You're good at it and you can do it."

"Just like that? What do you think I can do? The department's already got this thing marked solved and closed. As of three this morning."

"Reopen it," she said.

He laughed, but not with humor. "Easier said than

done. I'm not God Almighty, or even the commissioner. And you know precisely the kind of clout I have.''

''You've done harder. When you had to.''

''Oh yeah, sure.''

''Come out to the coast,'' she said. ''I'll arrange it for you to talk with Abby, talk with other people who know Steve.'' She kept her eyes on his face. Then she stopped. There was something in his expression. ''You don't think he did it, do you?'' she said suddenly.

''I don't know,'' he said slowly, not looking at her, keeping his eyes on the road. ''One thing I do know, there are too many loose ends, too many things that don't add up. It's like somebody gave you a bunch of loose pieces and told you to put them together and they'd make a whole. But when you try, what you find out is they're from different puzzles so there's no way you can make them fit. I'm not the only one who feels that way, for your information. Carlos Rodriguez has the same uneasy feeling, and so does a fed I know who used to work for Morrison, a guy named George Strickland. We tossed it around late last night. No answers, just a lot of questions.''

''So you will look into it.''

''Strictly on my own. The department wouldn't like it, nobody would like it.''

''I don't care. Just do it. You've got vacation time, and a lot more that's owed you.''

''I'll think about it,'' he said.

''Don't think. Do.''

The ride into the city was easy. After all, it was the middle of a hot summer weekend, so the people who had gone to their summer places wouldn't be returning until Sunday night at the earliest, and those who had gone to beaches for the day were staying until the last minute. Even death, assassination, couldn't keep people in the city to swelter unless they had no choice. Plans made were plans kept. So the Long Island Expressway had far fewer cars than usual, no tie-ups anywhere, and they were through the Midtown Tunnel and pulling into the garage a couple of blocks from their house in less than an hour.

Rogers turned off the motor, left the key in the ignition, waved to the garage attendant, and then reached over and retrieved Melissa's overnight case from the back seat. Together they set out for home. As they approached the building, Rogers saw somebody camped out on the stoop. The guy looked up, saw Rogers, rose, and started forward. George Strickland.

"Where the hell have you been?" Strickland said. "I've been waiting for a couple of hours. I figured you couldn't have gone to Timbuktu." He saw the suitcase in Rogers' hand, and then saw Melissa and did a double take. "Well, well," he said. "I could be wrong." He looked at her again. "I know you," he said.

"I don't think so," she said.

"I'm sure. I never forget a face."

Rogers grinned at him. "Go to the movies?"

Strickland took another look at Melissa. His face brightened. "So that's it," he said. "I knew I'd seen that face somewhere."

Rogers introduced them then. Melissa studied Strickland and nodded.

"You've got taste, Ben," Strickland said with a smile.

"Maybe I'm the one with taste," Melissa said.

"Hanging around with Ben?" Strickland said. "Not bloody likely."

"You guys," she said. "You think it's always the man

who takes the lead. You never give a woman credit for anything."

Strickland laughed. "I'm just a throwback to my youth," he said. "Women's lib passed me by. I still stand up in the subway and give a lady my seat."

"Not such a bad thing," Melissa said. "It's other things that count."

"Why the hell are we standing out here in the street?" Rogers said. "Come on upstairs. We'll turn on the air conditioner and get cool."

Upstairs, the air conditioner did its work and the apartment cooled off quickly. Melissa took her case into the bedroom, dropped it on the bed and returned.

Rogers and Strickland settled into the cool of the living room. "Where the hell have you been?" Strickland said. "I've been trying to reach you all day. Left a message here and in the office. You didn't return them."

"I've been around," Rogers said. "Here and there. There were things to do, things to think about."

"I told you last night," Strickland said, "two heads are better than one. Besides, I've been doing some checking, found out a few things."

"Is this private or can anyone join in?" Melissa stood in the doorway, watching them.

Strickland looked across at her. "Join the fun," he said. He turned back to Rogers. "I think I've found some answers. You're not going to like them, not after what we were thinking."

"She knew him," Rogers said.

"Who?"

"Gold."

Strickland turned and stared at her. "How?" he demanded. "Where? When?"

"Out on the coast," she said. "He produced my first picture."

"That's all?"

"No. We got to be friends. His wife is an even better friend. I saw a lot of her, and him."

"So you think you know them," Strickland said.

"I don't think. I know."

"Nobody knows anybody," Strickland said. "The guy had a secret life. Everybody does. I wonder if he ever told his wife. I kind of doubt it. It's not a thing you're likely to talk about."

"What are you talking about?" she asked.

"I'll tell you. I never forget a face, and I never forget a name. When I got home, I couldn't get to sleep. That name, Steven Gold, kept rattling around, and I kept trying to remember where and why. At first I dismissed it. There are lots of guys named Steven Gold. But when I saw his picture on the news this morning, I knew it was the same guy. Maybe he was a lot older, dressed different, but he hadn't changed all that much. Nobody really does. First thing, I started to do some checking, went back into my old files, punched up some stuff on the computer, and bingo, I hit the home run. Maybe they had the right guy after all. We know he had the means. For chrissake, he had the goddamn rifle. We know he had the opportunity. He was in the room with a clear view of the street. What we didn't know was why the hell the guy would do it. The motive. Well, now we've got that."

Rogers stared at him. "What are you talking about?"

"I'll tell you. It's a long story, and not a very pretty one, and it goes back a long way. You remember—no, you wouldn't remember, you're too young, both of you. But anyway, about twenty-five years ago, back when I was still pretty new—remember, I was NYPD in those days, before I went to Washington and got honest—I was working on the DA's squad. One of the assignments they threw at me was to work with the vice squad, which was a lousy assignment, and, when you come to it, not a thing I'm particularly proud of, but that was what they threw at me, so I did it. So there we were, with crime in the streets, the Mafia running a million rackets and not much competition except among themselves, teenage gangs wherever you looked, and horse all over the place. They used to call that strip along Broadway Needle Park in those days, what with everybody sitting on those benches and shooting up, right in plain view, and the pushers wandering around like they had public pushcarts. But what were we doing to fight the crime wave, as they used to call it? Busting hookers and queers. That was the big thing, bagging fairies." He looked across at Melissa. "I know. We don't call them that anymore. It ain't politically correct. But in those days, they were queers and fairies and faggots and a lot of other names, and the way we went after them you'd have thought they were public enemies number one through one hundred, and anything you could do to get them was all right with the public out there. It wasn't like they were infecting everybody with AIDS then; hell, nobody had even heard of that, it didn't exist. It was just that they were perverts, and people thought maybe they were right in Salem and they ought to be burned at the stake or something, or at least put away."

"How people live their lives, their sex lives if you insist, is their own damn business, isn't it?" Melissa said.

"Sure," Strickland said, "at least these days. They

don't even have to stay in the closet anymore. But back then, even the closet wasn't a safe place."

"Some people," she said, "thought the world was going to come to an end if they let gays into the police department or the army or anyplace, but it was all right to have guys running around tearing the clothes off every woman they met. That showed they were all-American boys."

"Times haven't changed all that much," Strickland said.

"They haven't, have they?"

"What the hell do gays have to do with all this?" Rogers said.

"That's what I was about to tell you," Strickland said. "Back then, I was part of the fairy patrol. I was just a green kid and I suppose I must have looked like a punk. My job was to circulate, act like I was one of them, and when they came on, the backup would move in and that would be that. In those days, there were all those bathhouses. A lot of them were just what they were supposed to be, places where people who lived in the tenements and the cold-water flats could go once a week, get clean, real clean, even get a massage and all the rest. But some of them were places where fairies met other fairies, went into private little rooms and did their thing.

"There was a bathhouse on the west side over near the theatre district. That was a joint people in the arts used to frequent. We knew it and the high muckety-mucks decided to close it down, and in the process make a good haul of some very important people. There were guys in the department who figured those people might be very useful some day. They wouldn't want this kind of thing to come out. You got to remember, it wasn't like today.

Everybody was in the closet and you were screwed good and proper if people found out you had peculiar appetites. I got sent in, checked my clothes, grabbed a towel and began wandering about. In about five minutes I must have stumbled onto twenty guys in what they used to call *in flagrante delicto*. I got the word out and five minutes later the place was swarming with the vice squad. The paddy wagon backs up, and those twenty guys, half of whom were still in the altogether, got marched out and hauled off to night court.

"One of the guys we bagged that night was a kid from the theatre. He couldn't have been more than twenty-two, twenty-three. The thing is, his name was Steven Gold, and he was none other than our Steven Gold. And the ADA who drew the case that night was John Morrison, our future mayor. You looking for the motive? There it is."

"That's ridiculous," Melissa said.

"Not back then," Strickland said.

"What happened to them?" Rogers asked.

"I'm not sure," Strickland said. "My files don't say. My job ended when I told the judge that night what I'd seen. I don't think I ever did learn how it came out after that. Except from what I read, Gold blew town right after."

"So Steve Gold waited twenty-five years to take revenge on the man who prosecuted him? I said it before, I'll say it again, it's ridiculous," Melissa said sharply. "Kids the age he was then experiment with all kinds of things. And then they drop them. Steve was married. He has children. There's never been a whisper about him, even among the gay crowd. Even if he did swing both ways, what difference would it make, why would he kill somebody?"

"You get tarred with a brush, the tar doesn't come off easy," Strickland said. "Maybe it's okay with young kids, but when you get to be middle-aged, with a reputation and a wife and a family, it wouldn't be a nice thing to have come out. I think a guy like that would do just about anything to protect what he'd built up over the years. And there was one other thing. That night in the bathhouse, he was with another kid. The kid was younger, only about eighteen. When we put them in the lockup, before the arraignment, that kid put his belt around his neck and hung himself. I know, somebody should have taken the belt, but they didn't. Nobody figured on what happened. But I'd say that thing must have really hit Gold hard. It had to. What person wouldn't be shattered by something like that?"

"Maybe you're right," Rogers said. "But why the hell wait twenty-five years?"

"Like I said," Strickland said, "you never can tell what eats away at people. Maybe it ate away at him. Maybe watching Morrison rising to the top, about to grab the brass ring, was too much. Maybe somebody was putting a little pressure on him, letting him know the story was going public. It could have been Morrison himself, for all that. You know how he squirreled the dirt away and pulled it out when he needed it. It could have been somebody with him who had access. Who knows? According to what people say, he was a big booster of the mayor, talking him up, making nice, tossing money every which way into the campaign war chest. I'd say he was doing that as entry, to get close and do what maybe he'd been thinking about all through the years, do it at the moment when it would mean something. Wait until the revenge is sweetest. I say now it looks like they got the right guy after all.''

''So now you buy the official line,'' Rogers said.

''Until I hear something better,'' Strickland said.

''It's an interesting theory, I'll give it that much,'' Melissa said. ''But it won't wash.''

They turned and stared at her.

''You're saying Steve Gold planned this whole thing, came to New York to do it, sat in his hotel window, aimed a rifle, and killed the mayor who was at least a hundred feet away with one shot? It couldn't have happened in a million years.''

''How do you know?''

''For one thing, he hated guns. One of his causes was not just gun control but outlawing guns. Perhaps you could argue with that, say it was all a pose. But there's something else you can't argue with. Steve Gold was practically blind. He wore glasses so thick you could barely make out his eyes. Abby told me he was scheduled for a cataract operation. The man couldn't see five feet in front of him.''

Rogers watched her carefully. ''You know this for sure?''

''For a certainty,'' she said. ''I was with him often enough to see how he fumbled even to find a light switch.''

Rogers turned to Strickland. ''What does that do to your theory?''

Strickland shrugged and gave a resigned laugh. ''It sounded good. It played,'' he said. ''But you never know. There's always the unexpected, something you couldn't figure.''

''You still buy it?''

"Let's say, I'm open to suggestions. You got any?"

"At the moment, I don't have anything definite. Just a few ideas."

"Like I said, two heads are better than one. Don't forget, I'm available."

"Make me a drink," Melissa said as soon as Strickland was gone. "That was more than I could take."

9

In the dusk of Sunday, Rogers drove Melissa to the airport and put her on the plane for California. They had had less than twenty-four hours, but they had been good and necessary hours. Once Strickland left, they had erected a wall around themselves to keep out the world of assassinations and rumors and accusations and questions that could not be answered. They had risen late, and over breakfast read through the papers, all the stories about the assassination and about Morrison and Gold, and the sidebars about Harry Gondolian, finding in them all speculation, attempts that failed to find a motive for Gold as the assassin. There was little Rogers did not already know, and there was nothing about the old story that Strickland had recited the night before. But then it was a weekend and old files were hard to come by, even if anything did exist in them.

In the late afternoon on the way to JFK, they stopped at Gracie Mansion and joined the parade of the politicians, VIPs, and others of enough importance to gain admittance. Janet Morrison was in the middle of the long main room, greeting those who had come to pay their condolences, accepting their uncertain words, if she even heard them, with a regal grace. She was stoic, though perhaps the stoicism was more shock than anything else. She kept looking around, toward the doors, as though expecting Morrison to appear at any moment.

Rogers and Melissa moved with the procession that approached her and passed by. When they reached her, she took Melissa's hands and held them tightly. "It's so nice of you to come," she said. Then she looked closer. "I thought you were still in California."

"I flew in last night. Just for the day. I'm flying back tonight."

Janet Morrison nodded, reached for Rogers' hands and held them tightly. Her palms were hot and dry. She looked directly into his eyes. "Why would anyone do it, Ben?" she said. "I can't understand it. All he wanted was to do the best for people. Why would anyone do such a thing?"

Rogers only shook his head.

As he started to move on, she stopped him. "Ben, would you be a pallbearer? He would have wanted that."

He could only nod.

"The funeral will be on Tuesday. I wanted it at Trinity Church. He loved that place. It had memories. But they said it was too small. So it's going to be at the Cathedral of St. John the Divine. I'll have someone call you with the details."

They moved on then, and a few minutes later were back in the car and heading over the bridge. At the airport gate, she held him, then stood off and looked into his face. "Don't wait long," she said. "Come out to the coast as soon as you can. Talk to Abby."

''As soon as I can,'' he agreed. ''There are things to do first. I'll let you know.''

The trip back from the airport took nearly two hours. It was Sunday night, the end of a summer weekend, and the returning traffic moved at a slow crawl, when it moved at all. It was late when he reached the apartment and unlocked the door. As he closed the door behind him, he saw a plain white envelope on the floor. Inside was a short note. ''Santangello has made a deal with the federal government.'' That was it.

He went to the phone and pressed the buttons, waited. After the fourth ring, Carlos Rodriguez answered.

''Carlos,'' he said. ''Sorry to disturb you on the weekend.''

''There aren't any weekends,'' Rodriguez said. ''Not now. You know it. What's up, Ben?''

''Santangello. He made a deal with the feds.''

There was a pause. ''I heard it, too,'' Rodriguez said. ''One of my stoolies. He's trying to pin it down. Where'd you hear it?''

''From somebody who ought to know.''

''Okay. I won't ask who. He tell you what feds?''

''No. Just the feds in general. Not even what kind of deal.''

''My stoolie's supposed get back to me, maybe even tonight. I hear anything more, I'll be in touch.'' It sounded as though he was about to hang up, then decided otherwise. ''About the other thing,'' he said.

''Yeah.''

''You read the papers?''

''Of course.''

"Nothing we didn't already know. They bought it, hook, line, and sinker."

"So did Strickland. Almost, anyway."

"What do you mean? I thought, the other night, you know . . ."

Rogers laid it out for him.

There was a long pause while Rodriguez absorbed the information. Then, "So your lady friend says he couldn't possibly have been the shooter."

"That's what she says. And I believe her."

"Strickland believes her, too?"

"When he left, yeah. At least I think so."

"We got to get together," Rodriguez said. "Lunch tomorrow?"

"I'm on."

There was one more call to make. Strickland's answering machine picked up. Rogers left a message: call when you can.

10

Monday morning the lines moving in and out of the City Hall rotunda had thinned. It was, after all, the beginning of a new week, a work week, and the world goes on. In the afternoon, the casket would be moved to the Cathedral in preparation for the service the next day. Now, in the last few hours of public display, the citizens of the city he had served still moved slowly past the closed coffin containing the remains of John Morrison.

Rogers skirted the line, not pausing this time, just taking a glance as he went up the stairs and entered the mayor's office. Iris Ferguson, Morrison's secretary, who had served him in Washington when he had been a deputy attorney general, who had followed him into private Wall Street law practice, and then into City Hall, sat behind her desk looking lost, trying to find some order and meaning in a world that had lost its center and its focus.

She looked up as Rogers entered. "Ben," she said, spread her hands and shook her head.

He made a meaningless remark, then, "Iris, can you

lay your hands on the mayor's logs? The phone logs, going back to the spring?"

Her expression at first said she didn't understand, that words weren't quite getting through. Then slowly she nodded. "I have them somewhere," she said. "When do you need them?"

"Now," he said. "As soon as you can get them."

"I'll look," she said. She rose and moved away, opening a door and disappearing. Five minutes later she was back, carrying the books. She handed them to him, not asking why he needed them, not asking anything. "You'll bring them back," was all she said.

"In a couple of hours," he said.

Cradling the logs under his arm, he walked out of the office, along the hall, down two flights and opened his office. It was the same as always. He switched on the air conditioner and went to his desk. The red light was glowing on the answering machine. He ignored it.

He spread the logs open and began to go through them slowly, carefully, making notes on a yellow legal-size pad. It took him more than an hour. He went back over them again, until he was satisfied. Then he looked down at the notes.

Steven Gold had called just before noon on a Wednesday in the middle of April. Morrison had been in conference. Gold had left his number in Los Angeles. Gold called again at five that afternoon. Morrison took the call. The call lasted ten minutes.

Steven Gold called on May 3. The mayor took the call, and they spoke for fifteen minutes.

Gold called on May 21. He spoke to Morrison for ten minutes.

Morrison called Gold's number in Los Angeles on June 3. The call lasted twenty minutes.

Morrison called Gold in Los Angeles on June 14. They spoke for five minutes.

There were four other calls in June and July, two from Gold to Morrison, two from Morrison to Gold. They lasted from five minutes to a half hour. One of those calls from Gold was local. The New York number was written on the page.

Rogers went over to the bookcase and pulled out the reverse telephone directory. He found the number. It was that of a small hotel in the east 50s just off Park. He had heard of it, though he'd never been inside. It was a place very important people in the movies, from California and Europe, stayed when they were in the city. It wasn't cheap.

There was no mention in the logs about the subject of the calls.

Rogers went back to the logs and examined the other calls on those days, trying to find a pattern. He found one. It had to be. It wasn't just coincidence. Immediately after the first call from Gold, Morrison had placed three separate calls, all brief in duration. One had been to Melvin Rasmussen. The second had been to Moishe Weinstein. The third had been to Harvey Jessup. After every conversation between Gold and Morrison in April, May, June, and July, Morrison had called Rasmussen, Weinstein and Jessup.

And then there was one other item that held Rogers. He kept staring at the name on the pages. In May, after the third conversation between Morrison and Gold, Harry Gondolian called Morrison. The call lasted seven minutes.

Harry Gondolian called Morrison three more times. Every time was within hours of a Gold-Morrison conversation.

What was it the note from Gondolian said, the note passed to him that day a few weeks before at lunch by Annie Kendall? He unlocked the desk drawer, fished around and found it. "Rasmussen. Weinstein. Jessup. What do they have in common besides the obvious? Find out."

Was this it? Was Steven Gold the link?

Rogers closed the logs, put the yellow sheets and Gondolian's note in his desk and locked the drawer. As he was rising from his chair, the phone rang. He let it ring twice, then picked it up before the answering machine took it.

"Ben," Rodriguez's voice came through. "Are we on for that lunch?"

"Yeah. When and where?"

"Say about one." Rodriguez named an outdoor cafe overlooking the Hudson just north of Battery Park City.

"It's a long walk," Rogers said.

"Well. You know . . ." Rodriguez let that hang.

It was obvious. Nobody wanted to be seen with Ben Rogers. It might give the wrong people ideas, wrong ones or right ones, it didn't matter. Even Rodriguez didn't want to risk that.

"Okay," Rogers said. "See you then."

He rose then and carried the logs back up to Iris Ferguson and handed them back to her.

She looked a question at him. "Did you find what you were looking for?"

"I'm not sure," he said. "I'm not even sure what I was looking for. But I found something. More than something. I don't know what the hell it means, but I'll find out." He spread the logs open before her and pointed to the pages. "Do you have any idea what these calls were all about?"

She looked. Her mouth fell open. "That's the name of the man who killed him," she said.

"The guy they say killed him," Rogers said.

She peered up at him. "What do you mean? You don't think he did?"

"I don't know for sure," he said. "But right now I'm not buying simple explanations." Then he asked again, "Do you have any idea what they talked about?"

She shook her head. "He had so many calls, every day. Some times he told me about them so I could make notes. Some times he didn't. These calls, he never said a word about them. I don't think so, anyway."

"If you remember—anything at all—let me know. One more thing. Has anybody else come in here and asked to see the logs?"

"No," she said.

Giving himself enough time, he left City Hall by the back way, avoiding the lines that still crept up the stairs at the front, and headed west. The noon crowds in the Wall Street area were thick, and heat from the pavement rose in shimmering waves. He felt like he was creeping through a viscous haze, the sweat dampening the back of his shirt. It took him longer than he had estimated. He reached the cafe a little after one, looked around and spotted Rodriguez at a table in the shade over by the water. Rodriguez had a plate of greens in front of him. The guy always ate what the books said was good for you. Rogers greeted the homicide detective and sat.

Rodriguez looked up. "You're a little late," he said.

"Couldn't be helped. You know what the mobs are like this hour."

"Yeah. You want to order?"

Rogers motioned to a passing waiter, who dropped a menu in front of him. He studied it. He looked around, caught the waiter's eye. The waiter strolled over, in no hurry.

"Can I tell you the specials of the day?" he said.

"Don't bother. Bring me the chef's salad and iced coffee."

"Right away." The waiter strolled away.

Rodriguez looked at him. "I got an answer," he said. "My stoolie called this morning. And then I made a couple of other calls to guys what owe me favors. They backed him up, in spades."

"Yeah?"

"Your guy was right, and so was the stoolie. According to people who know, Santangello made a deal with the feds, which is why he's out. He's supposed to be protected, like thirty-six hours a day. With what he's supposed to be giving, they ought to have an army protecting him forty-eight hours a day."

"What's he supposed to be giving?"

"Everything. And more. They don't even have to ask and he gives. Things they never dreamed about. You'd think he knew who done every fuckin' unsolved crime for the last twenty years, for chrissake."

"What's he supposed to get in exchange?"

"When he finishes his song, they're gonna ship him wherever he wants to go, just so long as it's outside the lower forty-eight, with Hawaii and Alaska thrown in. Maybe he's got hisself a little island paradise in the South

Seas, with native broads and everything else to make the livin' easy."

"That figures. One more question. What feds?"

The waiter moved toward them carrying Rogers' lunch, and he set it in front of him. "Will there be anything else?"

"No, this is fine."

The waiter turned and moved away. Rogers looked at the salad, took a sip of the coffee, looked back at Rodriguez, who was finally starting his own lunch. "I asked," Rogers said, "what feds?"

Rodriguez paused and grinned broadly. "You wouldn't believe it."

"What wouldn't I believe?"

"All of 'em. The whole fuckin' government, the way I hear it. The FBI. The T-Men. The Secret Service. Even the goddamn CIA. They all want what he's got. And like, I figure, he's playin' 'em off, one against the other, and he's got enough for every one of 'em."

"But they've got him secure, right?"

"They're supposed to. They've got him stashed in some fancy hotel, a fuckin' suite for a grand a night. They got a couple of marshals watchin' over him all the time, like he was precious cargo that'd go rotten if they didn't wrap it nice and careful and keep an eye on it. Not that the son of a bitch isn't rotten from the start, all the way through. But you say somebody, one of your stoolies, saw him on the loose. And my guy says other people have seen him in places where he oughtn't to be with people he shouldn't be with, and not a babysitter in sight. I figure maybe he's got ways and there are greedy guys out there who'll do just about anything so long as you make it worth their while."

It had happened before, so maybe it was happening again, even if the guy was Victor Santangello who shouldn't even be out of the slammer, no matter what he had to give. But if Victor Santangello was doing whatever he wanted to do in exchange for giving up what everyone seemed to want, and given what Victor Santangello felt about Jack Morrison, then that threw a new piece into the puzzle.

Rodriguez was watching him, reading his mind. "You thinkin' what I think you're thinkin'?" Rodriguez said.

"What am I supposed to be thinking?"

"What we was talkin' about the other night. Santangello was good with weapons. All kinds. He was more than good. He was a fuckin' expert."

"It bears looking into, doesn't it," Rogers said.

"Fuckin' a. The thing is, how do we get to the bastard?"

"For the moment we don't. We probably aren't even supposed to know he's anywhere but Atlanta. So, we'll just have to start nosing around and see what we smell."

"A goddamn rat, that's what."

"In more ways than one. You put your lines out and I'll put mine out and we'll see what fish, dead or alive, we pull in."

"We could ring in your buddy, too, that guy Strickland. He's a fed, so maybe he can find out things we couldn't. Three heads are better than one."

"I'll talk to him," Rogers said.

Rogers rode the subway uptown. The platform was stifling, a steam bath. The air conditioning inside the train was going full blast for a change. It brought a chill to the flesh. He got off at Bloomingdale's. The faint scent of all the perfumes on the first floor drifted out as he climbed the stairs. He ignored it, turned out onto the street and walked south a couple of blocks, turned west and turned into the hotel, ignoring the doorman who held open the door.

Inside, the lobby was small and in refined good taste, everything arranged neatly, everything expensive, everything spotless. A guy with a small broom and a covered dustpan wandered through the lobby, cleaning side tables, brushing away dust, picking up invisible litter. A couple of men were lounging on wing chairs upholstered in a tasteful blue fabric. One, in a lightweight dark summer suit, was reading a book, occasionally reaching for a cigar that was poised on the edge of an ashtray on an antique table next to his chair. The aroma drifted. It smelled like Havana. It smelled expensive. The way he looked was expensive. The other, a heavyset guy in a neat tan suit, relaxed over the *Wall Street Journal*. Rogers watched him for a moment and grinned. The elevator door opened and a woman in a stylish gray suit that didn't come off of any rack stepped out into the lobby. She looked better and younger than her photographs. As she crossed the lobby, her eyes picked up Rogers. They moved on and then returned. The look said, I know you from somewhere. She couldn't place the somewhere and moved on toward the door. He had met her at a party out on the coast with Melissa. She was a hot screenwriter who had begun directing, and that night she had been wooing Melissa to read her latest script; there was a part that was just right. Rogers wasn't about to remind her of that meeting. He had been just an addendum, somebody nobody really noticed because he didn't belong.

He crossed toward the guy behind the newspaper. ''Hello, Frank,'' he said. ''Right in your element, *Wall Street Journal*, expensive suit and all the rest.''

The guy looked up. His name was Frank Gianfrido. He was a sergeant in the Two-Nine precinct. He and Rogers had gone through the Police Academy together. They'd been kind of friends until Rogers went to Internal Affairs. They hadn't spoken or even seen each other in a few years. ''Ben,'' Gianfrido said, ''what the hell are you doing here?''

''Slumming,'' Rogers said. ''You?''

''Moonlighting,'' Gianfrido said.

''You been here long?''

''Three, four years now. It's a cushy job. They supply the rags and all the rest so I look like I belong. The food's good, better than I get at home, let me tell you, and the job's a breeze. All I got to do is sit around and look like

I'm a regular, and then make the rounds every hour or so."

"You know the people who stay here?"

"The regulars, yeah. The transients? Who the hell knows them?"

"You going to be around long?"

"A couple more hours. Why?"

"I might want to talk to you."

Rogers turned and headed for the desk. A clerk in morning clothes looked at him, examined him up and down, the expression saying he wasn't a regular, probably didn't belong here, and probably couldn't afford the tab. Rogers asked to see the manager. The clerk gave him the fish eye. Rogers sighed, reached into his pocket and flashed the shield. The clerk's expression changed. It wasn't welcoming, and it wasn't respectful, but at least it wasn't dismissive any longer. The clerk turned and went through a door behind the desk.

Rogers waited. A couple of minutes later, the door opened and the clerk returned with an older man, middle-aged, neat gray hair, neat, expensive gray pinstriped suit. The manager looked at him and waited.

"Can we go somewhere and talk?" Rogers said.

The manager continued to examine him, then slowly, with just a trace of reluctance, nodded, came out from behind the desk, and started across the lobby without looking back. Rogers followed. They reached a door. The manager opened it, held it for Rogers, and then followed him into a small windowless room with a desk, a love seat, and a couple more wing chairs. The manager sat behind the desk, motioned Rogers into one of the chairs.

"How can I help you?" the manager said.

"Steven Gold stayed here when he was in New York?"

The manager put on a stern expression. "We do not divulge information about our guests. You know that a subpoena is required to examine the records."

"Steven Gold's dead," Rogers said, "so he doesn't have privacy any more. Now, give."

"Mr. Gold's dead?" He looked shocked, stunned.

"Don't you read the papers? Don't you watch the tube? Yeah, Gold's dead."

"I didn't think that was our Mr. Gold. I couldn't believe it. I was sure it must be somebody who happened to look like him."

"It was him all right. Now, let me repeat the question. Steven Gold, that Steven Gold, stayed here when he was in New York?"

"Yes."

"How often?"

"Two or three times a year for the last four or five years."

"When was the last time he was here?"

"I'd have to check our records."

"I'd appreciate it if you'd do that."

The manager rose and walked out of the room. He was back in about five minutes, carrying a printout. He sat behind the desk again and spread the paper in front of him, read through it and then looked back at Rogers. "The last visit was just a week ago. He checked in at ten A.M. on Monday and then checked out at noon on Tuesday. The time before that he arrived at ten A.M. on June 20 and checked out at three P.M. on June 25. I can give you the dates of his previous stays."

"I imagine all your rooms have direct-dial phones so the calls don't go through the switchboard?"

"That's correct."

"I'm sure you have a list of the long-distance calls he made, since you obviously charge for them. But there's no way you have a list of the local numbers he called while he stayed here. Right?"

"Well, as a matter of fact, we do have such records."

Rogers sat up, surprised.

"You're correct that all our rooms have direct-dial phones. The guests merely dial a nine prefix and then the number and they're connected automatically. However, for their protection, and ours, our computer records the numbers dialed, both long-distance and local. No one can listen in, but we do have those records. Of course, we have no records of the calls he received."

"That figures. But I'd like a list of the calls he made while he was here."

"It will take some time to compile. We'd have to have the computer check and then print out."

"That's okay. I've got the time."

The manager picked up the phone on the desk, punched a couple of numbers, waited, and then gave instructions to whoever answered to print out Gold's room charges. "When you leave, stop at the desk and the list will be ready. Now, is there anything else?"

"Did he have visitors while he was here?"

"I wouldn't know that."

"Who would?"

"We guarantee our guests privacy. They come and go as they please."

"This is an exclusive place, tight security and all the rest," Rogers said. "People just don't go in and out, ride up the elevators, wander around without getting clearance from the desk and the person they want to see. I don't figure you could tell me everybody from every visit. Just the last couple."

"I still wouldn't be able to do that. I'm back in the office."

"How about the desk clerk?"

"He might. If he could remember, which I doubt. Our guests have visitors, and there would be no reason he'd remember people who arrive to see a guest. Unless there was something exceptional about them. Then he might remember. But this hotel caters to many famous and well-known persons, they come and go, both as guests and visitors of our guests, so I doubt whether the clerks would remember one in particular."

"I'll buy that. Get Gianfrido in here."

The manager gave him a puzzled look.

"The house dick."

"Oh, you mean the security officer. Is that his name?"

"Frank Gianfrido, yeah. If he hasn't changed, he has a memory like an elephant."

The manager picked up the phone and gave the orders. Gianfrido knocked at the door in about thirty seconds, and then walked in and looked around, looked at the manager, looked at Rogers. The manager waved him into a seat.

"Lieutenant Rogers would like to ask you some questions," the manager said.

Gianfrido nodded. "Shoot."

"Frank," he said, "you know the people who stay here on a regular basis, right?"

"Sure. I remember faces, so I see somebody who's in and out all the time and doesn't check at the desk every time he comes through the door, I know he's staying, and I know who he is, name and all. I get photos of the people who are staying here. Every day when I get here, they give me the pix of the new people and put a name to them. Not that it's necessary a lot of the times. All you got to do is go to the movies and you see them, or pick up the papers and read the columns."

Rogers looked over at the manager.

"A security precaution," the manager said. "We have a camera in the wall behind the desk and we photograph people when they check in. It's for their protection, and ours."

"Sure," Rogers said. "I believe it." He looked back at Gianfrido. "How about people you don't recognize?"

"Somebody comes in I haven't seen before, I watch him close. He goes to the desk and asks for somebody, they call up. Usually, I make it my business to be somewhere near so I can hear. If it isn't too busy, I'll ride up the elevator with him, like I'm one of the people staying here, get off at the same floor and make sure he's going where he said he was going and that he's expected. That kind of thing."

Rogers looked back at the manager. "For the guests' protection, and ours," the manager said.

"Okay. Now, one of the regulars here was a guy named Steven Gold."

Gianfrido gave him a look, as though he was about to say something, then held it and just answered the question. "Sure. Big time Hollywood producer. He seemed like a nice guy, from what I saw. Quiet. Never made trouble. Not stuck on himself, like some of the people." Gianfrido paused, his mind working. He looked back at Rogers. "It's hard to believe, Ben, the stuff in the news. He didn't hit me like the kind of guy who would blow people away, especially people like Morrison. But you never know, do you?"

"You never know. Everybody has a secret life. So, you knew Gold pretty well?"

"Not really. I saw him around when he was here. He got used to seeing me. We exchanged a few words. He seemed pretty smart, and I figured he knew just what I was doing. It didn't bother him."

"People came to see him?"

"Sure, like everybody here. They all have people coming. Meetings, making deals, that kind of thing. And sometimes a little hanky-panky. Strictly high-class though, not the usual."

"You recognize any of the people who came to see Gold?"

"Let me think about that one. I'll have to search back." Gianfrido paused, reflected, then brightened. "Some of the people, they came maybe once, and I probably wouldn't be able to pick them out in a lineup. A couple of people showed up whenever he was here."

"Who?"

"The reason I remember them is 'cause they stood out. I mean, they weren't the usual crowd that comes into a place like this, so right away you sit up and take notice. One I couldn't put a name to. Beard down to here, big fur hat no matter what the weather, black suit, long black coat, like they used to wear maybe a hundred years ago. You know, the works. Hasidic. I figured a rabbi. The other two I got names for, 'cause they're in the news all the time. One was that black preacher, Rasmussen. They don't have a whole lot of blacks in this place. And then every time there's a little trouble anyplace, his puss is all over the TV. The other, he was that gay guy, what's his name, Jessup? That's right, Jessup."

"Anybody else?"

Gianfrido grinned. "Hollywood people, like from the movies. Glamour pants and macho guys you see on the big screen all the time. Nothing unusual in that. A lot of people here have those types in. It was the other three, they weren't the usual, which is why I remember."

"Anything else you want to tell me?"

"Not unless you've got questions."

On his way out, Rogers stopped at the desk and retrieved the list of Gold's telephone calls. He would study them later, checking in the reverse directory to match numbers with names.

He was back at City Hall by late afternoon. The lines of people were gone, the viewing over. The flags still flew at half-staff. They would continue there probably for another month. The area was quiet. It wouldn't come alive again until after the funeral. He went in by the side entrance, unlocked the door to his office, turned on the lights and air conditioner, took the reverse directory from the bookcase and then sat at his desk and spread Gold's phone records in front of him.

The red light on the answering machine glowed brightly, demanding. He continued to ignore it.

He turned to Gold's phone records and the reverse directory. The man had made two calls the past Monday, during that one-day visit. There was a long distance to a number in Los Angeles. The second was to a number that wasn't in the reverse directory. It had to be unlisted. Rogers made a note of it.

When Gold was at the hotel in June, he had called that

same number. He had also called the Los Angeles number every day, usually late in the evening. He had called several other L.A. numbers, too. Rogers would ask Melissa if she recognized them, have her check them out. One of the local numbers Rogers knew. It was Morrison's direct line at City Hall. Gold had called it once. Rogers recognized another number. It was Morrison's direct line at Gracie Mansion. Gold had called there once, too, in the evening.

Now he began to go down the list. It looked like the man spent half of every day on the phone. The going was slow and tedious. A lot of the numbers were production companies and distributors around the city. One belonged to a Wall Street broker. There were half a dozen unlisted. One was the same unlisted number he had called on his final stay. He'd have to use some clout to get those. And there were three others. He had called all of them twice, one after the other, three days apart. He went down the reverse directory and found them. One was to Rasmussen. One was to Weinstein. One was to Jessup.

He picked up the phone, dialed a number he knew by heart and reached the phone company security office. He asked for Jane, identified himself and read off the numbers. Five were those of movie stars. That figured. It was the sixth.

"I'm sorry," Jane said. "I'm not supposed to give that out, not to anyone. You'd need a subpoena."

"Come on," Rogers said, "I've done you enough favors. And this is important."

"I'm not supposed to, under any circumstances."

"Break the rules. Just this once."

There was a long pause. "Just this once. But for God's sake, don't tell anyone where you got it." The number was that of a company called Phoenix Trans-World Shipping. He wrote the name, stared at it. Why the hell would a shipping company have an unlisted number?

"You got an address?"

There was a long pause. "You don't just want to get me fired. You want to get me locked up. Just the name. Be satisfied with small favors." Jane hung up.

Rogers reached for the business directory. There was no listing for Phoenix Trans-World Shipping. There was no address.

He dialed the number. After a half dozen rings, just as he was about to hang up, somebody picked up the phone. A male voice said, "Phoenix."

"I'd like to make arrangements to ship some merchandise," Rogers said.

"Call Allied Van Lines," the voice said, and hung up.

He stared at the phone.

Somebody was knocking at the door. A voice followed the knock. "Ben, are you in there?"

"Come on in," he said.

George Strickland came through the door. "Where the hell have you been? I've been trying to reach you all day."

"I've been around, in and out, here and there."

Strickland noticed the red light on the answering machine. "For chrissake, don't you ever pick up your messages?"

Rogers grinned. "Most of the time. Today, I wasn't in the mood."

"You never know. Maybe there's something important."

Rogers shrugged, pressed the button and the machine

began to play back. Strickland stood beside the desk and listened with him.

There were two calls from Strickland, wondering where he was and why he hadn't gotten back. There was a call from a Ralph Smithers. The name didn't register. The message did. Would Mr. Rogers please call as soon as possible to obtain instructions for pallbearers at the funeral? There was a message from Annie Kendall. Some people were going to get together and raise a glass to Harry Gondolian the next day, Tuesday, about six. They would be at Geary's, a newspaper hangout in midtown. If Rogers wanted to come, he was welcome, and she'd see him there. There was a message from Chief O'Bannion. It wasn't polite. The chief sounded mad as hell. He had been trying to reach Rogers at home and at the office. He wanted to see Rogers. Call for an appointment. The sooner the better. No please. There were a half dozen other calls that he ignored, pressing the fast-forward button when he heard the voice or the name.

He looked at Strickland, reached for the phone and called the number Smithers had left, identified himself and got instructions for the next day. The funeral would be at noon. He should be at the church no later than eleven, earlier if possible. He should wear a dark suit.

"Satisfied?" he said to Strickland.

"Who the hell is Annie Kendall?"

"A kid who worked for Gondolian. She says she was his gofer. He said otherwise. I agree with him. She knows what he knew. Of that I'm positive. And she's got his goddamn records."

"That's important?"

"Damn right. I'm sure of that."

"Why?"

''He gave me a message the last time I saw him. Three names. Said I ought to check them out.''

''What the hell does that have to do with Morrison?''

''There's a link. There's more than a link. They keep popping up everywhere I look. Like what I was doing today.''

''You were doing what? I thought we agreed to work together.''

''That's right. What I've been doing is backtracking Gold.''

''For chrissake, why? I thought we wrote him off, after what your lady said the other night.''

''Yeah, we wrote him off. But I figure somebody set the poor bastard up. What we have to do is find out who, why, and how.''

Strickland turned that over, and nodded. ''I'll buy that. Give. What did you pick up?''

Rogers told him.

''I don't get it,'' Strickland said. ''What's the connection? A big shot Hollywood type, a rabbi, a black rabble-rouser and a fairy? And where does Morrison fit in?''

''That's what I'd like to know.''

''And this thing, Phoenix whatever? What the hell is that all about?''

''You tell me.''

''What else?''

He thought for a moment, then looked at Strickland. ''A thing came up which could be down your alley.''

''Everything's down my alley.''

''This in particular. You ever heard of a real bad dude named Victor Santangello?''

''Of course. Who hasn't? Morrison sent him away for ten lifetimes. I worked on the damn case.''

"The ten lifetimes have passed and the bastard's out."

Strickland stared at him. "Bullshit."

"No bullshit." He spelled out what Rodriguez had told him earlier, and what Max, his stoolie, had told him even before that. "You one of the people Santangello's singing to?"

Strickland shook his head slowly. "Not so as I know. I'll check on it."

"Carlos thought you ought to."

"I will. Now, where do we go from here? I've talked to my people, told them what we know. They talked to your people. Your people buy Gold. My people aren't so sure, after what I said. They think we ought to take a close look at it. I said that was fine with me. I said you and me and maybe Rodriguez were ready to run with it and see if we reached the end zone. They gave the green light."

"They tell the department?"

"Like hell. Does Macy's tell Gimbel's? When was the last time we told NYPD anything we didn't have to, especially when they had different ideas? My people said they'd call and say they wanted you two guys released to us on a special assignment, strictly hush-hush. If we have to, we'll invent something plausible."

"Not necessary. I've got time coming. Six or seven weeks. Vacation and overtime. I'll take it now, before they ship me off wherever they're going to ship me to. Carlos will find time. Besides, why create the possibility of trouble when there's no need?"

"If you say so, agreed," Strickland said. "Now, where and when do we start?"

"The funeral's tomorrow, then the thing for Gondolian, and then I suppose I have to see the chief and find out where in Siberia he's sending me. That takes the next couple of days. After that, we'll pick up the ball."

Later, as he was getting ready for bed, Melissa called. "I talked to Abby," she said. "I told her you were going to look into this and clear Steve's name. She wants to talk to you, she wants to see you."

"Good work," he said. "I'll try to get out there as soon as I can."

"Sooner," she said.

"When I can," he said. "Meanwhile, do me a favor."

"Anything."

He fished out the list of L.A. numbers and read them to her. She laughed. "The first one," she said, "the one he called every night, that's his home. The other one he called all the time, that's his office. I'll find out about the rest and call you tomorrow."

"Do that," he said.

"I miss you already," she said.

"Same here."

"And I love you."

"Same here."

"Please get out here soon."

"I will."

12

They buried John Morrison in a manner befitting a man of power and stature.

For a dozen blocks around the vast, unfinished, perhaps never to be finished Cathedral of St. John the Divine, on the corner of Amsterdam and what was called Cathedral Parkway but which, east and west, was 110th Street, the city was cordoned off, lined with saw horses, patrolled by cops on foot and on horseback. Security was tight all over the city, but especially tight north of the cathedral to the wall around Columbia and south into Spanish Harlem, and east and west from Broadway to the northern perimeter of Central Park. There were too many very, very important people to take any chances.

Outside, the crowd of ordinary citizens spilled down Cathedral Parkway toward Broadway, and north and south along Amsterdam. Inside, the cathedral was packed to overflowing, a rare event, but then this was a rare event. The President, Vice President and most of the Cabinet had flown up from Washington along with the state's two senators and the city's congressmen. There were governors from around the country. If somebody had dropped a bomb on the cathedral, the power structure of the nation would have been wiped out in an instant.

The service lasted more than an hour. There were prayers by the Episcopal archbishop, the Catholic cardinal, one of the most important Jewish rabbis. There were eulogies from half a dozen men who had known and worked with Morrison at one time or another from early in his career until his death. There were twenty-five honorary pallbearers, men who stood at the pinnacle of power in government, politics, business, and the law. The real pallbearers, like Rogers, were men who had been Morrison's friends and closest advisors and compatriots, who had served him loyally.

The funeral procession to the small cemetery in Westchester County where generations of Morrisons were laid to rest was half a mile long, and wound slowly north along Broadway and into the suburbs until it reached its destination. The burial itself was over before the last limousine arrived, before the last dignitary had made the long walk down the neat, groomed, hedge-lined gravel path to the graveside.

As he was leaving the cemetery, Rogers felt a hand on his arm. He turned. Chief O'Bannion was glaring at him. "Where the hell have you been?"

Rogers shrugged. "Around."

"I want to see you."

"Now?"

"Tomorrow will do. At my office. Be there by ten." The chief turned and strode away.

Rogers moved on toward the drive and the limo that would take him back to the city. Just as he was climbing in, Tom Scanlon walked toward him.

"Well, well, Rogers," Scanlon said, and he was grinning. "It sure as hell looks like everybody's plans are in the garbage can."

Rogers gave him a sour look. "You don't look like you're one of the mourners, Scanlon."

Scanlon grinned even broader. "Can't say I'll miss the bastard."

"Not down in Florida, or up in New England."

"Who said anything about that?" Scanlon said. "Everything's changed. I've reconsidered my plan about retiring."

"I wouldn't if I were you."

"But you're not me," Scanlon said and walked on.

Rogers watched him go. Another bastard with a real motive, he thought, then dismissed it. Scanlon might be a lot of things, but Rogers was sure the old politician didn't have the balls for murder. Besides, if push came to shove, Rogers knew what Morrison had known about Scanlon, and he had the proof, too. When Scanlon thought about it, maybe Florida wouldn't seem so bad after all.

The memorial to Harry Gondolian was something else. Geary's, a small, dark saloon with sawdust on the floor, was filled with reporters and editors, male and female, ten deep around the bar, all with drinks in their hands when Rogers arrived a little after seven. The walls, smoke-stained, were filled with photographs arranged haphazardly. Rogers had been in the place a couple of times before and had noticed them, but nobody had ever said who they were or why they were there. Now he saw Gondolian's photograph, new and clean, the smoke not yet clouding the glass, at the end of a row. It was an old picture, taken maybe twenty or thirty years ago. Still recognizable—he'd looked like an old ferret then. He looked like an old ferret the day he died.

Somebody put a glass in his hand. He took a sip. Scotch. He looked around to pay somebody, but nobody was looking like he wanted money. He saw Annie Kendall. She was wearing a sheer white summer weight dress. Her face was flushed and she looked like she had had a few already, a few too many. She had a glass in one hand. She saw Rogers and threaded her way through the mob toward him.

"You made it," she said.

"I wouldn't have missed it," he said. He gestured toward his glass. "Who do I pay for this?"

"Nobody," she said. "It's on the house."

"Then the next one's on me."

She laughed. "You can't pay. It's already paid for. And you'd have a hard time finding the host."

He gave her a questioning look.

"Harry. He made all the arrangements when he found out he was going away for good. He didn't expect it so soon, but he made his plans. He made plans for everything."

"Even his funeral?"

"No funeral," she said. "He didn't believe in any of that crap. Cremate me, he used to say, and dump my ashes somewhere around City Hall. When nobody's looking. He had it in his will."

"Where he had his best days."

"Where he had all his days, all his grown-up life. Now he'll be there forever, haunting the damn place." There was a catch in her voice.

He motioned toward the pictures on the wall. "He's here, too," he said.

"Yes. With all the rest."

"All the rest who?"

"All the rest of the reporters who got killed covering a story. It goes back to the Spanish-American War, I think. The original Geary hung the first one. And they just kept it up. Every time somebody got killed, they hung his picture. It's one way of remembering."

He took a long look at all these pictures, some a century old of guys with muttonchop whiskers, and on to guys in the dress of their time on through the ages. "It's hard to believe," he said. "There's an army of them."

"That's right," she said. "Why can't you believe it?"

"Newspaper guys? You know . . ."

"I don't know," she said. "Reporters get killed all the time. Every time there's a war, the roll call mounts. Sometimes in places nobody ever heard about and nobody but a guy out for a story cares about. There's trouble in the street, a reporter's there, and he's not carrying a gun like you guys, he's carrying a notebook and a pencil, or maybe a tape recorder these days, and when he goes down, the only people who care are other guys who do the same thing. Only they don't bury reporters at Arlington and nobody gives big funerals, like they gave for your boss today. The president doesn't show up. Nobody shows up but a few friends, and then everybody goes back to work." She sounded mad. She was.

"You know a lot for a kid," he said mildly. "And you care a lot."

"I do. I was brought up with it."

She turned and headed for the bar, not quite steady on her feet. He followed. There were conversations going on all around them. Nobody was talking about Harry Gondolian. They were talking about Morrison's funeral, which a lot of them had covered. They were talking about Russia, about China, about Africa, about anything in the news. They were cracking raunchy jokes. It wasn't a mournful crowd. It was a crowd of people who shared careers, who had seen too much and were cynical about everything, who always seemed to look for the worst, and always to find it. They were never surprised by anything, not by life and not by death. They accepted what happened and moved on. They would raise a glass to Harry Gondolian and drink the booze he had provided for them, and that was that.

Rogers had another drink, listened to the talk, said a few things of little importance to some reporters he knew and who accepted his presence, after a hesitation, not as if he belonged but as if there was nothing wrong with his being here.

About eight thirty, he moved toward the door. Annie Kendall was leaning against the wall right beside it. She was pale, the expression on her face vague, her eyes not focusing. He stepped up to her. "Are you okay?"

She tried to focus, gradually recognized him. "Rogers," she said, the voice slurring. "Harry's buddy," she said. "Okay? Sure, okay. Drunk is what I am. Harry would like that. He never saw me drunk. Always said he wanted to see me have more than a wee little glass of wine. I had more than a wee little glass of wine." She laughed bitterly, reeled away from the wall, then leaned back against it. "I loved that man," she said.

Rogers looked at her, nodded. "Sure," he said.

"Goddamn you. It's not the way you think. I loved the man. Oh, the son of a bitch. I loved him." She looked at him archly. "You ought to love him, too," she slurred.

"Sure," he said. "I loved the guy."

"Mean it," she said. "Told me he solved your puzzle."

Rogers looked at her. "What puzzle?"

"Didn't say. Said you'd know."

"You ought to go home," Rogers said.

She peered at him through half-closed eyes. "Go home? Sure, I ought to go home. Would. Only don't think I can make it."

"I'll find somebody to take you."

"Nobody'll take Annie. Not when there's another drink on the house."

"Okay, then I'll take you," he said. He took her arm. She didn't resist. He led her outside, into the hot night, moved to the curb and looked for a cab. One of those August storms had been threatening all day. When it came, it would break the heat and the humidity for as long as it lasted, maybe a half hour, and then the heat would be back, and the humidity worse. But for that little time, there would be some relief. A slash of jagged lightning cracked across the sky, turning the world garish.

A cab rolled by, saw him in a sudden flash of lightning and braked. Rogers pulled open the door, helped her in, and climbed in after. He looked at her. "What's your address?"

She had to think about that, then murmured an address just off Riverside Drive in the eighties. He repeated it to the cabby.

Halfway there, the rain came, not in a drizzle, but in a sudden deluge. The water drummed on the cab's roof, turned the windows opaque so that the cabby had to creep slowly northward, the windshield wipers slashing frantically and ineffectually.

Finally, they reached her building, just in from the corner. It was an old five-story brownstone that had been completely renovated. A sign outside said that apartments inside were for sale. He imagined the prices had undergone some renovation, too. He helped her out of the cab. The rain and the wind hit them with a force that sent them reeling back. He gripped her arm, held her steady and fought against the storm's fury toward the stairs. They reached shelter, stepping just inside the door. His clothes, soaked, clung to him like a second skin. He looked at her. Her dark hair was matted around her head, her face shining with water. Her dress had nearly disappeared in the wetness and her body was revealed as clearly as if she was wearing nothing at all. She seemed oblivious to that, though the pummeling of the rain seemed to have washed away the worst of the alcoholic haze that had enveloped her.

Just inside the door a tenant board listed two apartments to a floor. Hers was on the third floor, the rear apartment. He looked at her. She was leaning against the wall, trying to orient herself. He asked if she had the key. She fished uncertainly in her small purse, came up with it and held it out triumphantly. He took it and unlocked the door, led her down the carpeted hall toward the stairs. He spotted an elevator at the rear and moved that way, pushed the button and in half a minute the door opened. The inside was paneled, the walnut wood glowing. He pressed the button for three. The elevator moved up, and then the door slid open.

He steered her down the hall toward her apartment, examined the keys, found the right ones, unlocked the dead bolt and then the lower lock, and opened the door. Fumbling against the wall just inside, he found a light switch and flicked it. Lights bathed the apartment hall, and at the end of the hall softer lights went on.

She touched his arm and pointed toward a closet beside the door. "Alarm," she said. "It's in there. Better turn it off."

He opened the closet door, saw the electronic alarm and switched it off.

They moved down the hall and reached the entrance to the living room. They stopped and stared.

It was a mess.

Books, a library of them, that had lined one wall were strewn across the floor. The twin doors in a credenza gaped open, the contents littering the area in front. The glass doors in a stereo rack hung from broken hinges, the CDs and tapes scattered about the room. The drawers in a wooden filing cabinet were pulled out, emptied, the papers everywhere. It was chaos.

Annie Kendall stood frozen, suddenly sober. "My God," she said. She took one step into the room, then leaned against the wall. She closed her eyes, as though trying to banish the sight. She opened them again, hoping it had been a nightmare and now things would be as they had been. Her hands went to her face, the knuckles rubbing her eyes. She kept shaking her head.

Rogers moved quickly across the room toward an open door. It was dark beyond. He found the light switch. In the glare, the bedroom was as much a ruin as the living room.

He turned back toward Annie. She was still leaning against the wall, staring with disbelief. Water was dripping off her onto the floor. She seemed unaware of it.

Rogers moved quickly toward her, took her by the shoulders, gripped her. She stared at him. "First," he ordered, "get out of those wet clothes. Then start looking around and see what's missing."

She continued to stand there in shock.

"Do it," he said. "Now."

Slowly she nodded. "Yes," she said. "All right." She moved toward the bedroom, froze at the entrance as her eyes took in the devastation. Then she edged her way inside. He stepped toward the two windows at the end of the living room and checked them. One had an air conditioner. It had not been disturbed. He turned it on. The other window was locked.

He moved toward the bedroom and stepped inside. Annie was kneeling at an open closet, picking through the clothes that had been dumped on the floor. She was naked. He ignored that, moved quickly toward the windows, checked them. They were locked.

He turned toward her. She had found a pair of jeans and was pulling them on. "Any other rooms?" he asked.

She shook her head. "No. Just the living room and bedroom. And the kitchen."

"Any windows in the kitchen?"

"One," she said, fastening the jeans and reaching for a t-shirt, pulling it from a pile. Without makeup and dressed that way, she looked about twelve.

He spun, left the room, crossed the living room toward an archway, went through it and was in the kitchen. He turned on the light, went to the window. It was locked.

There was a phone on the wall. He picked it up, and dialed a number.

Ten minutes later, the apartment was filled with cops. There were half a dozen in blue and four in plainclothes from the precinct's burglary squad. Rogers didn't know any of them. They didn't know him, but they knew who he was. They were wary, constantly looking sideways in his direction. Every time they asked a question they cast a glance at him, as though trying to avoid stepping over some line.

Rogers filled them in rapidly. The windows were latched. No sign of any tampering. The door had been double-locked, both the regular lock and the dead bolt, and there was no sign that the locks had been picked, though it was hard to tell these days. There was an alarm system hooked to the door and windows. It had been set when they arrived. Rogers had checked and it was in working order. There was, then, no sign of a forced entry, but there had been an entry nevertheless, as they could see. Miss Kendall had done a quick search while they were on the way. They could ask her what, if anything, she had discovered. Then he stepped back and let them do their job.

They were gentle with Annie Kendall. And she was sober now.

"You live here alone, Miss?" the lead detective asked.

"Yes."

"Anybody else have a key?" There was that sidelong glance at Rogers. They weren't certain just what his relationship was, why he was here.

"No," she said. Then, "Yes. My mother and father. They have keys."

"We can rule them out?"

"Of course."

"Could you give us their address, anyway?"

She gave an address on Fifth Avenue.

"Lieutenant Rogers said you've made a search?"

"Just a very quick one. I'd have to spend a lot more time."

"As far you could see, is anything missing?"

She nodded. "Yes. My jewelry. It was in a lockbox in

the bottom dresser drawer in the bedroom. The box is gone. And about three hundred dollars in cash. That was in the top drawer, under some clothes.''

One of the detectives made notes.

''What kind of jewelry, Miss?''

She thought, her mind working, picturing it. ''A string of pearls,'' she said. ''Five or six pairs of earrings. Two rings. A few bracelets. Brooches, pins, necklaces. A lot of things like that. Oh, my passport and birth certificate and some other papers were in the box, too.''

''The jewelry, was it valuable?''

''Yes. The pearls were real. I think they must be worth two or three thousand dollars, at least. They were a graduation present from my father. One of the rings had some diamonds in it. It used to be my mother's, so I have no idea what it was worth, but I think a lot. A lot of the stuff was gold or platinum, some with precious stones. Most of the things were gifts. But, yes, they were quite valuable.''

''You could give us a complete list and a description?''

''Probably, if I thought about it. But the insurance company would have all that. You can check with them.'' She gave them the name of the company.

''Anybody know you had valuable jewelry in this apartment?''

''Probably, I never discussed it, but I wore it. I don't think anyone thought I went to the bank, to a safe deposit box every time I put on a ring or a bracelet or anything.''

''Didn't you ever think it might be an invitation to keep stuff like that around?''

''No, I never thought about it. I wear my jewelry when I want to. Why else have it?''

''Is there anything else missing?''

She hesitated for just a moment. Rogers caught it, the

other cops didn't. He watched her closely now. "I'm not sure," she said. "I was just starting to look around this room when you got here." She gestured toward the filing cabinet. "There were file folders in that, and other things all around. But they weren't worth anything to anybody but me. And they didn't touch the paintings." She motioned toward five oils that still hung on the walls.

It went on like that for another hour. As the cops were leaving, they said that she should take her time and make a careful search of the apartment and then be sure to get them a complete list of everything that was missing together with the insurance company's description and valuation.

Then they were gone.

She stood in the middle of the living room, staring around helplessly. "I'll have to clean up all this," she said to Rogers.

"Yeah," he said. "But not right now. It can wait. What you ought to do is go to bed and get some sleep. Tomorrow's soon enough." He hesitated. "What's missing from the file cabinet?"

She gave him a veiled look, and shook her head. "Nothing," she said.

"Something," he said. "What?"

She thought about it, then nodded slowly. "Harry's files."

"You're sure?"

"Yes. They were in orange folders. Look around. Do you see any folders like that?"

"How come you had his files?"

"I knew where they were. Saturday I went and got them. I brought them here."

"He must have had files going back fifty years. There must have been more than one drawer of them."

"He did and there were. The cabinets were labeled. I just took the ones he had marked active. I was going to have somebody get the others later. But I thought there might be something in those, so I took them."

"Did you have a chance to look through them?"

She hesitated, then nodded.

"Did you find anything?"

"I'm not sure. I have to think about it."

"Fill me in. I'll help."

She shook her head. "Not right now. Later."

"Still not sure about me?"

"That's not it. I just want to think about them. I'll share what I know, but not right now."

"Have it your way. I think you're making a mistake."

"Maybe. But I don't think so. Besides, it's late." She looked at him, closely, and for the first time in hours smiled. "You're soaked," she said. "The rain. And you haven't dried out yet. You're going to get sick."

"Don't worry about it," he said. "When I get home, I'll take care of it."

"Don't leave," she said suddenly, seriously.

He looked at her closely.

"I'm scared," she said. "I don't want to be alone."

"It's just the shock," he said. "You'll be all right."

"No, I won't. What would have happened if I'd been here?"

He'd thought about that, and he didn't like the thoughts. He tried to banish her fears. "They'd probably have left."

"No," she said, shaking her head. "That isn't what happens. They'd have hurt me, wouldn't they?"

He waited, then nodded slowly. "They might have. It happens. But you weren't here."

"I'm scared," she said. "What if they come back?"

"They won't."

"How can you be so sure?"

"I am. They won't. They got what they came after, so there's no reason for them to come back."

"You don't know," she said. "I want you to stay. Please."

All he had to do was look at her to know she wasn't kidding. She was frightened, very frightened. At that moment, she needed someone to lean on. Maybe anyone would have done, but he wasn't so sure about that, not the way she was looking at him.

"They weren't really after my jewelry, were they?" she said. "That was like a cover."

"Why you do think that?"

"Whoever it was wanted Harry's files. That was the real reason. If they took the lock box, maybe they thought nobody would notice. I'll bet they didn't even look inside the box. I'll bet they don't know what they got. And I don't think it was important."

He tried to persuade her she was wrong. There wasn't a way. She wasn't buying. He gave up, and nodded slowly. "Smart girl," he said.

"I am," she said simply. "You're staying." It was a statement, not a question.

"Do I have a choice?"

"No," she said. "Now, get out of those clothes and take a shower. You'll feel better."

"You have something for me to wear?" He grinned. She was a foot shorter than he.

She laughed. "I'll find something."

While he was in the shower, he thought he heard the bathroom door open. Then the shower curtain parted and she stepped in with him.

He woke early. She was sitting up in bed watching him. "Good morning," she said. "You sleep hard."

"Have you been awake long?"

"No. I just woke up." She continued to stare down at him. "Thanks," she said.

He wasn't sure how he was supposed to answer.

"For everything," she said. "No strings," she said. "You've got enough strings already, don't you?"

He nodded. "All tied up."

"Don't feel guilty," she said. "I needed you last night. And I wanted you."

"It works two ways," he said, "and I feel guilty as hell."

"Just an old fashioned guy," she smiled.

"I suppose so, in some ways, at least. I made a commitment, and I believe in commitments, and I believe in loyalty. So, yeah, I feel guilty."

"You'll get over it," she said. "We all get over everything."

"The voice of experience?"

"Maybe. You don't know a lot about me. Let's leave it that way, shall we?" She turned, dropped her legs over the side of the bed and rose, moving away unselfconsciously. She picked up a robe that had been tossed across a chair and put it on, tying it loosely around her waist. "I'm going to make breakfast," she said and walked out of the room.

In the bathroom, his clothes had been hung over the shower rod. They were dry now and he put them on. In the small dining alcove just off the kitchen she had set a table for two, had put out glasses of juice, muffins on plates and there was coffee in large mugs.

"Sit down and eat," she said, and took a seat across from him. "What now?" she said.

"I have to see the chief this morning."

"Why?"

He shrugged. "A new assignment. The old one ended last Friday."

"It did, didn't it? I suppose I have to talk to my editor about my, well, my future."

"You taking over for Harry?"

"That's what he wanted. But I doubt it. Two things against me. One, they think I'm too young and that means they're sure I don't have enough experience. Two, I'm female. They'll find something for me. Society page more than likely."

"I thought those days were over."

"In theory. Not in practice."

He looked at his watch. "Look," he said, "I've got to run."

"Naturally."

"No, not naturally. I have to get home, change, and get down to headquarters. I'm supposed to be there first thing."

She nodded. "Good luck."

"You, too."

"It was fun," she said. "Maybe more than fun. And I'm truly grateful."

"I still want to know what's in Harry's files."

"You will. Count on it. I just have to sort them out. Now, get out of here. I have to start getting this place back together."

"You'll be all right?"

"Now? Yes. Don't worry about me."

He didn't tell her to change the locks. If whoever had broken in had been able to defeat a dead bolt and an alarm system without leaving a mark, it would have done no good. All he could do was tell her to be careful and not take any chances.

13

e reached One Police Plaza at ten and rode the elevator to the chief's office. The secretary motioned to a chair and said she'd tell the chief he was there. He sat. At eleven, the intercom on her desk went off. She picked it up, nodded, looked at Rogers and said the chief would see him now.

Chief O'Bannion was behind his desk, examining a stack of papers. He didn't look up immediately. He let Rogers stand and wait. Finally, he glanced up, his eyes moving over Rogers, and he pointed to a chair. "Sit down," he said.

Rogers sat and waited.

O'Bannion took his time. "What are your plans?" he said.

"That's up to you. I think I'd like to go back to Internal Affairs."

The chief shook his head. "I've given it some thought," he said. "IAD's got all the people it needs right now. What you need is a change of scenery. They need a lieutenant on the overnight out at the Six-O. I think you're the man for the job."

Sweet revenge, Rogers thought. Back in uniform and working nights, out on Coney Island. Just what he needed. "I think I'd be more use somewhere else," he said.

"No," O'Bannion said. "The Six-O is the right place. They've got some problems out there, bad morale, rumors of corruption, and more. Look into it. It's your kind of thing."

Rogers sighed. "When do you want me to start?"

"As soon as possible."

"Look, I've got time coming. Vacation, overtime, six or seven weeks, maybe more. I'd like to take it before I go out there. Settle some things, get my head together. You know."

"No objection," O'Bannion said. "Make it eight weeks and we'll be square."

"Fine." He waited. O'Bannion looked down at the papers on his desk, dismissing him. Rogers started to rise, then settled back. "One other thing," he said.

O'Bannion looked up. "What?"

"This guy, Gold."

"The shooter?"

"I'm not so sure about that. That's what I want to talk about."

A disgusted expression passed across the chief's face. "That's settled, lieutenant. It's a done deal. It's history. The guy was the shooter, all right, and we nailed him dead to rights. As far as the public's concerned, it's case closed. Unless a better explanation comes along, and right now we don't see one, Gold was the guy and he did it alone."

"There are a lot of questions," Rogers said.

"You and the damn feds. They've been on my ass about this. Well, they're wrong and you're wrong. I've heard all the questions. To me, they don't add up. The guy did it, all right. He was in the right place at the right time and he had the means. And he had a reason, which maybe you haven't heard."

"You mean that thing at the bathhouse?"

"The thing at the bathhouse. I don't know where you picked it up, but it's there. Damn it, Morrison chased the bastard out of town. I'd say he's been plotting his revenge all these years. Last Friday, he took it. In spades. And there's a lot more you don't know about, nobody knows about. It won't come out unless it has to."

"I still don't see a motive," Rogers said. "If you look at what he's done since, I'd say Morrison did him a favor."

O'Bannion sighed. "I've already assigned people to look into this thing from every angle. Maybe they'll turn up something, maybe they won't. But this is our case, not the feds', not anybody else's. It took place in our city, and we'll handle it ourselves, and we sure as hell don't need outside help."

"I want to be part of it," Rogers said. "I'll pass on my vacation."

"Forget it," O'Bannion said. "You take your time off. You've earned it. I want you to stay clear of this thing."

"I was close to him," Rogers said. "I knew him. I think I can help."

"That's the problem," O'Bannion said. "You were too close. You'd just get in the way."

Bellevue loomed like a grim, forbidding fortress over along First Avenue. Rogers went inside, down the stairs to the basement, and along the corridor until he reached pathology. He stopped at the desk. "Is Dr. Sadowsky around?"

The nurse at the desk examined him. He reached into his pocket, pulled out his wallet and flashed the shield. She studied it. "I'll see," she said. She picked up a phone and pressed a couple of numbers. "Dr. Sadowsky? There's a Lieutenant Rogers from the police here to see you." She waited, then pointed toward a door. "Through there," she said. "He's in the fourth office."

Rogers went through the door and along a corridor. He knocked at the door of the fourth office. A voice told him to come in.

Sadowsky was over at a table against a wall, a microscope with a slide in it in front of him. He looked at Rogers. "It's been a while," he said.

"It has."

"What can I do for you this time?"

"You people do the autopsy on Steven Gold?"

"As a matter of fact, you've come to the right window."

"How did he die?"

"You crazy? Bullet through the brain, up through the mouth. All the rest. It was in all the papers, for chrissake. We just had to confirm it. All you people like things official. Neat and proper, no loose ends."

"Did you do a complete autopsy, or did you just look at the wound?"

"You ought to know me well enough by now to know that I never do things in a half-assed way." He studied Rogers for a moment. "Why?"

"You're certain the bullet killed him?"

"Absolutely. No question about it."

"And that he fired it?"

"He had powder burns on his hands. In the right places. It added up."

"Was he conscious when the shot was fired?"

"You ever hear of an unconscious man firing a shot? What kind of crap is this?"

"I'm serious. Was he conscious?"

Sadowsky didn't answer right away. He looked up at the ceiling, then back at Rogers. "No way of knowing," he said at last.

"You found something, didn't you?"

"Barbiturates," he said. "In the blood stream. I'd have to do a complete analysis to say which one, but I'd guess chloral hydrate, you know, the classic Mickey Finn."

"How much?"

"Enough."

"To knock him out?"

"Yeah."

"Fast?"

"It would depend. If he wasn't used to them, probably. If he took them all the time, it might take longer."

"He take them by mouth or injection?"

"I didn't find any punctures. My guess is by mouth."

"So he could have been unconscious at the time of death."

"Could have been. No telling for certain now. He could have taken them right before he shot himself, to sort of settle himself down. That way, he wouldn't have gone immediately. They take a little time to work, say twenty minutes or so."

"Or somebody could have given him some, in a friendly drink or something like that, and he'd never have known, but he sure as hell would have gone under, and then whoever did it could have blown him away with no fuss. Right?"

Sadowsky looked away again. "You inventing a theory?" he said.

"Maybe. Right now, I'm just exploring."

"You think somebody else was the shooter and set him up?"

"I'm looking into that."

"Official? How come we haven't heard it?"

"Because it's not official. I'm doing it on my own. Me and a couple of other guys who have some doubts."

"I want to take another look at my notes," Sadowsky said.

"Do it."

"I'll get back to you."

"Leave a message on my machine if you can't reach me. At this number." Rogers gave him his home number. Sadowsky took it.

From Bellevue, Rogers headed across town to the Statler Hilton. Most of the barricades were gone, the few that remained stacked along the sidewalks. There was no sign of the yellow crime scene ribbon that had ringed the area that Friday night into Saturday morning.

Inside the hotel, he went to the desk and waited. A clerk approached. "Can I help you?"

Rogers displayed the shield. The clerk looked at him warily. "Were you on duty last Tuesday about noon?" Rogers asked.

"We had a lot of clerks on duty," he said. "The place was very busy. People were checking in for the convention, you know."

"I know. What I'd like to know is who checked in Steven Gold?"

The clerk stared at him. "It could have been anybody."

"If you were the one, would you recognize him if I showed you his picture?"

The clerk shook his head. "I doubt it. We were very busy, as I said. People checking in all the time, the lobby full. We had our hands full just trying to keep things moving. I don't think anybody would remember anybody who checked in that week."

"Then it wasn't you?"

"I have no idea."

"Would you ask the other clerks who were on duty?"

"I will. But I don't think they'd remember, either."

"Try."

The clerk wandered away. Rogers watched him. There were four other clerks behind the desk. The clerk approached each in turn, and Rogers saw all of them shake their heads. The clerk returned. "None of them remember," he said.

"Anybody else on duty that day?"

"No," the clerk said. "The five of us were handling everything. They should have had more people, but they didn't."

"Thanks anyway," Rogers said and turned away.

He took the subway down to City Hall. There was a lot of activity now. The city was returning to normal, the new mayor taking charge. About the only sign that things had changed was the flag flying at half-staff.

In his office, he looked around, trying to figure what to pack, what to save, what to get rid of. He didn't have that many personal things here, so it wouldn't be too hard to empty out the place and leave it for the next tenant.

He picked up the phone and dialed. Rodriguez answered on the first ring.

"Carlos," Rogers said.

"Right here, Ben. What's up?"

"When you found Gold, did you search the room?"

"Damn right. Why?"

"You find any pills? Prescription bottles, that kind of stuff?"

There was a long pause. "Why?" Rodriguez finally said.

"I'll tell you in a minute. You did a thorough sweep?"

"We always do."

"And no prescriptions?"

"I didn't say that."

"So you did find some."

"Aspirin. Eye drops and a dropper. The eye drops were in a prescription kind of bottle with a label from some drug store out in L.A. Another bottle with some pills in it. Looked like prescription but you couldn't be sure because there wasn't no label. We'd have to check."

"Where's the stuff now?"

"In the property room, where else?"

"Can you get to it and have someone check that unlabeled bottle?"

"Why? What the hell is this all about?"

"Gold had barbiturates in the blood stream. No needle mark on the arm. The M.E. says he probably took them by mouth."

"You kidding?"

"No."

"Where the hell does that leave us?"

"Looking for the real shooter. Where else?"

14

Max squatted in a couple of packing cases linked together under the Williamsburg Bridge. He had attached a makeshift door and fastened it with a padlock he'd probably scrounged out of some scrap heap, the kind that anyone could have opened by just breathing on it. Most of the time nobody did. The homeless might scrounge the city, might hassle ordinary citizens, but they tended to leave each other alone, respect each other's meager possessions, not that those possessions were worth much. When Max was out, the padlock was secured, not that it really offered much security; it was just a sign that he wasn't home. When he was in residence, the lock dangled, unfastened, from the hasp.

It was dangling when Rogers and Strickland approached it in the early evening.

"Jesus," Strickland said. "What a way to live."

"All the comforts of home," Rogers said, gesturing toward the electric lines that stretched from the shelter toward a Con Ed power line nearby. Max was stealing electricity from the utility. So were the people living in other packing crates and cardboard boxes nearby. Con Ed might complain, but nobody else did.

Rogers knocked on the flimsy door. "Max, are you in there?"

"Who the fuck wants to know?" a voice replied from inside.

"Three guesses."

There was a groan, the door opened. Inside was Max's home. There was a castoff day bed he'd found somewhere, a low table, a couple of chairs. There was a lamp, connected to the electric line, and it was lit. There was a TV, also connected, and it was going, the evening news flickering in black-and-white. There was a hot plate, also connected, glowing red under a pan filled with something that didn't look edible. The cords leading from the appliances were a jumbled mess, some of them frayed, bits of copper wiring visible in places. A little overload, anything at all, and Max's abode would be a memory, nothing but a small mound of ashes. Rogers had warned Max about that in the past, and Max kept saying not to worry, one of these days he'd get himself some of that black electrical tape and do some repairs. He just never seemed to get around to it.

"Lieutenant Rogers," Max said. He saw Strickland and froze.

"It's okay, Max," Rogers said. "This is Mr. Strickland. He works for the government."

"What fucking government?"

"Federal."

"What's he doing, conducting a survey? How the other half lives, that kind of shit?"

"Not that kind of shit, Max," Rogers said. "Invite us in."

"When did I ever say no? Come in, try to find room."

The top of the packing crate was only about an inch over their heads. They felt as though they ought to stoop to protect themselves. Max gestured toward the day bed. Rogers and Strickland sat. Max poised on the end of a lopsided kitchen chair covered in torn and faded green plastic.

"So?" Max said. "What brings you to my castle?" He kept looking at Strickland, his mind working. "I know you from somewhere," he said.

"Not likely," Strickland said. "I've never been here before. I spend most of my time in Washington."

"No," Max said. "I seen you someplace. It'll come to me."

"Mr. Strickland would like you to tell him about your meeting with Victor Santangello," Rogers said.

Max shook his head vigorously, a nervous look on his face. "Meeting? What fucking meeting? I only said I saw the bastard. That's all."

"It's okay. Don't worry, Mr. Strickland's on our side. I've known him for years. Just tell him where you saw Santangello."

Max did.

"Are you sure it was Santangello?" Strickland asked.

"Sure as I'm standing here," Max said.

"How can you be so sure?"

"Tell the man, Lieutenant," Max said to Rogers.

"In the bad old days," Rogers said, "before Max got religion, and discovered it was better to squat in a packing case than live the high life that could only lead to the slammer in the end, he was a runner for Santangello."

"The motherfucker ever finds out I talked to you, that

I been workin' for you, there won't be enough of me left to fertilize the weeds in the Jersey meadows," Max said.

"Max was one of the informants who supplied evidence against Santangello," Rogers said. "His identity was kept secret."

"What name did they give him?" Strickland said.

"Alphonse D-Three," Max said. "One of fuckin' Morrison's fuckin' jokes. You know, after you, Alphonse. A couple of the other guys they called Gaston."

"Oh," Strickland said, "you're the Alphonse D-Three. You had some good stuff."

Max looked at him. "How the hell would you know?"

"I was working with Morrison then, on the Santangello case," Strickland said. "I didn't have anything to do with the informants, but I heard all about the four Gastons and the six Alphonses and the rest. Morrison never told most of us their real names."

Max looked at him a different way. "What d'ya know," he said. "The bastard really kept his word. I wondered. I was sure he had a big mouth like most of you guys, which is one of the reasons I ran like hell when I saw Santangello that time up on Columbus."

"Okay," Rogers said. "You were supposed to get back to me if you heard anything more."

"Yeah. Only, I figured you was kinda busy, and it could wait. Maybe I was wrong."

"Why?"

" 'Cause I seen Santangello one more time."

"When?"

"The day Morrison got his."

"Where?"

"Down around the Garden. I figured the pickin's would be good around there, what with all the tourists and the rest, you know, and one minute I look up and I seen Santangello comin' out of the hotel where Morrison had his headquarters. I did the invisible man before he could spot me."

Rogers and Strickland both stared at Max with renewed interest.

"What time was this?" Rogers asked.

"Afternoon sometime. I ain't got a watch and I don't give a fuck about time, so I can't be too sure. Like I said, I didn't hang around after that."

"Was there anybody with him?" Rogers asked.

Max's face worked. He shrugged. He shook his head. "How the fuck would I know? I wasn't checkin'. There must have been a million people around. All I know is I spot Santangello and I make like I was Carl Lewis."

As they walked away from the squatters' village, Strickland said, "I wouldn't have believed it."

"No? You've got it from the horse's mouth."

"I'm going to have to press."

"You couldn't find out anything?"

"They stonewalled. I put out the lines and the answer that came back was nobody was saying anything. It was like one of those press conferences where the guy keeps saying, 'no comment.'"

"Which usually means you're on the right track and they don't want to answer."

"Most of the time. But not always."

"But this time, yes. What I want to know is, where have they got Santangello stashed?"

"I'm going to find out. You can bet your life on it."

"Maybe Morrison's life, and some others."

"Maybe. Because now it looks like we've got another strong possibility."

"Someone who had it in for Morrison. Real bad. And somebody who wouldn't think twice about blowing him away."

Strickland said, "What's our next move?"

"One, I want to talk to the girl, Annie, again. I'm going to press her to come through with Gondolian's files."

"You told me somebody took them."

"Yeah. But she read them first. And she's got a good memory. And then I'm going to pay a visit to the three musketeers. Want to come along?"

Strickland hesitated, then shook his head. "You do it and let me know how you make out. I'm going to track down Santangello. Then we'll compare notes."

15

At home, Rogers picked up the messages off his machine. There was one from Annie Kendall. She wanted to thank him for all he'd done. She'd been doing a lot of thinking. He should call so they could get together. There was one from Melissa. She missed him. She wondered when he was coming to California. Abby Gold was anxious to talk to him. There were a couple of others he ignored.

He called Annie Kendall. Her voice answered, saying she wasn't home at the moment, but if the caller would leave his name, number, and a message, she'd return the call as soon as she could.

He left a message. He wanted to see her. They had things to talk about. He'd call in the morning.

He called California. Melissa's answering machine picked up, reciting nearly the same greeting as Annie's.

At the beep, he said he missed her, too. He said he loved her. He said he had a few things to finish and then he hoped to fly out to the coast by the beginning of the week.

He didn't make any other calls. He had no desire to talk to another answering machine. He went to bed.

As he was having breakfast, Carlos Rodriguez called. "I hear you're on sabbatical," Rodriguez said.

"The word spreads fast," Rogers said.

"You can't keep secrets around here," Rodriguez said. "What're you doin'?"

"Getting ready to pay a few visits."

"Can they wait?"

"Why?"

"There's someone you ought to meet."

"Who?"

"Charlie Westerman." Charlie Westerman was the cop Max had seen in the Cuban restaurant on Columbus with Victor Santangello.

"You've talked to him?"

"Briefly. Grab your running stuff and meet me at the reservoir in Central Park in an hour."

"What the hell is this?" Rogers said.

"Charlie's a jogger. Every morning at the same time. Like he's got a time clock. We run into him there, we can talk and get some exercise at the same time. What the hell, you're a runner, too."

"Yeah. But I run early, or I run late. Not in the middle of the morning when it's this hot."

"So, today you make an exception."

Rogers changed into shorts, a t-shirt and running shoes and left the house. He felt a little stupid walking around the city dressed like this, but he wasn't the only guy in the subway wearing shorts, a t-shirt, and running shoes. He blended.

It was about ten when Rogers reached the Engineer's Gate at Central Park, moved around the wooden horses that closed the park to traffic during the summer, and headed for the reservoir. Rodriguez, dressed for a run, was waiting at the stairs leading up to the track. The muscles in his arms and legs bulged. He looked like he not only ran but pumped iron, which was the truth. There weren't many other runners. The temperature was already approaching ninety, and the humidity was close to that. Most had already finished and gone their way, or wouldn't start until dusk. Midday in this kind of weather was for mad dogs and people who had slept late and were compulsive about never missing a day.

"Let's go on up," Rodriguez said when Rogers reached him.

"Where's Westerman?"

"He's on his first lap," Rodriguez said. "We'll pick him up when he comes around."

About five minutes later, they saw Charlie Westerman moving at a slow jog along the middle of the path. Westerman was a medium-sized man in his late thirties. He looked as though he was in fairly decent shape, no pot belly, not much extra fat. Running helped. Westerman had a Walkman strapped around his waist, the earphones around his head. His eyes were half closed. He was listening to whatever he was listening to and not paying much attention. He reached the stairs and passed by.

"Let's move it," Rodriguez said.

He and Rogers started out at the easy jog, caught up with Westerman and moved alongside, Rogers to the right, Rodriguez to the left. At first, Westerman didn't notice them, concentrating on what was coming from the walkman. They had run about a half mile, reaching the northern pump house, before Westerman sensed that he wasn't alone. His head turned, first left, then right, and he saw

Rogers and Rodriguez. He nodded with recognition and kept going.

"Must be good listenin'," Rodriguez said.

Without breaking stride, Westerman turned his head slightly and nodded. "The best," he said. "Old Blue Eyes." He kept going.

"Run off to the right, Charlie," Rodriguez said as they reached a side path heading away from the track.

Westerman looked startled.

"You heard me, Charlie," Rodriguez said. "Do it. Toward the tennis courts."

Westerman broke stride, nodded slowly, and took an oblique turn, moving down the path. Rodriguez and Rogers stayed with him. The courts were crowded, games going on at every one. Like always. They reached a grassy spot overlooking the courts. There was nobody on the grass.

Rodriguez took Westerman's arm and stopped him. "Take off the 'phones and sit down, Charlie," Rodriguez said.

Westerman stared at him, then did as he had been told. He was sweating, which was natural, given the heat and the exercise. They were all sweating. But Westerman's sweat had a kind of unhealthy sheen, and there was a scared look on his face.

"You run nice, Charlie. Nice and smooth. The thing is, you can run but you can't hide."

Westerman didn't say anything. He just sweated.

"You know Lieutenant Rogers?" Rodriguez said.

Westerman nodded. "We've met," he said. He was sweating even more.

"He wants to talk to you."

"About what? You guys know I'm clean," he protested,

but not too vigorously. "There's never been even a whisper."

"I'm not Internal Affairs now," Rogers said.

"I know," Westerman said. "You were the mayor's boy. Poor fuckin' bastard. So, what's this all about?"

"Victor Santangello," Rogers said.

Westerman swallowed hard. "Heard of him. Don't know him."

"That's what he told me," Rodriguez said to Rogers.

"I hear you do know him, Charlie," Rogers said.

"Whoever told you that got the wrong guy."

"I think whoever told me that had the right guy."

"No way."

"I'll even tell you where and when." Rogers told him.

Westerman looked very unhappy.

"Charlie, Charlie," Rodriguez said, "you had such a nice clean reputation. Now, look what you done."

"I didn't do anything."

"No? Then explain it."

Westerman leaned forward, burying his face in his hands. He didn't say anything. Then he looked at Rogers, stricken. And there was a look in his face that said he'd been waiting for this, he had been expecting it, dreading it and hoping it would come, that it was a thing he could no longer live with, he only needed an excuse, a reason to rid himself of it. "I've got a sick kid," he murmured.

"I'm sorry about that," Rogers said. "But lots of guys have sick kids. Lots of guys have lots of excuses, lots of reasons."

"No," Westerman said, "I mean it. He's real sick. God, he's only seven, right at the beginning, and he's got something wrong with his heart. The doctors say he's not going to get better unless he has a transplant. You know how hard it is to find the right match, to even find a heart, and then you know what kind of money they're talking about.''

"Insurance pays for it."

"Sure, insurance pays for it. After everything else you've saved up is gone. And then they only pay a percentage."

"So Santangello got to you at the right time."

"I didn't even know the bastard was out until the day I picked up the phone and he said who he was. I thought he was in the slammer forever. He said he wanted to see me. If it hadn't been for the kid, I never would have listened. Hell, I never would have met the son of a bitch."

"But you met him."

"Yeah. I met him."

"What did he offer?"

"He said name it."

"And you named it."

Westerman didn't answer.

"What'd he want?"

"Where he could find some people."

"Who?"

"The rats who sang on him. He gave me four names."

"Give."

"Max Abromowitz, Terry Galvin, Willie Giovanetti, Pat Wylie."

"How did he know that?"

"He said the feds told him. He said this fed he had tied up nice and tight gave him a list of the rats who squealed on him, gave him the cover names, like Alphonse and Gaston with numbers after them, and the real names to match. He said the fed told him where he could find most of 'em, except for those four."

''Why did he come to you?''

''He said the feds claimed they didn't know where those four guys were. He tried, but they said they didn't know. He figured they were telling it straight since they pointed him to the other guys. He remembered me because I was in narcotics back then and I used to run into him. Hell, I used to hassle the hell out of him. And when the feds went after him, I worked with them. So he figured I must know the guys who ratted, what they were doin' these days. He also knew about my kid. I ain't got the slightest idea how he found out about that, but I guess he's got his way. So he put it to me straight. Give about the rats and he'd take care of things so my kid would get what he needed.''

''And you did. You sold out.''

Westerman nodded slowly. ''What I could find out.''

''What did you find out?''

''About Max and Terry. Max. He's a homeless guy now, lives in cardboard down by the river. Terry works as a night clerk at a flophouse just off the Bowery. The other two, I lost track of, they just disappeared and nobody knows where they went.''

''You told Santangello what you knew?''

Westerman nodded slowly.

''And he paid you off.''

Westerman shook his head. ''No. He said he would. He said he'd get the money to me. But he hasn't. And I haven't seen him or heard from him and I wouldn't know where to look for him. I saw him two times and that was it.''

''Twice?''

''Yeah. Once when he put it to me and once when I told him where he could find Max and Terry.''

Rogers and Rodriguez exchanged looks. "You believe him, Carlos?" Rogers asked.

Rodriguez thought about it, then nodded. "No reason not to."

"Even that he never got the bread?"

"I swear it," Westerman said. "It's the truth. Why would I lie when I told you the rest?"

Rodriguez stared at Westerman. "I guess he's telling the truth."

"What're you guys going to do?" Westerman asked.

"I suppose we ought to bring you up on charges," Rogers said.

"Oh, Jesus," Westerman said. "I never did anything before. I've always been straight. Jesus. I've had a million opportunities and I never fell."

"Not until this time."

"Not until now. I was desperate. You gotta understand. But I guess I've got it coming, don't I?"

"You do."

"One mistake's all it takes."

"Right."

"Jesus, what am I going to say to my wife? What am I going to say to my kid?"

"You should have thought of that before," Rogers said.

"Give me some time, will you?" Westerman pleaded.

"How much?"

"A few days. A week. I've got to think."

"Don't do anything foolish, Charlie."

Westerman didn't answer. He buried his head in his hands and his shoulders started to shake. Rogers and Rodriguez watched him, then rose silently and moved away, back toward the running track.

"Poor bastard," Rodriguez said.

"Yeah."

"You think he's going to do somethin'?"

Rogers nodded slowly. "Yeah."

"I feel sorry for him."

"Yeah. And I feel sorrier for Max and Terry."

Rodriguez, his car parked just outside the park in an illegal spot, gave him a ride downtown. Rodriguez had placed the police card on the dashboard where it was visible to the passing meter maids. They hadn't given him a ticket.

They didn't talk much on the ride. They both had come away with a bad taste, a sense that there were no winners in this, only losers. As Rodriguez let Rogers out in front of the brownstone in the Village, the detective said, "When I get in, I'm going to do some checking. I'll let you know."

16

About noon, Rogers called Annie Kendall. Her machine picked up and recited the same announcement as before. He left another message for her to call. He thought about that and then called her newspaper. The operator rang her extension and when there was no answer, connected him with the metropolitan desk. He asked for Annie Kendall.

"She's not here now," a voice said.

"Do you know when she'll be back?"

"She's on special assignment. She'll probably check in later."

He left his name and asked that she call when they heard from her.

Then he headed out. First stop was the Public Library on Fifth Avenue. He went up to the office of Sam Janosky, the head of research, a man he had come to know well in the past.

"You need some help, Ben? Again?"

"Always. Sam, I want to run a couple of names. Four to be exact."

"Read them off and I'll see what the computer comes up with."

"Harvey Jessup. Melvin Rasmussen. Moishe Weinstein. Steven Gold."

Janosky sat back and studied Rogers. "Not precisely nonentities," he said. "You got all afternoon? This will take some time. I'd guess the listings are as long as your arm. Just what do you want?"

"Background. Insights. Whatever."

Janosky turned to his computer, pressed some keys and the screen filled. Rogers stood at his shoulder, watching and reading.

"You want a printout?" Janosky asked.

"Not everything. I'll tell you what and when."

It went like that for most of the afternoon. Something would appear, Rogers would tap Janosky's shoulder. Janosky would mark the particular data and feed it to the printer. By five, Rogers was walking down the long steps, threading his way through the crowds that sprawled on the cement between the lions in the hot sun. He carried a bulging manila envelope filled with the printouts. He wasn't completely sure what he had. The pages had come off one after another about each man. There had been no chance to put them together and see what, if anything, developed. He'd spend the evening at home doing that, trying to make some order and sense.

There were two messages on his machine when he reached home. Call Carlos Rodriguez. Call George Strickland. Nothing from Annie Kendall. He called Rodriguez. Rodriguez recited his name after the first ring.

"You got something, Carlos?"

"Yeah. And it ain't pretty."

"Give."

"Terry Galvin. According to the record, somebody tried to rip off the flophouse the other day. The story is that Terry said no. The story is that the guy didn't like taking no for an answer and he put one into Terry's head, right between the eyes. Bye-bye, Terry. Only, for chrissake, what asshole would try to rob a flophouse?"

"Witnesses? Description?"

"Witnesses? Comin' out your ass. Half a dozen, maybe more. Winos, hop heads, junkies, you name it. Yeah, they gave descriptions. A white guy, a black guy, a Spanish guy, a dame dressed like a man, a short guy, a tall guy, black hair, blond hair. Some fuckin' composite. It was handled by the local precinct. We didn't draw it because who the hell cares about a clerk in a flophouse? A fuckin' file-and-forget."

Rogers digested that. "What else?"

"I went over to the squatters' digs under the bridge, you know, to look up Max Abromowitz. He wasn't home. His castle was locked up tighter than a drum. There was just one thing." Rodriguez waited.

"Okay, I'm all ears."

"He had a new lock on the door. Not from a dump. From a real, honest-to-God locksmith. Not cheap. I think maybe the guy's worried, he throws his bread around like that."

"If I was Max, I'd be worried."

"So would I."

"If I get a chance, I'll wander over there and take a look myself."

"You come up with anything?"

"Just background stuff from the library. I haven't put it together yet."

"A fuckin' scholar," Rodriguez said, and rang off.

He called Strickland. "You learn anything?" he asked when Strickland answered.

"I pushed, and they gave a little," Strickland said. "They admit Santangello is out. They admit they've got him holed up here. They admit he's talking and they say what's coming out isn't vomit but pure gold. They claim they've got him sealed away tight, no chance that he's taking a walk all by his lonesome."

"And just who's doing the protecting?"

"The marshals, working three shifts."

"Santangello got to them, at least two of them," Rogers said.

"I'd bet on it," Strickland agreed. "Some of those guys have itchy palms, sure. But not many. Every once in a while you'll find the bad apple. You say the right thing, and prove you can back it up, and they drool. And the hand goes out. Then they start looking the other way. But they're the exception."

"You find out where they've got him?"

"The Summit, the hotel right over the subway station on Lex."

"Take the elevator down, a short walk and you're on your way."

"You know it."

"Can we get to him?"

"I asked. They said no way."

"Use your influence. You got the clout."

"I'll see what I can do. But don't hold your breath."

"And, for chrissake, talk to somebody. See if you can persuade them to keep the bastard in one place for more than ten minutes."

"I intend to. Now, what have you been up to? You talk to the three musketeers yet?"

"Not yet. Tomorrow. Today was research day."

"And?"

"I haven't had a chance to digest yet."

"Well, good eating and let me know."

Rogers tried Annie Kendall again. The machine was still picking up. The same greeting. He was beginning to get worried. He debated whether to take a ride up to her apartment and check. He turned it over. The paper said she was on a special assignment, which could mean anything, which could mean she could be anywhere, could be out-of-touch. He didn't like it.

The other things could wait. He went down to the street and rode the subway up the west side, got off at Seventy-ninth Street and walked west and north until he came to her building. In the lobby, he pressed her button. There was no response. He pressed several more buttons. He got a rise out of at least one. A voice came over the intercom asking who was there, and it was followed almost simultaneously by a clicking at the door. He pushed the door open, walked down the corridor and rode the elevator to her floor. Her door was locked and there were no lights visible from beneath the door. He rang. There was no response.

He hardly debated before reaching into his pocket and pulling out some picks. He fiddled with the lock and in less than a minute had the door open and was inside. The apartment was dark. Switching on the lights, he looked around. It was just the way he'd last seen it. A disaster. The books were still all over the floor, the furniture shoved around, drawers opened and the contents scattered. The bedroom was a replica. She hadn't even bothered to make the bed. She must have left right after he did and not come back. She hadn't even picked up the messages on her answering machine. The red light was glowing.

He felt better now. He scribbled a note on a piece of paper saying he'd been there to check on things when he hadn't heard from her, so she wouldn't be worried if she noticed scratches on the locks, and please call. Then he left, relocking the doors.

Back in his apartment, he made himself a sandwich and coffee, carried them to the table and, while he ate, opened the manila envelope, spread out the pages and began to organize them. In a couple of hours he had a fairly decent picture, the outline, if not the depth, of the four men. And he had found links, more than one. Maybe not the one, or more than one, that Gondolian had discovered and so enigmatically directed him toward, but links nevertheless. And maybe it was just that he wanted to see the ties and so read more into it than was really there.

Rasmussen, Weinstein, Jessup, and Gold were all in their late forties, not a year separating them. Weinstein, who was called Martin in those days and not Moishe, Jessup, and Gold all had been born and raised in the Bronx, along the Grand Concourse. Rasmussen had been born and raised in Harlem, just across the river from the Bronx. All four had gone to Bronx High School of Science, graduating in the same class. All four had gone on to Columbia University as undergraduates, though each had a different major—Rasmussen's field was science, particularly chemistry; Weinstein's was philosophy; Jessup's history; and Gold majored in English.

A couple of years after graduation, Rasmussen had taken off for a Baptist seminary in the south, to study for the ministry. Weinstein had gone to Israel where he turned religious, very religious, orthodox religious. Jessup had gone west, to the University of California at Berkeley, where he had become an outspoken gay activist. After a time in the New York theatre, Gold had gone to Hollywood.

Within a decade, Rasmussen, Weinstein, and Jessup were back in New York. Gold remained in California and carved out an onward and upward movie career. Rasmussen took over a small Baptist church in Harlem, preaching the militant gospel of black power. Weinstein was installed as rabbi of a small ultra-orthodox synagogue in Crown Heights where he rallied to the cause of the Jewish Defense League, taking offense at any slight, real or imagined. Jessup founded GALEA, the Gay and Lesbian Alliance, and took to the streets and the pamphlets to press for equal rights for gays.

He kept shuffling the pages, lining them up, searching for something else, anything else. It came then that there was something he hadn't noticed. Maybe it meant nothing. Maybe it had a deeper meaning. But it was there. All four men had left New York about the same time. The three who had returned came back about the same time.

At ten the next morning, he set out for GALEA. The organization operated out of a small house set in a garden on a winding street in the West Village. You opened a wrought iron gate and walked along a narrow path between what at first glance looked like overgrown vegetation but, on closer examination, proved to be well-tended gardens of herbs, vegetables, and even some flowers. The house was brown shingled, the shingles in need of repair and refinishing.

Rogers climbed the three steps to the front door and

rang the bell. There was no answer. He rang again. A voice called from inside, "Come on in. It's not locked."

He stepped inside. Across the room, a slim, attractive young woman sat behind a desk, staring at a computer screen. She looked like a college kid on a summer job, which maybe she was. She had short blond hair which looked like it hadn't seen a comb or brush in months and wore no makeup. She was wearing a t-shirt emblazoned across the front, in large red letters, the motto, "Gay and Proud of It." There were two large buttons pinned to the t-shirt. One, red letters on a white background, said, "GALEA." The other, black letters on a white background, read, "AIDS" with a red slash across the letters, from the top left to the bottom right. She kept staring at the computer screen, typed something on the keyboard and then looked toward him. She started to smile, then saw he wasn't anyone she knew or recognized, and the face turned a little cold.

"Yes?" she said. "You want something?"

"Is Harvey Jessup around?"

She examined him. "He's in conference," she said.

"Any idea when he'll be free?"

"Next week," she said.

He sighed, reached into his pocket, pulled out a card and dropped it on the desk in front of her. She looked at it. "I knew you were a cop," she said. "You have the look. And the smell."

"That's okay," he said. "Just take that in to Jessup, will you?"

She picked up the card and held it. She put it down and turned back to the computer screen and began to work at the keyboard again. He waited and watched her. She ignored him for a couple of minutes, then pressed a button on the keyboard. The screen flickered, whatever she was working on vanishing and a menu appearing in its place. She reached out, turned off the computer, got up and, without looking at him or saying anything, stepped out from behind the desk, went to a door and through it.

He waited, his eyes moving about the room. There was an old sofa against one wall, a low, dark gray glass coffee table with some chips in it in front, and a couple of upholstered chairs. Nothing matched and repairs would have helped a lot. The walls were filled with photographs. Some had been there for some time, they were a little faded and curled, some were newer. Some of the faces were familiar, some famous and a lot just ordinary people. They all had something in common. They were all dead and they had all died of the same thing. It wasn't pleasant to contemplate.

The girl came back through the door. She went back behind the desk and turned the computer back on, pressed a button and whatever she'd been working on reappeared. She studied it. Then she looked at Rogers. "Harvey's in there," she said, nodding toward the door. "He'll see you." The expression said, it beats me why.

Harvey Jessup's office was a small, cramped cubicle made even smaller by a large, curving, rosewood pedestal desk, a dozen filing cabinets and a couple of chairs for visitors. There were a dozen framed autographed photos on the walls, good wishes and mementos from instantly recognizable men and women—the President, Mayor Morrison, a couple of senators and a few congressmen, authors and actors and even a business leader or two. An air conditioner in the window was going full blast. The room could have doubled for a meat storage locker. Rogers felt a chill run through him.

Jessup leaned back in a large leather chair behind the desk, holding a bulging notebook. Neither the chair nor the desk looked too big for him. He was a large, fleshy man in his mid- to late-forties, with a full head of long, wavy gray hair gathered in a ponytail at the back. He was dressed in a black polo shirt and tan trousers, the legs stretched out beneath the pedestal ending in worn running shoes. He set the notebook on the desk and looked up as Rogers came through the door. Rising, he extended his hand across the desk.

"It's nice to see you again, Lieutenant," he said.

"I wasn't sure you'd remember," Rogers said. "I was always in the background."

"I notice things," Jessup said.

Rogers took the offered hand. Jessup motioned toward a seat across from him, and sat back. "That was a dreadful thing," he said. "He was a good mayor, a good man. The city can ill afford to lose him."

"Agreed."

"How can I help you? I'm sure this isn't a social call. I imagine it must have something to do with what happened."

"A lot of loose ends," Rogers said. "I'm trying to tie off some of them."

"If I can help, fire away."

"How well did you know Gold?"

"You mean Steven Gold? The one they say shot him?"

"That's who I mean. How well did you know him?"

"Not well. I've seen him now and again over the last few years." The face was bland, the voice even. It sounded good. It sounded as though he was leveling, but Rogers knew better.

"I assumed you knew him better than casually."

"Not really," Jessup said. "We met about five or six years ago at an AIDS benefit, got to talking, and we've seen each other off and on since. Steven was very concerned about the AIDS epidemic. But who isn't? He wanted to do something to help. He gave money and he gave time." He reached for a pipe in an ashtray on the desk, filled it from a humidor, taking his time, then lit it and puffed slowly. He looked back at Rogers. "These are not just idle queries, are they? Are you just trying to put together a profile of Steven Gold, or do you have some reservations?"

"Do you?" Rogers asked.

"How could I?" Jessup said. "I only know what I hear and read. It certainly appears that he was the man who did the shooting."

"That's how it appears," Rogers agreed. He debated whether to face Jessup down, throw at him what he had learned. He decided this wasn't the moment to press all the way. He'd push just enough to worry the man. Maybe Jessup would start to wonder just how much Rogers actually knew, and then he'd start to sweat, and then it might be possible to get inside through those open pores.

"You know," Rogers said reflectively, "I've always been puzzled about something."

"What's that?" Jessup said.

"How come three guys who are so different could work together behind Morrison."

Jessup watched him closely. "Who are you talking about?"

"You, Rasmussen, and Weinstein."

Jessup gave a short laugh. "Politics makes strange bedfellows, as the old saying goes. Actually, if you really look at it, we didn't work together. We went our separate ways. It just happened that we agreed on one thing. That Jack Morrison was the best man for the city, and for the state."

"That's all?"

"That's all."

"I don't know," Rogers said. "Sometimes I used to see the three of you together with him and I'd swear there was more than that. It was like you three were joined hip and thigh, as they say."

"Your eyes deceived you. When you come right down to it, we actually don't like each other much. Marty, or Moishe, as he calls himself these days, is of the opinion that I'm a curse on the human race. He thinks homosexuality is not just an unforgivable sin but a disease that infects all of society. And, to tell the truth, I haven't got much use for people who are so narrow-minded, you know, people who are certain they have all the answers, that their way is the only way, which is Moishe to a T. As for Mel, well, he's a bigot in his own right. If you're not black, you're not worth two cents, and even if you're black, if you're not the right kind of black, which means his kind, then you're worth even less. And about people like me, he shares the same sentiments as Marty. So, if you think there was anything between the three of us beyond supporting Morrison, you couldn't be more wrong. And even that one thing is history now. I'm sure in the future you'll find us on opposite sides of the barricades."

"Maybe," Rogers said. "But it was a feeling I had. Besides, you guys go back a long way, don't you?"

Jessup thought about that for a moment. "Have you been checking up on us?" he asked finally.

"Is there something to check?"

"I'd say you've been doing some homework. I don't know what you think you've discovered, but it was one thing when we were a lot younger. We've taken different roads since then."

"And Steven Gold?"

Jessup's face, and the mind behind it, worked. He considered. "There was a Gold back in college. I didn't know him. I heard about him, but I don't think I ever ran into him. Is that the same Gold?"

"The very same. The one and only."

"I'll be damned."

Rogers decided then that he'd pressed as far as he wanted for the moment. He rose from the chair. "Well, thanks for the help, Mr. Jessup."

"No more questions?"

"Not for the moment. If I think of any more, I'll be back in touch."

Jessup nodded. "I hope I've been of some help, though I don't see that I've contributed very much."

"More than you know, sir. More than you know." He turned and headed for the door. As he opened it, he took a quick glance back. Jessup was reaching for the phone.

Rogers came down the elevated stairs at 125th Street and walked toward Lenox Avenue. There weren't many white faces around, and a few people gave him a look and then turned away. Some kids stared and made him. They had a way of recognizing a cop no matter how he dressed or acted. From them there were some sour looks, some sneers, and a few muttered comments. He ignored them,

turned north for a few blocks and eventually reached
Rasmussen's small church, a neat white frame building
in the center of the block, a sign over the door saying it
was Shiloh Baptist Church. He went up the steps, between
the white columns, and through the door, stood just inside
the church proper and looked down toward the altar. He
spotted Rasmussen sitting in a front pew, surrounded by
half a dozen other men. He moved down the aisle toward
the group.

Rasmussen saw him, stiffened, motioned toward the
group, which silenced them, rose and stood rigidly waiting, no welcome in his face or stance. He was a big man.
He looked as though he could have, in his younger days,
played an inside lineman for a professional football team.
His black hair and neatly trimmed black beard were
flecked with gray. His skin had the glow of highly polished
mahogany.

"Reverend Rasmussen," Rogers said when he was
within a few feet of the man.

Rasmussen ran his eyes over Rogers. "I recognize you,
young man," Rasmussen said. "You were Morrison's
errand boy."

"In a manner of speaking."

"What brings you to enemy territory?"

"Is that what this is?"

"In a manner of speaking," Rasmussen said. He smiled
just a little.

"I'd appreciate a few minutes of your time."

"Why?"

"There are some questions I'd like to ask."

"About the late mayor?"

"That, and some other things."

Rasmussen nodded slowly and turned. "In my office,"

he said. He started toward a door to one side of the altar. He didn't look back. Rogers followed.

The office was spacious and well-furnished. There were African masks and African woven tapestries on the walls, African sculptures on tables, a bookcase filled with books by American black and African writers, books about Africa, about slavery, about the state of blacks in America.

Rasmussen went behind a large desk and leaned back in a large leather chair. He motioned Rogers into a chair on the other side of the desk. "Now, young man, what can I do for you?" Watching him, Rogers had a feeling that Rasmussen knew precisely what Rogers wanted, that he was far from surprised when Rogers showed up, that actually he had been expecting him. "Tell me about Steven Gold."

"For a white man, he was okay." It was the kind of answer that could have meant something, or nothing at all. Rasmussen's face, and voice, were unreadable, so it was hard to tell.

"You knew him well?"

"I know no white men well."

"But, still, you've known him for a long time. You went to college together, maybe even high school."

"That was then and this is now."

"What does that mean?"

Rasmussen studied Rogers. He took his time with his answer. He was taking time with all his answers, as though he had prepared for this. Maybe he had. "We were one thing when we were young. We became another thing as we grew older. We went our separate ways and turned into other people."

"But you kept contact?"

"No. We lost contact. We only renewed our acquain-

tance two or three years ago. I gather Steven had heard
of my work. Perhaps, like some few white men, he felt
guilt and a desire to atone. In my mail one day, I received
a rather large donation from him. I wrote and thanked
him. He wrote back. Since then, he has contributed money
to my church and my cause." Rasmussen laughed as he
added, "We would, of course, accept money even from
the devil himself."

"And you've seen him often, right?"

"No," Rasmussen said. "Perhaps twice in that time."

"Talked to him on the phone?"

"I can recall three conversations. No more."

"Recently?"

"No. More than a year ago."

"You haven't talked to him in more than a year?"

"Neither talked nor seen." Rasmussen was watching
Rogers closely, through hooded eyes.

Rasmussen was trying to gauge the effect his answers
were having, trying to see whether Rogers was buying.
That was obvious. Rogers kept his face blank. "So you
haven't any idea why he would shoot Mayor Morrison?"

"None whatever. I assume, however, that you have
some questions about that. Otherwise, you wouldn't be
here."

"I'm just trying to get a picture of the man."

"In that, I'm afraid I can be of little assistance."

"Well, it doesn't hurt to try. I want to talk to anyone
who knew him. You and other guys who go way back."

"I repeat myself. That was then, this is now. We are
not the same men we were a quarter of a century ago.
The world is not the same and we are not the same."

"The more things change, the more they stay the
same," Rogers said.

"It is better in the French," Rasmussen said. "And it is no more true in English than it is French." He smiled a little, then made a dismissing gesture. "If you have no more questions, I have some important meetings. I interrupted one, and I must get back to it." He waited.

Rogers nodded and rose. "Nothing that can't wait until later."

"Now or later," Rasmussen said, "you will learn nothing from me that you don't know already."

It took more than an hour to reach Brooklyn. It was dark when he came up out of the subway into a different world, a different country, a different time. It was as though the clock had run in fast reverse during his underground ride. He emerged into a world that could have existed a century earlier, a place where the people spoke a strange dialect he could not understand, where the men and even the young boys wore large hats, felt and broad-brimmed or fur, all with side locks curling down in front of the ears. Many had full beards, and wore long black coats and trousers with white shirts buttoned at the neck and no ties. The women, even in the summer heat, wore long dresses with sleeves down to their wrists, dark cotton stockings, no makeup, and wigs covering their heads. Even signs on the storefronts were in a script he could not decipher.

Just off President Street he found the address he had written on a piece of paper, an old brownstone, Hebrew letters over the door. He climbed the stairs. The door was locked. He knocked. No one appeared. He stood just outside the door, looking along the street. Two young men, dressed so much alike they could have passed for twins, were walking toward him. He moved down the

steps and approached. They were in such an intense dis-
cussion they never noticed him until he blocked their
way. They halted and stared.

"Sorry," he said. "There doesn't seem to be anyone
here."

"It's late," one of the young men said. "The shabbos
services are over and everyone has left for the night."

It took him a moment to understand, to realize this
was Saturday, the Jewish sabbath. It was after sundown,
of course, so the sabbath was over. "I'm looking for
Rabbi Weinstein," he said.

The two young men talked to each other rapidly. It
sounded like an argument. It wasn't. One of the young
men turned to Rogers. "You go two blocks that way,"
he said, pointing, "then you turn right and go three blocks.
The rabbi lives in the middle of the block. Come, we
will show you, so you shouldn't get lost."

Rogers started to say that wasn't necessary, then didn't
say it because it probably was necessary. They started
off, went the two blocks, went the three blocks to the
right, and stopped in the middle of the block. "This is
the rabbi's house," one of the young men said.

"Thanks," Rogers said.

"Thanks are not necessary," one of the young men
said. "It is a commandment to help strangers who are
lost." They went on.

Rogers went up the steps to the front door and rang
the bell. The door opened. A woman in a long dress, a
scarf bound tightly around her head concealing her hair,
stood in the entrance staring at him. "Yes?" Behind her,
from the interior of the house, he could hear the sounds
of children.

"I'm looking for Rabbi Weinstein."

"The rabbi is having his meal," she said, blocking the way. "He has had a long day, and he is tired."

"I only need a few minutes of his time."

"The rabbi does not like to be disturbed when he is having his meal. He especially does not like to be disturbed at the end of the shabbos."

"I understand. But would you tell him that Lieutenant Rogers from the police would like to talk to him?"

"You are from the community relations department? I do not know you."

"I'm not from community relations," he said. "I used to work for Mayor Morrison. I think the rabbi may remember me."

"Mayor Morrison? Oi! A tragedy. May his soul rest." She turned and moved down the hall. He stepped just inside the door and waited.

He heard voices, in that other language, from a room off the hall. The rabbi came through the door, shrugging into a black coat, wiping his mouth with a large napkin. He was a man of medium height with red hair turning gray, a yarmulke on his head, and a red beard streaked with gray. He looked a little soft around the middle.

He walked toward Rogers, his hand outstretched. Rogers took it. The grip was firm. "Lieutenant," he said, "you have come to my home? You would like to see me? To talk about what?"

Rogers sighed. He was certain Weinstein knew precisely what he had come to talk about. "Steven Gold," he said.

Weinstein nodded. "Come to my study. We will be comfortable. You would like maybe a glass of tea?"

"Nothing, thanks," Rogers said.

Weinstein led the way down the hall, opened a door

and led him into a room filled to overflowing with books, some in English, most in Hebrew. The furniture was old and worn, and didn't look particularly comfortable. The chair the rabbi motioned him into wasn't. He didn't think the high-backed old fashioned chair Weinstein settled into was, either.

"Now," Weinstein said, "what is you would like to know?"

"Tell me about Steven Gold."

"What is there to tell?"

"You knew him."

"When we were young, yes. That was many years ago. As you can see, I am not young anymore."

"How about recently?"

Weinstein reflected. He answered slowly. "I had not seen him in years. He went west, I went elsewhere. We followed different roads, made different lives. Two or three years ago, I received money from him in the mail. He had heard of my work, he knew of our need, and he came to our help. I was grateful. We talked on the telephone. Since then, he has sent money now and then and we have talked on the telephone two or three times."

"Have you seen him?"

"Once."

"When was that?"

Weinstein appeared to think about that, as though trying to remember. "I cannot give you an exact date," he said. "It was about a year ago. He was in New York. I gather it had to do with a motion picture he was making. I don't know precisely. We do not go to the motion pictures, nor do we watch television. On that occasion, he appeared at my synagogue. We greeted each other and he donated more money. We talked a little, and I learned that in many ways he had not changed. He still did not believe. He still had not discovered the truth. He still did not know who he was, what he was."

"That was the last time you saw him?"

"That was the only time I've seen him since we were in college."

"Then you have no idea why he might want to shoot Mayor Morrison."

"No idea at all. I find it hard to believe. With all his faults, he was not a violent man in the old days, and I cannot believe he changed so much that now he would take a gun and shoot somebody. But you say he did. Who am I to dispute you when you must possess the evidence?"

"You don't know of any antipathy he had toward the mayor?"

"How could I know? Would he discuss such a thing with a stranger? And was I not a stranger to him?"

"Yet he gave you money."

"He was generous. But the money was not for me. It was for the people, for the things we believe."

"You said he wasn't a believer."

"Not in religion, no. But in the people and in the cause, yes."

"There's a difference?"

"Of course."

"You know what's interesting?" Rogers said. "Gold gave money to you, and he gave money to Melvin Rasmussen, and he gave money to Harvey Jessup. He gave that money to people he'd known a long time ago, or at least knew of, from what Jessup says, people he hadn't seen in years. I keep wondering why?"

"About that, I'm afraid I can't help you," Weinstein

said. "I'm sure he gave to many others, too. He was a generous man."

"So you said."

"Perhaps he was a man devoted to causes and a man who had a means to show that devotion."

"Perhaps," Rogers replied.

It was late when he reached home. The day had not been a wasted one. He had learned more than any of the three men had wanted him to learn or even thought he learned. What it all meant and where it would lead, he wasn't yet sure. But he was beginning to see signposts.

From the entrance to the apartment, he glanced toward the answering machine. The red light was on. He went toward it. The crystal display said he had one call. He pressed the button.

"Hi, this is Annie Kendall," came the voice. "Sorry I haven't gotten back to you before, but I haven't been home until now. I had lots to do. I think I've stumbled onto something. Let's get together tomorrow. Don't bother to call tonight because I'm not staying here. Why don't you come by about seven tomorrow night, okay?"

He took a deep, relieved breath.

17

The acrid smell of smoke lay heavy on the air even before he reached the area under the Williamsburg Bridge. There were three fire engines blocking the street, hoses stretching out under the bridge. A couple of police cars, roof lights flashing, were pulled up nearby. Several firemen were beginning to fold the hoses back into the engine.

Rogers moved quickly toward the scene, reaching into his pocket for his wallet and shield to gain passage through the crowd that had gathered. He spotted the fire commander, went to him.

"What's up?"

The commander started to order him away, saw the shield. "These idiots have been warned a hundred times about stealing the goddamn power from Con Ed. It was bound to happen," the commander said with obvious disgust.

Rogers waited. He knew what was coming.

"Well," the commander continued, "it happened. One of those shacks, if you can even call them that, went up. It must have taken about thirty seconds and there wasn't a thing left. By the time we got here, there were only ashes. Not even an ember.''

''Anybody hurt?''

The commander nodded. ''Guy trapped inside. Not much of him left.''

''Mind if I take a look?'' Rogers asked.

''Be my guest.''

Rogers threaded his way through the hose lines, stepped over pools of water until he reached the squatters' village. He made for Max's home. A morgue ambulance was pulled up alongside. Attendants were carrying a rubber body bag toward the rear of the ambulance. Max's house was now a small mound of ashes.

He went to that pile and, taking a metal pipe that lay to one side, began to sift through it. He knew what he was looking for. He found it. That new lock that Rodriguez had noticed lay in the middle of the ashes, the metal charred. He looked down at it, looked again. The lock was secured.

He turned away.

From a nearby phone, he called Carlos Rodriguez. It was Sunday, but Rodriguez was working. He was out on a case. Rogers left a message for Rodriguez to call him when he could.

Rogers was back in the apartment when the call came a couple of hours later.

''I got news,'' Rodriguez said.

''So do I,'' Rogers said. ''Yours first.''

''Charlie Westerman. The poor bastard did what you thought. The official report is going to say he was cleaning his gun when he had an accident.''

''He leave a note?''

''No note, no nothin'. Which is why they can log it accident. Now, what's your news?''

"They got to Max."

"You surprised? How?"

"Set his shack on fire, him inside, door locked. Do something?"

"What?"

"Ask for an autopsy. Tell them you want to be sure how he died. I'll bet the verdict's going to be he burned to death. Tell them to look for, say, a bullet."

Rodriguez didn't answer right away. Then, "You think . . ."

"Yeah, I think. What I think is that somebody wasted him, then locked the fucking door and set the place up. Who's going to take a close look at the body of a homeless guy?"

"I'll get back," Rodriguez said.

18

uring the afternoon, a cold front moved across the city, breaking the heat wave. In an hour, the temperature dropped twenty degrees, to a comfortable seventy-five. By seven, it was hovering around seventy, and some people, grown used to the heat, had put on sweaters and light jackets. Maybe the weather would stay cool and the start of the new work week in the morning would not be so unbearable.

It was just after seven when Rogers reached Annie Kendall's building just off Riverside Drive. Inside the front door was the tenant's board. He pressed the button next to her name and moved close to the house intercom, waiting for her voice so he could identify himself. Instead, there was buzzing at the front door, unlocking it.

Stupid, he thought, as he pushed the door open. After what happened, she damn well ought to find out who's downstairs before letting him in. It could be anybody, not necessarily somebody she's expecting. He'd have to tell her never to let anyone in without checking first.

He rode the elevator to the third floor, walked to her door and rang the bell. From inside, hard on the echo of the bell, he heard a muffled sound. It sounded like a shot. He froze for an instant, then reached for the door and grabbed the knob. It turned in his hand. The door opened. It was unlocked. He raced down the hall toward the living room lights, and started into the living room. He caught a glimpse of something lying on the floor across the room. Something hard came down across the back of his head. He felt himself falling. Something was put into his right hand. He tried to open his eyes, tried to focus, tried to make out who was moving near him, what was in his hand. Something came down across his face, and there was only blackness.

He had no idea how long he was out. He was sure it couldn't have been long. Feeling, sensation began to return. He struggled to his feet. And a voice shouted, "Freeze! Put it down nice and easy!"

He turned groggily to try to see where the voice was coming from. He made out somebody in blue, a cop, standing at the entrance to the living room, pointing a gun at him.

"I said, put it down, nice and easy," the cop repeated.

Rogers wasn't sure what the guy was talking about. He saw the eyes staring at him, saw where they were staring and he looked down. A gun dangled loosely in his right hand. He tried to focus on it, wondering what it was doing there, how it had gotten there. It wasn't his. He was sure of that.

The cop gave the order again, sharper, more threatening. He nodded slowly, bent, and felt a wave of dizziness pass over him. He reached out with his left hand and steadied himself against the wall, shaking his head, trying to clear it. The haze lifted just a little. He crouched slowly and set the gun down on the floor beside his foot.

"Now kick it over here," the cop ordered.

He shoved the gun across the room with his foot. It slid across the polished wood.

"Against the wall and spread 'em," the cop ordered. In a different voice, the cop said to his partner, "Frank, call for backup, then get the hell over there and see how bad it is."

"I called, soon as we walked in." The other cop was already moving across the room.

Rogers moved his head slowly, feeling pain across the back, to follow the cop. He knew what he was going to see, and he didn't want to see it. He saw it. Annie Kendall with a hole seeping blood in the middle of her forehead.

"You hear me?" the cop barked at Rogers. "Against the wall and spread 'em."

He did as he was told. He felt one of the cop's hands moving over him, shaking him down, while the other held a gun against his back.

"Well, will you look at this," the cop said, relieving Rogers of the gun in the holster on his belt. "A fuckin' walkin' arsenal, this son of a bitch."

"I'm a cop, a lieutenant," Rogers said, the words coming out not quite right. He was having trouble talking, trouble making sense.

"And I'm fuckin' J. Edgar Hoover," the cop said.

"Look in my wallet," Rogers said.

The cop pulled the wallet from Rogers' hip pocket, shook it open and took a quick look. "Son of a bitch, he's telling the truth." He looked closer at the photo ID card. "What the fuck do you know. The bastard's Rogers. You know, the rat squad, fuckin' IAD."

Suddenly the room began to fill. More cops in blue. Four guys in plainclothes. Rogers thought he recognized two of the detectives. They were the guys who had shown up the night the place was robbed. They stared at him. One of them said to the cop who was guarding him, "What's he doing here?"

"Fuckin' shooter is what. He was still holdin' the piece when we walked in."

The cops who had looked at him with a little fear and apprehension the first time they met, looked at him a different way now.

"I didn't shoot anybody," Rogers said.

"Sure," the cop said. "I believe you." He laughed sardonically.

"I'm going to read you your rights," one of the detectives said. "Then you can say anything you want." He recited the familiar Miranda formula. "Now, what were you saying?"

"I didn't shoot anyone," Rogers repeated. "Certainly not Annie Kendall."

"Noted. What were you doing here?"

"We had an appointment. I rang the bell downstairs and somebody pushed the buzzer to let me in. When I got up here to the door, I heard a shot inside. The door was unlocked. I ran down that hall and when I got to the end, somebody whacked me across the back of the head. I don't remember much after that."

"You two have an argument?"

Rogers looked at him. "No argument. I think whoever shot her waited until I got here to set me up."

"Sure. Let's go back over this nice and slow. Take it from the beginning again."

There was that look on his face. Rogers had seen it too many times. He had put it on often enough himself. He shook his head. "I think," he said slowly, "I ought to see a lawyer."

19

The lawyer he got was Harris Abelman. Abelman was the man to get if you were guilty or if, even if innocent, the case against you was so strong it didn't look like you had a chance. Abelman didn't come cheap. At least, not if you were well fixed. But there were times when Abelman made exceptions. When he was convinced of a client's innocence in the face of everything, when the challenge was enough to test all his legal acumen, when a close friend prevailed upon him, he might waive his usual six-figure retainer, might even waive his costs. In Rogers' case, the last two were the telling factors, at least at the beginning.

From the precinct, Rogers had made his one allowed call. He phoned Morton Solomon, a corporate attorney he had come to know a few years earlier. Solomon didn't handle criminal cases. Solomon said he would call the best in the business and persuade him at least to see Rogers. Solomon called Harris Abelman.

Just before midnight, Abelman appeared at the precinct where Rogers was locked in a holding cell until the time came to take him downtown for a preliminary arraignment. Two assistant district attorneys had already shown up. Rogers had refused to talk to them.

Then Abelman arrived. Rogers was ushered into a private office where the lawyer was waiting. He was in his early sixties, a short, portly man with a fringe of close cut gray hair circling a round head, thick black-frame glasses covering his eyes, a suit that looked about a size too large and needed a press (it was Abelman's costume; he used it to convince juries, if not judges, that he was just a poor hardworking guy, just like them), Abelman watched Rogers enter the room, his eyes as penetrating as an x-ray.

"Don't tell me if you're guilty," were the first words he spoke. "If you are, I don't want to hear a lie. If you're not, we can think about that later. What we have to talk about is the charge against you and how we defend against it, that is, if I decide to take your case."

"I'm not guilty," Rogers said. "I did not shoot that girl."

"At the moment," Abelman said, "I'm not interested in whether or not you shot her. Tell me your version of what happened."

Rogers did. Abelman listened intently, making notes on a yellow lined pad. When Rogers was finished, Abelman stared at him. "Why," he asked, "would someone want to set you up?"

"In this case? I don't know. Maybe I was getting too close, closer than even I know."

"Too close to what?"

"To a lot of things I still don't understand."

"Tell me and see if I understand."

"I worked for Jack Morrison."

"I already know that. Morton Solomon says you were his eyes and ears, and ferret."

"In some ways. I've been looking into his murder."

"Why? They already know who killed him."

"That's what they say."

Abelman took his time, the eyes piercing. "You doubt it?"

"I doubt it. So do a few other people."

"I see. And what have you unearthed?"

"A lot of pieces that don't add up yet. At least not to me. Maybe somebody else is worried that I'm getting close enough so they will."

"And just where does this young lady they accuse you of killing fit into this?"

"She's one of the pieces. I'm not sure where she fits. But she had Harry Gondolian's files. There was something in them. Somebody stole them from her. But not before she read them. She was going to tell me what she found. They got to her before she could."

"Slower, please. You'd better explain the sequence of events to me. Just the outline now. I'll want the details later."

Rogers nodded and did as Abelman asked.

Abelman made notes. He looked up from the paper and smiled just a little. "I think," he said, "I'll take your case."

"I'm not rich," Rogers said. "I've got my salary, but not much put aside."

"Don't worry about the money," Abelman said. "We can work that out later. The first thing is to get you out of here and back where you can continue what you've been doing, and where we can talk a little more privately and decide how to proceed."

Abelman rose and walked to the door, knocked on it and waited for someone to open it and let him out. As he left, he turned to Rogers. "I'll see you in court in the morning."

It was hard to believe all this was actually happening, and happening to him. For the first time in his life, he had cuffs fastened around his wrists, too tight, and the wrists pulled behind his back. He had spent a night in the lock-up, listening to the sounds that never ceased, the clanging of metal on metal, ringing in his ears, constantly aware of the lights that were never extinguished, that burned through his eyelids. He did not sleep. No one liked Rogers, certainly not the police and certainly not the criminals in the other cells.

In court the next morning, sitting at the table in the well next to Abelman, he was still in a state of suspended disbelief. He understood, as he had never understood before, just how the accused felt. Looking around, he spotted a middle-aged couple on the front benches, staring at him. They must be Annie Kendall's parents. He would have to explain it to them, try to ease their minds, try to set things right with them.

Al Goodhue, the assistant district attorney who had been tossed the case, one of the top prosecutors in the office, rose to argue that not only should the case against Rogers be bound over for the grand jury, but that the evidence against him was so strong that he should be held without bail. "This," he told the court, "is a capital offense, and if we still had the death penalty, the state would argue for its application in this matter. This was a heinous crime, the cold-blooded murder of an innocent young woman. The daughter of one of the city's most eminent families. As your honor knows, her great grandfather was a founder of the newspaper for which she worked, her uncle is its publisher, her father is senior partner in a leading Wall Street investment firm. She was a young woman with a boundless future, a young woman with her life ahead her, with unlimited prospects. And they were snuffed out as you would snuff out a candle. Without thought and without care. There can be no excuse, no mitigating circumstances. We feel that the evidence against the accused is overwhelming. We are certain Your Honor holds with us that the accused presents a clear and present danger to society. He is a police officer who has violated his oath, his uniform, his department, and all of society. Therefore, beyond peradventure of doubt, he should be remanded to custody until the grand jury indicts, which it will when it hears the evidence, and remanded until trial. This man should not be free to roam as he will the streets of the city he has despoiled.''

Abelman was good. He was very good. He earned his money, whatever money Rogers would eventually have to pay him, and a lot more, that morning. He opened with his trademark humble, man-of-the-people voice.

''Your Honor,'' he began, a bemused look on his face, ''in the normal course of events, I would waive responding at this preliminary hearing. However, after listening to my learned colleague, I feel duty bound to respond at this time. I listened to Mr. Goodhue, and I had to pinch myself to return to reality. You would have thought he was talking about John Dillinger, about Ted Bundy, about some mass murderer, some dangerous criminal, some public enemy number one who had made a career of preying on the innocent. In fact, Your Honor, he was talking about one of the most decorated police officers in this city, a man who has devoted his life to the elimination of evil wherever it may lie, a man who has spent the last years as the good right hand of the late mayor, John Morrison, in his noble effort to return this city to greatness. Is this a man who would attack a defenseless young woman in her home? Is this the kind of man who would murder in cold blood a young woman for whom he had the greatest respect? No, Your Honor, this is a man who has demonstrated time and again that he is a protector of the innocent, a defender of the city and its people against all enemies, no matter where they lurk.

"In his unceasing devotion to his calling, he has made many enemies, as your honor and my learned colleague fully realize, not only among the criminal element but among certain levels in the police department itself. There are those who would go to any lengths to bring him low. We must not let that happen.

"What does my learned colleague offer? That my client was having an affair with the deceased and when the deceased tried to break it off, he attacked her in a rage and shot her. What proof does he offer? None. My client has a perfectly reasonable explanation for his presence at the scene. My learned colleague says he lies. On what basis? Why? My client says he was attacked when he entered the deceased's apartment and was struck across the back of the head. Did the arresting officers, did anyone in a position of authority call a physician to examine my client? They did not. They were so anxious to write solved to this crime that they ignored that one simple, and necessary, step. Had they done so, they would have known that my client was speaking nothing but the truth. How do I know? Prior to our appearance here this morning, I had the eminent neurologist, Dr. Joshua Mason of the New York Medical Center examine Mr. Rogers. He found bruises and contusions at the back of Mr. Rogers' head. He found evidence that Mr. Rogers had suffered a minor concussion from those blows.

"Now, I say to my distinguished colleague and Your Honor, if the state seeks an indictment before a grand jury, we will present evidence to show that there is insufficient evidence to warrant the bringing of such an indictment. Meanwhile, I respectfully request that this court release the defendant on his own recognizance pending the dismissal of the charges."

Abelman turned and sat down.

"I trust, Mr. Abelman," the judge said, "that your client is pleading not guilty to the charges."

"Correct, your honor. Normally we would waive a plea at this time. But the circumstances are such that we are duty bound to enter that plea now."

The court considered. It agreed with the state that there was enough evidence to bind Rogers over to the grand jury. But it also agreed with Abelman that Rogers' record merited his release on bond. "The court," the judge ruled, "sets bond at $25,000."

Goodhue rose, his face purple. "The state must object," he shouted. "If this court is going to set bond for this defendant, which we strenuously protest, then the amount should be no less than one million dollars."

"I said $25,000, and $25,000 it is, Mr. Goodhue," the judge said flatly.

"Objection."

"Overruled."

"Then will Your Honor at least rule that the defendant must not leave the jurisdiction of this court?"

"I think we can expect that Mr. Rogers will appear at the appropriate time when necessary without restricting his movements."

"He could flee the country, your honor," Goodhue said.

"I seriously doubt that, Mr. Goodhue."

Rogers listened to it all, and turned to Abelman. "Where the hell am I going to come up with twenty-five grand?"

Abelman smiled benignly. "I could tell you to seek out a bail bondsman. I could tell you to mortgage whatever you possess. I could offer a hundred other suggestions. I will not. Instead, I will show you this." He reached into the breast pocket of his jacket and retrieved a check. He showed it to Rogers. It was a certified check for $25,000. It was drawn on the account of Morton Solomon.

Rogers just stared at it. "Why?"

"He feels he owes you a great deal. And he feels there is no risk."

"How the hell did you know how much?"

Abelman only smiled. "I expect you in my office tomorrow morning at ten," he said.

Abelman walked toward the bench and made the necessary arrangements. Rogers turned and saw Annie Kendall's parents glaring at him. He moved toward them.

"You're Annie's mother and father," he said.

They didn't answer. They continued to glare at him.

"Look," he said, "I understand how you feel. But I didn't kill her. There's no way in the world I would kill her. And I'm going to find out who did. I promise you that."

Mrs. Kendall thawed a little. "Annie liked you," she said.

"I liked her."

"She said people could depend on you. To do the right thing."

"I like to believe that."

"If you didn't kill her, find out who did. And why."

"I will. I promise you that."

Rodriguez and Strickland were waiting outside the courtroom when Rogers walked out.

"We just got here," Rodriguez said. "We missed it. What happened? You walk?"

Rogers shook his head. "Bound over," he said.

"You make bail?"

Rogers nodded.

"How much?"

"Twenty-five grand."

Rodriguez whistled. "Jesus. You got that kind of bread?"

"I've got the right kind of friends," Rogers said. "You know, a friend in need is a friend indeed."

"I should only have that kind of friend," Rodriguez said.

"Are you okay?" Strickland asked with concern.

"How the hell can I be okay, with this thing hanging over my head? No, I won't be okay until it's over. Now, let's get the hell out of here. I want to go home and take a shower and change my clothes. I can't stand my own stink after a night in the slammer."

Rodriguez sniffed the air, grinned a little. "I've smelled worse," he said.

"I haven't," Rogers said.

They went through the wide doors down onto the street and started walking west.

"What now?" Rodriguez asked.

"What we've been doing." He turned to Strickland. "Any luck with Santangello?"

Strickland shook his head. "Not yet. I'm working on it."

"I want to talk to the bastard."

"You really think he's the shooter?" Strickland asked.

"He's a shooter all right. The question is, who did he shoot? Maybe Morrison and Gondolian and Gold, or maybe not. Maybe Annie Kendall, too, or maybe not. I'm not sure about one goddamn thing. Anything's possible. It's just as possible somebody else took care of them. But he's a shooter. I figure he's got at least three notches in his gun in the last couple of days."

Strickland halted. "Three? You mean not counting Morrison, Gondolian, Gold, and the girl?"

Rogers held up one hand and counted off. "Terry Galvin. Max. And I'll give him that poor bastard, Westerman, too. There may be more if we look hard enough. But those three will stand for now."

"But you're not convinced about Morrison?"

Rogers shook his head. "No. I've got a gut feeling that was another party's doing."

"You got any ideas?"

Rogers took his time. "I'm getting some," he said.

Strickland and Rodriguez stared at him. "Who?" Strickland said.

"When I'm positive," Rogers said. "It's not just the who, there's the why. I keep asking myself what was in Gondolian's files? What was in Annie Kendall's head after she read them?"

"We'll never know now," Strickland said.

"Maybe not," Rogers said. "But I'm not so sure. One

thing I'm going to do is try to backtrack, try to remember just what Gondolian said, and just what Annie said."

"I thought," Strickland said, "they didn't say anything."

"Not anything I paid much attention to at the time. But there may be something there that I missed. If so, it'll come to me." He turned to Rodriguez then. "Carlos," he said, "there's something you can do."

"Sure."

"Have ballistics check the bullets that killed Galvin and Max. I assume they did find a bullet in Max."

"They did," Rodriguez confirmed. "In the brain."

"See if they match. And for good measure, see if there's a match for the one that killed Annie."

Rodriguez started. "You suggestin' something?"

"No. I don't think you'll find a match with that one. That slug probably came from the gun they found on me. But let's not close any doors before we have to."

"Okay. Will do."

"And, George, you'll get on Santangello."

Strickland nodded.

"And now I'm going home," Rogers said. He turned and disappeared down the subway stairs.

20

He was so tired that even his bones ached and his mind had stopped working. All he wanted was a shower to wash away the night and then the bed to sleep without dreams. The light was glowing on the answering machine. He was tempted to ignore it, let it wait until he woke. He sighed and pressed the play button.

He heard Annie Kendall's voice. It was like a knife cutting through him. He had forgotten to erase that message from her. It was all that was left, and he thought maybe he never would erase it now.

Her voice closed and another replaced it, a familiar one that still had the traces of a foreign accent. "I am distressed to hear of your troubles," the voice said. "Come to see me. Perhaps I may help." No name, no telephone number. They were not needed. Rogers knew whose voice it was.

Another call. "Benito, what's happened? I do not hear from you and then I hear on the television and read in the newspapers you are in great trouble. You must call me. You must come to see me." His grandmother, the woman who had raised him after his parents died. He would have to drive out to Queens to see her, or at least call.

And one more. Melissa. "Ben, when you pick this up, call me." That was all. There wasn't much warmth in the voice. He thought about it and decided not to call her just yet.

He stared at the phone, then picked it up and pressed the buttons for his grandmother. She answered immediately.

"Nònna," he said, "I got your call."

"Benito," she said, her voice nervous, "you are all right?"

"I'm okay. Don't worry."

"I read the papers. I watched the TV. They say terrible things."

"Not true," he said. "They just report what people tell them. Set your mind at ease. Everything will work out."

"Who was the girl?"

"A reporter," he said. "She worked for a friend of mine. She had information for me. Somebody got to her before she could give it to me."

"Terrible, terrible," she said. "A young girl."

"Terrible is hardly the word for it," he said.

"But you are all right?"

"Fine."

"You will come to see me soon?"

"Soon as I can."

"And Melissa? You hear from her?"

"All the time."

"She is well?"

"Of course."

She asked a few more questions and, apparently relieved for the moment, hung up.

The Kendalls' telephone number at their Fifth Avenue home was unlisted. It took Rogers about three minutes to get it. When the phone was answered, he asked for Mrs. Kendall.

"Who's calling?"

He identified himself.

There was a pause. "I don't think she'll want to talk to you."

"Ask," he said. "It's important."

He waited. In about a minute, he heard her voice. There were echoes of Annie's in it. "I hope you'll talk to me. I'm sorry to bother you," he said, "but I have a question."

"Yes?"

"Did Annie ever mention anything to you about Harry Gondolian's files?"

"Yes."

"I don't mean the ones that were stolen from her apartment. I mean the others."

"Yes, she mentioned them."

"Did she happen to say where they were?"

"No. But she said she was going to have them moved to her apartment."

"Do you know if she made those arrangements?"

"I know she talked to a moving company. I'm not sure, but its name was something like Phoenix. Phoenix something or other."

"It couldn't have been Phoenix Trans-World Shipping?" he said, holding his breath.

"That sounds like it," she said.

"Do you have any idea where she got that name?" he asked.

"I'm sorry," she said, "I don't." She paused, then, "Oh, I think she said something about Harry Gondolian using them, or recommending them once, or finding them in his notes. I'm sorry, I can't be certain."

"You don't happen to know where they're located, do you?"

"I don't. Is it important?"

"It may be."

"Annie left some things here, in her room. I'll look and see if she might have written it down and left it there."

"I'd appreciate that."

"If I find it, how do I reach you?"

He gave her his number and started to hang up when he heard her voice again. The words came in a rush, as though she was trying to control herself, keep the emotion out. "Annie's funeral is tomorrow. If you came, I would be grateful. I think Annie would have wanted that." Her voice broke on the last words.

"Then I'll be there," he said.

She told him the name of the church. The service would be at ten in the morning.

There was something that had eluded him, something Annie had said. He had been trying to remember, and now it returned, her voice, whiskey-slurred, at the wake, or whatever it was, for Harry Gondolian.

He picked up the phone. Rodriguez answered. "Carlos," he said, "how long have you been a cop?"

"Why do you want to know?"

"Just tell me."

"Twenty-three years," Rodriguez said.

"Turn your memory back, say fifteen or twenty years ago. You ever hear of a cop named Justin McCauley?"

"No," Rodriguez said after a moment's pause.

"You sure?"

"Positive. Maybe he was someplace I wasn't. But I never worked with a guy named that, never heard of that name. Why?"

"Somebody said that was the name of a cop who got killed in the line of duty."

"Bullshit," Rodriguez said. "That I know for sure. You want, I'll sing you every name of every guy got it since I've been around. And there ain't no Justin McCauley in the lyrics. Now, what the hell is this all about? Does it tie with what we're lookin' into?"

"Maybe. Just maybe. Something I said once to Gondolian, and something Annie Kendall said to me."

"Follow it up, for chrissake. And, oh yeah, that thing you asked me about. I got to ballistics. Same gun killed Terry Galvin and Max. Different gun for Annie Kendall. Not even the same caliber. They got it with an eight millimeter; the gun that got her was a thirty-eight, the one they got from you."

"I just wanted to be sure," Rogers said.

The morning was passing. He was due at Abelman's office, and that was a date he couldn't pass. Abelman didn't keep him waiting. A secretary ushered him into a conference room and Abelman, the sleeves of his pink striped shirt turned up, red suspenders holding his trousers, appeared immediately looking harassed.

"This," Abelman said, "is going to take a long time. We have to go over everything about ten times, at least. I've got a book full of appointments. So, what I want to do is give you an hour now, then you hang around. I'll try to get back here with you at every break. I think we may get through by five. At least, I hope so."

That's the way the day went. Abelman in and out, Abelman with that yellow pad making voluminous notes, Abelman asking questions, and not just about Annie Kendall, about every aspect of Rogers' life.

"Forget what I said to you the first night. Today, I want the truth. No shilly-shallying, no obfuscations. You tell me the truth and we'll deal with it. You tell me lies and they'll come back to haunt both of us. Now, did you kill that young lady?"

"No," Rogers said.

"All right. Were you having an affair with her?"

"Not precisely," Rogers said.

Abelman glared at him. "I said, no obfuscations. Were you having an affair with her, yes or no?"

"When I said, not precisely, that was the truth. We went to bed together once, the night somebody got into her apartment and turned it upside down."

"That one night, did you take advantage of her? And you know what I mean. She must have been a very disturbed young lady. Did you take advantage of that?"

"No," Rogers said.

"Your going to bed together, then, that was mutual?"

"In a manner of speaking, yes."

"Don't 'manner of speaking' me. Yes or no?"

Rogers thought about how to answer. "She was disturbed, yes. She was frightened. She didn't want to be alone. She wanted somebody around. I happened to be there. One thing led to another. That was it."

"All right. We'll go into that in more detail later. Now, did you have an argument with her?"

"No. There wasn't any reason for us to have an argument."

"Did you ever have an argument with her?"

"No."

"By argument, I mean words, disagreements, anything somebody could call an argument?"

"No."

"How many times were you in her apartment?"

"Twice. That night and the night she was killed."

"Was she ever in your apartment?"

"Once. The night Morrison and Gondolian got shot. I came home and she was waiting for me outside."

"All right. Now, I want you to go into detail about the night she was in your apartment. What she said and did, what you said and did. Then I want the same thing about both times you were in her apartment. Don't leave out anything. You never know what's important."

And so it went, and so the day passed, and by five Abelman said he had what he needed to start preparing. "I'll undoubtedly need you a lot more. Keep yourself available."

"When's the DA going to the grand jury?"

"Soon, I expect. He's got one impaneled now, so he can put the case before them any time. I imagine he'll want a week or two to put together the evidence to get an indictment. Not much longer than that. So, if you can fill in all the blank spots, solve this thing, the sooner you do it, the better. Then you'll be home free and the issue will be moot. No grand jury, no indictment. Understand?"

"Of course. Now, is there anything to stop me from flying to California?"

Abelman's eyes bore into him. "When?"

"Early next week, probably."

"Why?"

"For one thing, Gold's widow lives out there and she's agreed to talk to me."

Abelman thought. Then nodded slowly. "I don't see why you shouldn't go. Just don't stay away long. And check in with me every day, in case I have to have you back here."

"I will."

On the way home, he stopped at a restaurant where nobody knew him and had something to eat, the first meal since morning. He rushed through it, not tasting the food, scanning the newspapers while picking at what was on the plate and not liking what the papers were writing about him. On the face, the facts looked damning. He got up, dropped some money on the table to cover the bill, left the papers on the seat, and went home.

Back in the apartment, he poured himself a drink and stared at the telephone. The message light was on. A message from Strickland for him to call. Another message from Melissa. Just, "Why didn't you return my call?" That was all.

He finished the drink and made another, then went to the phone. He called Strickland first.

"They're not going to let us get to Santangello," Strickland said. "Especially not after what's in the papers about you today."

"That figures," Rogers said.

"Don't sound so down," Strickland said. "I think I have a way."

Rogers sat still and waited.

"The guy goes here and goes there. We know it. It's almost as though he doesn't have a leash on him. Most of the time he goes out about eight or nine at night and gets back whenever he feels like it."

"How do you know that?"

"I have my ways," Strickland said. "Now, what we'll do is this: we'll camp out across the street, in a bar or something, and watch. When he comes out, we'll move. First, let's just see where he goes. If we can get him somewhere nice and quiet, so much the better. If not, we'll take him wherever and whenever we can."

"Agreed," Rogers said. "When?"

"Tomorrow night's as good as any to start. I'll pick you up at your place about seven, and we'll move from there."

He knew he had to call Melissa. There was no way to avoid it. He stared at the phone, then finally reached for it and hit the buttons. Her answering machine picked up. He left a message.

An hour later, the phone rang. "You didn't return my call," Melissa's voice said.

"It was late when I got in," he said, "and then I was with the lawyer all day."

"You know you could have called no matter the hour. I waited up and you didn't call."

He mumbled that he was sorry.

"Who was she?"

He knew that was coming. "Harry Gondolian's assistant," he said.

"She was young enough to be his granddaughter."

"That's all she was, his assistant. She called herself his gofer. He was training her."

"And her family owns the paper."

"I only found that out yesterday. Maybe she was trying to make it on her own. She didn't talk about them."

"It was all over the news."

"I didn't read the papers until later. There were other things to occupy my mind."

"I don't have to ask if you killed her. I know you too well. But, were you having an affair with her?"

"No, I didn't kill her, and no, I wasn't having an affair with her. I hardly knew her." That was the literal truth, anyway. As he'd told Abelman earlier. Once didn't make it an affair. And normally you didn't know somebody well after only a handful of meetings. With Annie Kendall, it was different. He hadn't known her long and he knew nothing about her past, not that a kid her age could have had much past, or her background. Still, he had seen things in her, and he thought he had sensed a depth, and so he knew her. But he didn't want to go into that. You couldn't even begin to explain.

"I saw her picture. She was beautiful."

"I suppose so," he said. "Yes, I guess she was. She was very young."

"And you weren't sleeping with her?"

"No."

"Should I believe you?"

"Yes. I love you," he said, which was the truth, literal and otherwise.

"I wondered," she said.

"Don't wonder. It's true."

"And her?"

"I liked her. She was a nice girl. She was smart. Maybe she was too smart. She didn't deserve to get killed."

"Nobody does."

"Almost nobody," he said.

"Are you all right?"

"I suppose so. I've been too busy to think about it."

"Are they going to indict you?"

"They intend to. If I can come up with answers before they go to the grand jury, they won't."

"Are you going to be able to do that?"

"I'm going to try."

"Are you coming out here? I mean, will they let you leave New York?"

"Yes, and yes. Yes, they'll let me leave. And, yes, I'm flying out there."

"When?"

"Soon. Over the weekend, or the beginning of next week. It depends."

"I love you," she said. "And I miss you and I believe you and I believe in you, and I can't wait to see you."

She hung up without waiting for him to respond.

21

It rained during the night, and by morning there was a
fine mist coating the air, dampening the city. People were
hurrying through the streets carrying umbrellas. Rogers
forgot his, but the rain felt good on his face, clean and
fresh, and he needed that.

The church was crowded, people standing at the back
and along the sides of the sanctuary. There were a lot of
older people, and there were a lot of kids in their twenties,
Annie's friends. Looking around, Rogers could almost
tell who had come out of friendship or obligation or
some other reason to Annie's parents and who had come
because of Annie, because they had known and cared for
her. There were a lot of tears, girls holding onto each
other and crying, even some of the young men seemed
to have wet eyes and wet cheeks, and nobody was wiping
away the tears, and nobody seemed ashamed to be seen
crying.

He found a vacant spot against the rear wall near the
aisle, wedged himself in between a couple of young men
and focused on the altar. There was a coffin just beneath

it, closed, covered with banks of flowers, mainly roses, white and red. He spotted Annie's parents in the front pew. Her mother, in black, sat erect, not moving, not looking around. Her father was slumped and his shoulders were shaking. Next to them was a boy about eighteen, his dark suit looking a little too large, the shoulders too high, as though the last thing he was used to was wearing a suit. He must be Annie's brother. Rogers hadn't known Annie had a brother; there was so much about her he hadn't known, and now wished he had. But he figured, from the proximity, it must be her younger brother. He noticed people whose faces were in the newspapers all the time scattered around the room. And everywhere there were the kids.

Morrison's funeral had been a ceremony to mark the passing of a fallen leader, attended by the rich and powerful, by men who did not know him well. Harry Gondolian's wake had been a celebration of a life and a dedication to the future. Annie Kendall's funeral was a time of tears and sorrow and mourning not just for what she had been and for how she had died, but for all the things she might have been, for a life ended at its beginning.

The minister, her minister he guessed, spoke as if he knew her well, spoke without notes, spoke of the things she had done and believed and hoped, and several times he had to pause, and take a drink and shake his head and remove his glasses and wipe the back of his hand across his eyes. A girl in her early twenties gave a eulogy, a rambling and not quite coherent reminiscence of her best friend, a friend since they were small children. She choked up several times, and finally just gave up, stumbling away from the altar. Her sobs echoed throughout the church.

When it was over, Rogers didn't move until the casket,

wheeled on its dolly, the pallbearers, six young men, their hands touching the top, walking slowly alongside, passed by. The Kendalls walked with a stricken dignity behind.

And then Mrs. Kendall saw Rogers. She made a motion with her head as she passed. He joined the departing mourners, saw her outside standing by a black limousine, the first in a procession of thirty or forty cars that would move on slowly to the cemetery. He stepped toward her.

"Mrs. Kendall," he said. There was nothing more he could say. He was struck again by the resemblance, thought that was what Annie would have looked like if she'd had twenty-five more years.

She opened her purse, drew out a piece of paper, and handed it to him. "This may be what you wanted," she said. "I found it in Annie's room." She turned and climbed into the limousine.

He stood on the sidewalk watching as the casket was placed in the hearse, as the procession slowly moved out onto the avenue and away. Then he looked at the paper. The name Phoenix Trans-World Shipping was written on it, along with the phone number he had once dialed, and now with an address and a suite number in Chelsea. And there was another address as well, a private mini-storage warehouse over by the Hudson on one of those abandoned piers, along with the room number, a lease-identification card and a key taped across the bottom with transparent tape. The key was a Medeco-type, the kind used in locks that couldn't be picked. At least not with a hairpin.

By noon, as he came up from the subway at Twenty-third Street, the sun had burned off the mist and the clouds and the heat and humidity had returned. Not many people were on the street, some women carrying supermarket bags, a few men with briefcases, some kids, and nobody seemed in hurry. He walked west to Eighth Avenue and then south a couple of blocks until he reached a five-story building that had obviously been renovated, including a new steel and glass facade.

A guard stationed at a desk just inside the door watched him, then went back to the book he was reading. Rogers looked like he knew where he was going, like he belonged. He walked directly to the elevator at the rear of the lobby, pressed the button, waited, got on, and pressed five.

The suite was at the end of the corridor, just a number on the door, no name. He tried the door. It was locked. He pressed the buzzer beside it. After a moment, there was a clicking and the door opened.

A middle aged woman in a severe gray jacket and skirt to match, both matching the color of her hair, sat behind a desk watching him closely as he approached. "Can I help you?" she said, and the voice said she didn't know him, and what was he doing here, and he'd probably come to the wrong place anyway.

"This is Phoenix Trans-World Shipping, right," he said.

She didn't say anything.

"I'd like to talk to somebody about a consignment," he said.

"I think you've come to the wrong place," she said.

"You do moving and shipping, don't you?"

She didn't answer.

"A friend gave me your name and address and said you did rush jobs."

"I think you were misinformed," she said.

"You don't?"

"We only handle customers who have been recommended. Mainly large corporations."

"Well, you were recommended to me."

"By whom?"

"Actually, by two people. Harry Gondolian and Anne Kendall." The lady didn't look like someone you'd say Annie to.

She studied him, then reached for the phone. She talked into it quietly, covering the mouthpiece with her hand. He couldn't hear what she said. She hung up, then looked back at him. "Have a seat over there," she said, pointing to a couple of chairs on the other side of the room. "Someone will be out to see you shortly."

The someone who appeared through a door in the wall behind the receptionist, or more likely the guardian, was dressed in a dark business suit, white shirt, striped tie, with brown hair cut close and one of those faces that had "fed" engraved all over it. Rogers caught just a glimpse of the world behind him, got a glimpse of a line of computer terminals, the screens flickering with images. They looked like they had nothing to do with shipping, moving, and storage, at least not the kind you'd expect.

The guy looked at Rogers. "What can I do for you, Mr. Rogers?" he said.

Rogers rose, took a moment, said, "You know my name?"

"Your picture's been in all the papers. Now, can I help you?" It was obvious the guy wasn't even going to pretend, not for a second, that he was a shipping executive, and that this was a usual shipping company. Maybe that had been his original intention. But recognizing Rogers, combined with the names Gondolian and Kendall, had washed that away.

"Maybe," Rogers said. "I hope so. Who am I talking to, by the way?"

The guy looked at him for a moment. "John Doe," he said.

Rogers grinned. "Or Richard Roe?"

"Or John Smith or Sam Jones. It doesn't matter. Now, what can we do for you?" It didn't sound like Doe/Roe/Smith/Jones or whatever was about to do anything for Rogers.

"You did some work for a couple of people I know."

"I doubt it."

"Harry Gondolian and Anne Kendall."

"No," the guy said.

"You know the names."

"I read the papers."

"They gave me this address."

"From beyond the grave?" the guy said.

"Let's say they left it."

The guy thought a moment "Anything's possible."

"So, you know them."

"No."

"Then what makes you think they might have given me your name?"

"Let's stop playing games, Mr. Rogers. Just what do you want?"

"Annie Kendall called you to ask about moving things."

"If she called, and I don't know that she did, she was referred someplace else."

"She wasn't the kind to be put off. And she had your address. To me, that means she showed up here."

"People show up here all the time."

Rogers grinned. "Sure. Like Gondolian." He paused, then, "And like Steven Gold."

The expression didn't change. "I think, Mr. Rogers," he said, "it's time for you to leave."

"A question before I do. Just what the hell do you do here? Or do I need to ask?"

"Our business. Not yours."

"Right now I think very much mine."

"A word of caution, Mr. Rogers," the man said. "There are things and places where you shouldn't put your nose. It could make for a lot of problems. This is one of them."

"What agency do you work for?" Rogers said.

"Not your concern."

"Don't bet on it."

"If I were a betting man, that's a bet I'd win. Now, if there's nothing more, and there is nothing more for you here, I'd suggest you leave." He turned his back on Rogers and moved quickly back through the door, closing it behind him.

Rogers stared at the door. The woman behind the desk stared at him. "You're leaving now," she said. It was a statement, not a question.

He grinned at her. "Do I have a choice?"

"No," she said.

22

There was a message on the machine from Rodriguez. "Ben, about that question you asked. I checked with the PBA. No Justin McCauley ever got it. No benefits ever paid to the family of a Justin McCauley. As far as they know, the guy never existed. What now?"

Strickland was at his door precisely at seven. "I brought this along," Strickland said, holding a gun out to Rogers. "They must have lifted yours, along with the shield, and I figured you might need it."

Rogers shook his head. "No, thanks. I've had a couple stashed away in case of emergency." He pulled back his jacket to reveal a pistol in a holster on a belt around his waist. And then he smiled and pulled his wallet out, opened it and showed a silver shield. "And I've kept this one, as a souvenir. I never thought it might come in handy until the last couple of days."

Fifteen minutes later, they were perched on stools against a window facing the hotel on Lexington Avenue, sipping club soda. It was a quiet hour, a few late commuters around the bar, the last stragglers moving down Lex toward Grand Central Station, not many people in the street. In the dim light of the bar, in the waiting, it seemed a time for reflection, a time to share confidences, to talk of the past, the way people in bars do.

"You know," Strickland said in a soft, reminiscing voice, "I miss the son of a bitch."

Rogers knew he was talking about Morrison. "Don't we all."

"Sure," Strickland said. "Everybody who knew him has to. He was one hell of a guy."

"He knew what he wanted, and he knew where he was going, that's for sure."

Strickland shook his head a little. "You didn't really know him, Ben."

Rogers looked at the club soda. He would have liked something a lot stronger, but not now. "I think I did, George," he said. "About as well as anybody around him."

"There were things in that man that most people missed," Strickland said. "You have to go way back to see it. He kept most people at a distance. He didn't really open up. With me, it was different. We shared a hell of a lot over the years. People came and people went. He used people for a time, and then they went their way. But I was with him from way back. I got to know him while I was working vice, right after I joined the NYPD, and he was one of the up-and-coming ADA's. We were both sort of starting out then, feeling our way, and it made for a bond. He asked for me and I got assigned there, and I worked with him, went undercover for him, made his cases, until I got honest and went to Washington. And when he went to Washington, he recruited me to work with him there. God, the nights we used to spend together. I could talk to him. He was one guy I could always talk to. He was, I guess, kind of like an older brother. Even when he came back here, we never lost touch. We used to meet every month or so somewhere, and spend all night talking. You really get to know a guy, get close at three in the morning with a half-empty bottle of scotch on the table. There wasn't anything I wouldn't have done for him. I guess there wasn't anything I didn't do for him. All he had to do was ask. And the thing was, it went both ways. The world feels kind of empty now that he's gone."

Rogers studied Strickland. There was a depth of feeling he had never seen before. There was something else, too, that he couldn't fathom, a sorrow that went beyond the loss of a friend, a mentor. If they'd been drinking, he could have credited the booze. But they weren't drinking.

Strickland gave a little laugh. "What the hell's gotten into me?" he said. "I sound like a barroom philosopher, a falling-down drunk."

"It's okay, George," Rogers said. "Sometimes it helps."

"Doesn't it."

About nine, someone strolled out of the hotel. He didn't look hurried and he didn't look worried. He strolled like he had all the time in the world and nothing hanging over him. He was a little guy, not much over five foot six or seven, but the swarthy face was hard and unforgiving, and there were bulges in the sleeves of his jacket that could only have been muscles on muscles. Victor Santangello was on the move, Victor Santangello dressed for a night on the town, maybe, Victor Santangello looking like he'd just walked out of a men's fashion magazine, tailor-made suit, pastel shirt, paisley tie, black polished shoes that matched his hair.

Strickland touched Rogers' arm, and together they moved out of the bar and onto the street. Santangello crossed the avenue and headed south toward Grand Central. He wasn't walking fast, and he wasn't walking slow, he was just walking like a guy out for a stroll on a nice evening. He turned into the station at the Lexington Avenue entrance and walked toward the main waiting room. Strickland and Rogers moved after him, mixing with other people entering the station, keeping close to the shadows of the wall so that Santangello wouldn't make them if he glanced around.

"Do you believe it?" Strickland said. "The bastard's not even looking back. He's one confident asshole."

They moved up a little, about fifty feet behind Santangello. Inside the station, Santangello turned toward a rack of lockers, stopped at the end, reached into his pocket, pulled out a key, and inserted it into the lock. He reached inside, pulled out a parcel wrapped in brown paper, tucked it under his arm, reached in again, and pulled out a paper bag which he stuffed into his jacket pocket. It made a bulge, destroying the line of the suit. As he moved on, his right hand fiddled in that pocket, then came away holding the paper bag. He dropped it on the floor, turned and started toward the ramp that led to the subway.

"Stay close," Strickland said. "We don't want to lose him. But be careful he doesn't make us."

Santangello went down the escalator, through the turnstile and headed for the downtown train. They followed. An express pulled in. Santangello ducked his head into the car in front of him, looked around, stepped back.

Rogers and Strickland watched from the shadows of the stairs, ready to move when he did.

Another downtown express pulled into the station. Once more, Santangello stuck his head inside the door, looked around and then backed away.

"Son of a bitch has got a date," Strickland said.

Rogers nodded. "Smart bastard," he said. "He's going to make a switch."

"Yeah," Strickland said. "I'll bet a hundred that parcel's got his laundry."

"Dirty laundry," Rogers said.

About five minutes later, a third express arrived. Santangello moved to the door, stuck his head in, and looked around. He stepped into the car.

Rogers and Strickland moved fast, boarded the car just behind as the doors were closing. They edged up to the door between the cars, watching through the glass. Santangello's car had about a dozen people in it. He was just taking a seat next to an old lady. She put her shopping bag on the seat between them.

"Watch," Rogers said. "Any minute he's going to make the switch."

Strickland kept his eyes on Santangello. "You've seen it before," he said.

"Too often," Rogers said.

"An old lady?" Strickland said.

"What else? What could be more innocent?"

The doors closed. The train started with a sudden jerk, the shopping bag between Santangello and the old lady tipped, the packages in it tumbling to the floor. The old lady looked distressed and helpless. Santangello leaned forward, gathered the packages, and put them back in the shopping bag. The old lady smiled her gratitude.

Santangello leaned back, his brown paper–wrapped parcel tucked under his arm.

"Neat," Rogers said. "Helpful little bastard, isn't he?"

"If I hadn't been watching, I'd never have made it," Strickland said.

"The guy's good," Rogers said.

"What's in the package?" Strickland said.

"Junk or money," Rogers said. "Right now, I'd bet money."

Strickland nodded. "The way he's spreading it around, undoubtedly."

The train pulled into Fourteenth Street. The old lady got up, picked up her shopping bag and left the train. Santangello kept his seat, left hand hugging the parcel, right hand in his pocket. He wasn't so casual now. He appeared alert, his eyes moving around the car, examining the passengers who got on and the passengers who continued on the train. The eyes kept checking.

Four kids, maybe fifteen or sixteen, not much older, got on, laughing, shouting. One of them carried a boom box. It was going full blast. Even in the next car, even over the rattling and rumbling of the train, the rap music blasted against the ear drums. Santangello was watching them carefully, waiting. He kept his right hand in his jacket pocket. The arm was tensed.

A man with a briefcase looked toward the kids, annoyed. The kid with the boom box turned the volume up. The man said something, but the kids laughed and turned the boom box up another notch. Everybody in the car was staring at them now. The man said something else, not pleasant, and made a gesture. One of the kids stuck the middle finger of his right hand up in the air in the man's direction.

Santangello was watching with a concerned look. The last thing he wanted was trouble on this train at this time.

The man with the briefcase looked around for support. Most of the people in the car looked away. Nobody wanted trouble, nobody, perhaps, but the four kids, who were now moving toward him. One of them grabbed the briefcase and when the man lunged for it, the kid tossed it to one of his friends. The briefcase flew from one kid to the next. One pried open the latch, reached inside, and came away with a fistful of papers, which he started throwing around the car.

The man tried to get up, but one of the kids shoved him back into the seat. Another kid punched him in the face, bloodying his nose. The other passengers cowered in their seats. Santangello watched.

In the next car, his eyes on the scene through the window, Strickland said, "Leave it."

Rogers nodded. "Nothing we can do."

Strickland said, "We intervene, he makes us."

The train slowed as it pulled into the Brooklyn Bridge–City Hall station. The doors opened and a transit cop got on. He halted in the door as his eyes caught the devastation, then his hand went to his waist and his gun came out. He turned just slightly and shouted toward the platform for backup. He yelled to the kids to stop where they were.

The kids reached the open door. One threw the briefcase at the transit cop, hitting him across the chest. His gun went off, and the man without the briefcase fell off the seat onto the floor, blood spurting from his chest. The other passengers cowered in fear and panic.

The kids scattered onto the platform. The transit cop yelled for them to stop. They kept running. Two more transit cops came racing down the platform, guns out, ordering the kids on the platform heading for the stairs to stop. One of the transit cops fired a shot over their heads. There was a second shot and the kid with the boom box went down. The other kids reached the stairs and started up, as fast as they could go.

In Santangello's car, the first cop was bending over the man without a briefcase, trying to give mouth-to-mouth resuscitation. He was shaking his head and crying. The other people in the car were trying to crowd their way out the doors. Santangello was in the middle of the shoving mob. He wanted out in the worst way.

The first transit cop shouted something down the platform and before more than a couple of people had gotten through, the doors shut, sealing the train. Santangello reached the door just as it was closing. He tried to force it open. The door wouldn't budge. His foot was caught between the two closing doors. He was trapped for a moment. He pulled his foot free and just stood there.

From their vantage, Rogers and Strickland had a clear view. "They've got it under control," Strickland said. "We just wait."

The two transit cops who had chased the kids up the stairs returned. They had nabbed one kid, cuffed his hands behind him, and were shoving him ahead. They unlocked one cuff and attached it to a steel railing, then one moved up alongside the train. The other went to the kid who had gone down and bent over. The kid was moaning. There was blood on his jacket. The cop looked down the platform and shouted, "Backup! Medics! On the double!"

Inside the train, the speaker hummed, clicked, buzzed. "We're sorry for the delay. There has been an accident on the train. All passengers are requested to remain where they are until the police arrive. Thank you for your patience."

Nobody on the train was very patient, especially in the car where the man lay bleeding on the floor. Perhaps in the other cars nobody knew what was going on, but in that car they were all too aware. They were scared and they only wanted out. Santangello especially wanted out. "Are you thinking what I'm thinking?" Rogers said.

"Yeah. I think," Strickland said, "maybe we ought to rescue the poor bastard."

Strickland moved toward the exit door. He rapped on it hard. The transit cop standing beside the next car looked his way, then moved slowly toward the door. He looked at Strickland. Strickland pulled out his wallet, opened it and held it against the door window where the cop could see it. The cop studied it. "We need out," Strickland said loudly.

The cop nodded. He went quickly down the platform. He was back with a subway technician in a minute. The technician used a large key and opened that one door. The cop stood in the doorway, blocking exit. "These two are cops," he said, pointing to Strickland and Rogers. "The rest of you stay where you are."

Strickland and Rogers stepped out onto the platform. The doors closed again before anybody else could move.

"You're federal," the cop said to Strickland. Strickland nodded.

The cop looked at Rogers. Strickland said, "He's with me." Rogers pulled out the old shield and flashed it, then put it away before the cop could get a good look.

"We're tailing a guy in the next car," Strickland said, moving adjacent to it. "Now we'd like to have a little talk with him."

"Which guy?"

"The one in the fancy suit." He pointed. "Can you let him out?"

Santangello was watching the door. He spotted Strickland. He didn't look happy.

"We're supposed to hold everybody until help gets here."

"I'll take responsibility," Strickland said. "He had nothing to do with it. It was those kids. If you want a statement, you can get in touch with me at my office." He reached into his pocket and handed the cop a card.

The cop looked at it, nodded, and put it into his pocket. He motioned toward the technician with the key. The technician opened the door of Santangello's car. The cop stood in the doorway. "Everybody stay calm," he said. "Help is on the way."

"There's a guy bleeding to death in here," someone yelled, watching the first cop still trying to give mouth-to-mouth resuscitation.

"A doctor's on the way," the cop said.

"It's not going to do him much good. He needs help now."

The cop looked toward the fallen man. The other cop, the one bent over him looked up and shook his head, then went back to his futile efforts.

The cop in the doorway motioned toward Santangello. "You," he said. "Come along. This man would like to talk to you."

Santangello held back, glaring at Strickland.

"Come on," the cop said. "Move it."

Reluctantly, Santangello moved past the cop and out onto the platform. The doors closed behind him.

"*Buenos dias,* Victor," Strickland said.

"Fuck off," Santangello said.

"We want to have a little talk with you," Strickland said.

"I got nothing to say."

"Your choice," Strickland said. "You come with us or you go back in there and wait for the boys in blue."

It took Santangello about half a second to make his choice. He glared at Strickland. "Where?"

"Just come along. We'll talk later." Strickland reached out toward Santangello. Santangello backed away.

"Hands off," he said, and started to move toward the stairs.

Out on the street, there must have been a dozen police cars and ambulances, lights flashing, filling the street around the subway entrance, and more cop cars were racing toward the subway entrance. Strickland, Rogers, and Santangello didn't pause. Strickland ordered Santangello to keep moving.

"Where we goin'?"

Strickland pointed east. "That way. Just keep walking."

Santangello looked like he was about to chance it, to make a break, then a look at Strickland's face made him think better of it. He hugged his parcel tighter against his chest. He kept glancing back toward Rogers, who was a step behind. "I know you," Santangello said. "Cop. You stink like a cop." He gave a short bark of a laugh, looked back again. "It's more than that. I seen you someplace."

"Just keep moving, Victor," Strickland ordered. "Save the talk for later."

"Screw you," Santangello said. "You can't do nothin' to me. I'm protected."

"Sure. And you're supposed to be protected all nice and neat in a hotel suite. How come you're wanderin' around on the loose?"

"Fuck you."

They kept walking, turned south a couple of blocks, moved along the silent, empty streets before moving east again until they reached a deserted warehouse near the Fulton Fish Market. The smell was rank. "In there," Strickland said, pointing toward an empty loading dock barely visible in the darkness. Santangello gave a look and decided the best course was to do as he was told. He moved. They backed him against the loading dock and stood facing him.

"Now," Strickland said, "we'd like to have a little talk."

"I got nothin' to say to you. I do my talkin' to other guys."

Strickland looked toward Rogers. "I want to ask you about Charlie Westerman," Rogers said.

"Never heard of the guy."

"How about Max Abromowitz?"

"Don't ring no bells."

"Terry Galvin?"

"Ditto. Now fuck off."

"Let's play it again," Rogers said. "This time, let's have some answers. Charlie Westerman?"

Santangello studied Rogers' face. There was something in it he didn't like. Besides, he was sure no matter what he said, there was nothing they could do to him. After all, he was protected. After all, he was valuable. "Dumb asshole cop," Santangello said.

"Max Abromowitz?"

"Motherfucker with a big mouth."

"Terry Galvin?"

"Ditto."

"You shoot them, Victor?"

"Westerman shot hisself, what I hear."

"How about Max and Terry?"

"Who gives a fuck about them?"

"What about John Morrison?" Strickland said suddenly.

Santangello glared at him. "What're you tryin' to do, pin every fuckin' crime in the book on me? The bastard got what was comin' to him, and the guy what done it, whatever the fuck his name was, done everybody a favor."

"You were right in the area a few hours before. Who's to say you didn't hang around and wait for your chance?" Strickland said.

"Bullshit," Santangello said. "If I could've, I would-'ve. But I didn't. There was marshals watchin' me every second. You think they would've looked the other way while I stood in a window with a fuckin' rifle an' blew Morrison away? Bullshit."

Strickland looked at Rogers. "You buy?"

Rogers nodded. "Yeah. I guess I buy. Max and Terry, and Westerman. But not Morrison."

Santangello gave a short laugh. "You assholes done? 'Cause I'm leavin'."

Rogers looked toward Strickland. "I don't think so," Rogers said. "One more thing, Victor. We're going to relieve you of your burdens now."

Santangello looked at him, puzzled. "What the fuck are you talkin' about?"

Strickland pointed and started toward him. "We'll take that package you're holding onto like it was a million bucks."

"Hands off," Santangello said, pressing ever closer to the loading dock. "Don't touch me."

"And we'll take what's in your coat pocket," Rogers said. "I think I'd like ballistics to take a look."

"Up yours," Santangello said. He shoved himself away

from the dock suddenly. His right hand went down fast
into the pocket, came out with a nine millimeter.

"Ben!" Strickland shouted, reaching for his own gun.
Rogers dropped to one knee, drawing his pistol.

Santangello got off a shot. Rogers felt the breeze as it
skimmed by his head.

The report from Strickland's gun echoed in the deserted
stillness of the loading dock. Santangello reeled back, a
dark stain discoloring his pastel shirt. As he fell, he fired
again. The bullet went harmlessly into the air. Strickland
fired a second time. Santangello's head exploded.

They stood looking down at him. "There's going to
be hell to pay," Strickland said. "Let's get the fuck out
of here. Let somebody else find him in the morning."

Rogers motioned toward the parcel Santangello had
been holding so tightly. It was on the ground near his
body now. "What about that? Shall we take a look?"

Strickland bent and picked up the parcel, undid the tape
that held it together. Inside were bills, fifty dollar bills,
hundred dollar bills. He looked at Rogers. "I said the bastard
was holding onto this like it was a million bucks. Maybe
not that much, but close. You want to count?"

"No. Whatever it is, it is."

"What do we do with it? If we leave it here, whoever
finds him in the morning's going to walk off with it. You
can bet on that."

"Agreed," Rogers said. "I think what we'll do is wrap
it up and send it to Charlie Westerman's widow."

23

The mini-storage warehouse filled what had once been the shed of a bustling shipping pier on the Hudson River south of Fourteenth Street. That pier and so many others along the five-mile stretch along the Hudson from the Battery north to Fifty-seventh Street had been rotting, abandoned shells until some enterprising businessmen got the bright idea that, after all, they could be turned back to profitable ventures. They turned some into parking garages and some more into mini-storage where people who live in the city could find a place to put all the detritus they couldn't bear to throw away. The one Rogers headed for was just south of Fourteenth Street.

The guard in a bulletproof Plexiglas cage just inside the entrance took a quick and not particularly careful look at the lease-ID card Rogers flashed and buzzed him through the steel mesh gate. Gondolian's storage room, up a steep flight of metal steps, was midway down an aisle on the second floor, a large box with a steel door nestled among an endless row of similar boxes. The lock was a Medeco. The key that Annie Kendall had taped to the card fit. The lock turned. He found a light switch by the side of the door and flicked it on.

The room was empty, except for a lot of dust. There were clear, clean marks where perhaps a dozen filing cabinets had once stood, and from the dust around those spots it was obvious that those cabinets had been there up until a day or so earlier. And there were a lot of swirls where the cabinets had been moved, lines of dollies and scuffed prints. Rogers swore softly, looked around, then turned and went back the way he had come.

The guard was still at the desk in his cage reading a newspaper. He didn't look up until Rogers rapped at the glass. He looked up quizzically and didn't say anything.

"Room two thirty-seven," Rogers said.

"What about it?"

"Somebody emptied it out."

"So?"

"Who and when?"

"What business is it of yours?" the guard asked. "You're not the guy who rented the room. I never seen you here before."

Rogers sighed, reached into his pocket and pulled out the wallet with the old silver shield. "My business," he said.

The guard looked at the shield. "I'll have to check," he said.

"Check," Rogers said.

The guard pulled out a large ledger, turned some pages and studied the writing. "The room was rented by somebody named Gondolian. Harry Gondolian," he said.

"I know that," Rogers said. "What I want to know is who cleared out the room and when?"

The guard studied the ledger some more. He turned

and reached for another book and opened it. His lips moved as he read. He looked up at Rogers. "Cleared out the day before yesterday," he said.

"Who by?"

"According to the book, it was done under court order number 7787-95. All proper. The people who showed up showed the papers and we did what we had to do."

"What people? What official orders?"

The guard looked back at the book. "Federal government," he said. "The book says there was a tax lien and they had the right to remove everything in the room to cover it. The agents brought it and they cleaned out the place. They had a right."

"Were you the guy on duty at the time?"

"Yeah."

"So you saw the order?"

"You bet. It had an official seal, notarized, the whole works. What was I supposed to do?"

"What you did. You notice anything about the agents?"

The guard didn't like the question. "What's the matter? You sayin' they were phonies, or somethin'? They looked like agents. You know what I mean. Suits, white shirt, all the rest."

"I'm not suggesting anything," Rogers said. "It's just we had a claim on the stuff, too. I guess they beat us to the punch."

"Tough shit," the guard said with a grin.

"One more thing."

"Yeah?"

"How did they move the stuff? I mean, from what we understand, there were something like a dozen file cabinets and other stuff in there. They must have had a truck and some moving guys, right?"

"Right. They had a truck. Pulled it right in here. And they had a couple movers in uniform and dollies and all the rest of that crap."

"You notice anything about the truck?"

"What was there to notice? I mean, it was a truck, like a moving van."

"Did it have a name on the side? Anything to say it was, say, government property?"

The guard thought. "Give me a minute. I think I wrote it down somewhere, so the owner would know who took the stuff so he could contact them. I mean, not just the government but the guys the government got."

"Can you look it up?"

The guard fished in a drawer beneath his desk, pulled out a batch of papers, went through them. He pulled out one and held it up. "Here it is. Name on the side of the truck was Phoenix Trans-World Shipping. I said something and this one agent, he says they had a contract with that outfit to do this kind of job. Yeah, now I remember that."

So John Doe or whatever his name was and whoever he worked for had moved fast. Gondolian was dead and now so was Annie Kendall, and they had been the only ones who knew what those files contained. Maybe the answers to all the questions rested there. Or at least the sign posts to point the way to the answers. But it was too late. They were both dead and the files were gone, and wherever they had gone, they were out of Rogers' reach.

There were some bills in his mail box, some junk mail, and a post office notice of a registered letter that he hadn't been home to receive and sign for. He stared at it. There was nothing on the notice to say who it was from. The only way to find out was to go to the post office and retrieve it.

He walked the few blocks to the post office, went to the right window, signed the return receipt form and was handed a large manila envelope. In the upper left corner was a name and a return address. Anne Kendall, 357 West 82nd Street. He stood by the window staring at it, unable to move until somebody tapped him on the shoulder, asked if anything was wrong and if not, would he kindly get out of the way and let the next person pick up his mail.

He left the post office, carrying the envelope carefully. There was a temptation to open it immediately. He resisted. He wanted to be alone when he read whatever she had written. He would wait until he was home, the door closed, a drink in his hand to prepare him for whatever it was. It would not be easy to read, whatever it said, knowing she had been alive then and was dead now, that these were the first and only written words of hers that he would ever see.

He took that drink first, and then he opened it carefully. There was stiff cardboard protecting the inside. He pulled out several sheets of paper and another piece of paper wrapped around something hard. That something hard turned out to be a number of computer disks.

He turned to the paper. She had typed the letter, her handwriting only the last word.

Dear Rogers:
    I decided to send these to you for safekeeping. I'm scared, which is the reason I'm doing it. I have a feeling that somebody's been following me ever

since I left the apartment after you the other morning. That's the reason I haven't been back there. Instead, I've been staying with my parents. I swore when I moved out that I wouldn't ever go back. You know, you can't go home again. I felt safe with you that night, but I don't think I could ask you to do that again, and I feel I need some protection, even if only from some imaginary shadows. I hope that's all they are and that I'll get over this soon. But there are times when one's parents come in handy, and this is one of them. I haven't told them anything about what happened. It would upset them too much. I just told them that I was feeling sort of lonely, and sad, after what happened to Harry, and I thought staying with them would help. They've been very sympathetic and haven't asked many questions, which helps. My mother said that if I wanted, she'd call the paper and ask for them to give me leave to get over it. If she did, they'd do it. I don't know whether you know, but my uncle's the publisher and my mother owns a lot of stock. That sounds lousy, doesn't it, as if I'd used their influence to get my job? I didn't. I swear it. Harry found me on his own and they were as surprised as anyone when they found out I was going to work for the paper. They didn't even know that I was interested in being a reporter. I don't know what they thought I wanted out of life, but certainly not that.

I've been doing a lot of thinking about what Harry told me and what I read in the files that I took from his mini-storage room. You see, there were things in those files that referred back to older ones, partic-

ularly some going back 20 to 25 years ago. Today
I went back to the warehouse to look. The problem
is I knew there were dozens of files dating that far
back and I couldn't possibly go through them in
one afternoon.

I did something else. I brought along my laptop
and a scanner, and I just sat there on the floor
and scanned all the files I thought pertinent onto
computer disks. So whatever happens, they're safe.
I haven't had time yet to go through them, but I've
copied them on the floppies I'm enclosing with this
letter. I think you ought to print them out as soon
as possible, read them, which I intend to do, and
we can compare notes when we get together—when
I have nerve enough, that is, to go back to my
apartment, and nerve enough to call you again (and
don't think it won't take a lot more nerve for me
even to begin to think about doing that. It's not that
I'm ashamed of what we did, or of how I leaned
on you; I'm not. It's just that you're taken, and I
don't want to come between you and what you're
sure is right and special. I don't know your friend,
but I can tell how you feel about her. So I guess
she must be special. But the way I feel about you
at the moment, I just might try, and then I would
be ashamed. Sorry for gushing on like this.).

There were some things in the files that, shall
we say, vanished from my apartment, that you'll
probably need to know as reference for what's in
the old files, which are on the floppies. At least I
imagine so. Harry wrote that those three men whose
names were on the paper he had me give to you—
Rasmussen, Jessup, and Weinstein—were each get-

ting a lot of money, he said between $100,000 and $200,000 a year for the last four or five years from somebody named Steven Gold (who they say shot Morrison and Harry, isn't that right?) He said he didn't think it was blackmail but something else. He didn't say what. He just said it goes way back. Maybe there's something in the old files. There was also something about a woman named Caitlin, but he didn't say what. It seemed to be just a note to himself, because it had a question mark next to it. And there was also both a question mark and an exclamation point next to Morrison's name, which was in the same file. There were some other names, too, but there were so many I can't remember right now what they were. He, Harry that is, must have known what it all meant, and how it ties together. But I don't. Not yet, at least. Do you have any idea?

One more thing. About that puzzle you presented Harry, something about a cop who got killed. Did I mention to you that Harry told me about it and said he thought he'd solved it? He said you had the wrong name, but the right initials (I remember that clearly) and the wrong reason he died. It was such a strange statement. He said that's all he'd tell me. The rest was for you and he'd explain it the next time he saw you. Did he?

That's all for now. Print the floppies and read them and I'll read them and then we can compare notes. I'll work up the nerve to call you very soon. And, please, forget all the soppy stuff at the beginning of this and let's just pretend, not that it didn't happen but that we can put it somewhere and not always have it out in front when we meet. Let's just pretend we're just friends and no more. Isn't that the way you want it?

I won't sign this, love, I'll just sign it

Annie

The name was written in blue ink. It was the only handwriting on the pages. He picked up the manila envelope and examined it. She had mailed it on Friday. If it had been delivered the next day, then maybe she'd still be alive.

24

Sol Melman ran a small computer operation on Park Avenue South, the name the city fathers had given years ago to what had once been Fourth Avenue in an effort to upgrade that avenue's image. The office, combination retail, repair, and expert advice operation, was just south of Fourteenth Street on the second floor of a rundown building. The building notwithstanding, Melman, a one-time hacker, was a computer genius, and people with problems brought their troubles to him. When they left, he had usually solved those problems, though he didn't come cheap.

That was where Rogers headed with the computer disks. He had known Melman for years. Melman lived only a block away and when Melissa bowed to the inevitable and sprang for a computer, he was the guy who designed and set up the system. For Rogers, bytes and bits, RAM and ROM, autoexec.bat and config.sys, and the rest of computer jargon still seemed a foreign language beyond his comprehension. Maybe grade school kids were becoming masters of computerese, but every time he looked at one of those thousand-page handbooks that lined the shelves above Melissa's computer, he froze. When a computer was involved, he had long ago learned to turn to Sol Melman.

He pushed the buzzer on Melman's office door. In about a minute, a clicking response unlocked the door. Melman was like too many other people, Rogers thought as he pushed the door open. He never asked who was there, he just pushed the unlock button. Rogers had warned him about that a dozen times, and Melman never listened. He'd already been robbed twice, and still he persisted in letting anybody in who rang.

Melman was at a table staring at a glowing computer monitor, the screen filled with incomprehensible numbers, letters and images. He looked up. "Ben," he said. "Long time no see."

"Solly," Rogers said, "could you do something for me?"

"Anything," Melman said. "Hey, I've been reading about you."

"You and everybody else," Rogers said. "I didn't do it."

"Who said you did? What's the problem? I thought the PC was Melissa's and you wouldn't touch it with a ten-foot pole."

"I don't," Rogers said. "Which is why I'm here." He reached into his pocket and pulled out the disks. "Could you print what's on these?"

Melman stretched out his hand and took them. "No problem," he said.

"The person who made them," Rogers said, "said that she copied them from a hard disk and they were files she had scanned, whatever the hell that means. Does that present a problem?"

"What it means is that she used a scanner to transfer the images on those files to her hard disk. Printing them out is just like printing anything else out." Melman looked at the disks. "There's a lot of stuff here," he said. "When do you need it?"

"How soon can you do it?"

"Tomorrow okay?"

"If that's the way it's got to be, then that's the way it's got to be."

"Come by late tomorrow," Melman said, "or, better, I'll drop it off at your place on my way home tomorrow night."

"How much is this going to set me back?" Rogers asked.

"For you, nothing."

"Come on."

"You've done enough favors for me, now I'll return one."

By the middle of the afternoon, he was in Sam Janosky's office at the public library. Janosky was somewhere back in the stacks. Rogers waited. About twenty minutes later, Janosky strolled in, carrying an armload of papers. He saw Rogers.

"You again," he said. "What is it this time?"

"I need information."

"Every time you show up here you need information. What do I look like, a research librarian?" Janosky laughed.

"Isn't that what you pretend to be?" Rogers grinned back at him.

"That's what my degree says," Janosky said. "Okay, what kind of information?"

"A list of cops who died twenty to twenty-five years ago. The thing is, their names have to start with a J and M."

Janosky stared at him. "What is this, anagrams?"

"I don't know. It's something somebody said. He used to talk in riddles, but when you figured them out, they made sense."

"Have you got all night? We close in a couple of hours."

"The list I want is of cops who died not in the line of duty. Some other way. Cops with those initials."

Janosky studied him. "Just what are you up to?"

"Research," Rogers said. "Which is why I came to you."

Janosky sighed. "All right, so I'll work late."

"Put in for overtime."

"You think this is the police department with an unlimited budget? Overtime? Whoever heard of such a thing around here? If I stay late, it's on my own time." He shook his head. "So I stay late."

It was after nine before they finished. The names came up, Rogers studied them, studied how they died, and, in most cases, passed them up. He figured he could rule out the cops who had gone to their reward in traffic accidents or heart attacks or some other natural causes. He also figured if he had the right reading of Gondolian's cryptic comment to Annie Kendall, there was some tie to Rasmussen, Jessup, Weinstein, and Gold, and maybe even to Morrison. That meant the cop probably worked in Manhattan. And there was that one other thing. Initials. He came away with clippings about five cops.

John Malone had been stabbed by his girl friend in what was officially called a domestic dispute. Malone had been a patrolman on the force for twelve years, assigned to Manhattan North precinct. The girl friend said she had killed him in self-defense when he came home drunk and attacked her. It was rumored that he was a bagman, collecting protection money from local illegal gambling operations. Nobody could call that line of duty.

Jason Myles, a ten-year veteran, a detective assigned to a Manhattan narcotics unit, had drowned in his backyard swimming pool. The story noted that Myles' unit was then at the center of a wide-ranging corruption investigation. There was nothing about Myles being implicated. But then there was nothing to say that he wasn't. His death certainly wasn't in the line of duty.

Jerome McKenzie, on the force for four years, working as an undercover cop assigned to the Manhattan District Attorney's office, had jumped or fallen from a window while under investigation. The story didn't say what he was being investigated for. It didn't say, either, what he had been investigating while working undercover. Going out the window was certainly not line of duty.

James Macklin, a cop for seven years, assigned to the bomb squad, was blown to pieces in the basement of his own home. According to the story, the police said Macklin was then under investigation by both the Manhattan district attorney and the FBI. It was said that he not only defused bombs but used his expertise to make them for sale to people willing to pay his price. The story didn't say who those people might be. Apparently, an explosive device he was constructing went off, and that was the end of Macklin. Certainly not a line-of-duty death.

Joseph Montefiore, a cop for eleven years, was a detective working out of headquarters. His assignment was investigating organized crime. It turned out that he was an expert at his job. An expert because he was on the payroll of one of the families. An informant gave him up. Montefiore was suspended, and he was told that an indictment would be sought unless he agreed to cooperate. Montefiore decided not to cooperate. He decided, instead, to hang himself in his basement. Not a line-of-duty death.

In the morning, Rogers called Carlos Rodriguez. "Carlos," he said, "the thing about the cop who died in the line of duty."

"You mean Justin McCauley? I told you, there's no such person."

"I agree. Now, can you do this? Check five names, John Malone, Jason Myles, Jerome McKenzie, James Macklin, and Joseph Montefiore. They were all cops. They all died twenty to twenty-five years ago. And not in the line of duty."

There was a pause, then, "And they all got names with J and M, right?"

"Right."

"You know you could throw in a sixth," Rodriguez said.

"I know," Rogers said. "But Morrison wasn't a cop."

"Close, though," Rodriguez said.

"Close, but no cigar."

"What do you want to know about these guys?"

"The real stories on how they died. I've got what was in the papers at the time. I want to know what the record says. And I want next of kin, families, that kind of stuff, and, if you can dig it up, what happened to those families and where they are now. Anything at all you can dig up about them."

"Jesus," Rodriguez said, "all you want is the cheese the moon's made of. What do you think I am, a fucking fortune teller with a crystal ball?"

"I know you. You can do it."

"Yeah, I can do it. It'll take a couple of days."

"Sooner. Like tomorrow. Put your mind to it."

"The guy wants miracles. I'll see what I can do. Soon as I get something, I'll let you know," Rodriguez said. "Do I ask how all this ties?"

"You can ask, but I don't have an answer. Not just yet."

Strickland answered the phone on the first ring.

"George, Ben Rogers."

"Ben, would you believe it? I had my hand on the phone to call you. The shit really hit the fan about that thing the other night."

"I believe it."

"There's a major investigation in progress. The two marshals who were supposed to be baby-sitting Santangello are in deep shit. Santangello was paying them two grand a week to look the other way."

"What a surprise," Rogers said. "They got any theories about how he met his sad demise?"

"They're looking into it. Right now the theory is that he was off doing his thing, and he must have been doing it with the wrong people. They asked me what I thought, because they knew I'd worked on the case back when. I said I thought they were on the right track."

"I'd say you said the right thing and the theory's about what it should be."

Strickland laughed. "Now, what's up with you?"

"Did you ever hear of an outfit called Phoenix Trans-World Shipping?"

"Like rising from the ashes? Not that I can recall," Strickland said. "Why?"

"They're a front of somebody who works for the same firm as you."

"Not my agency, at least not that I've ever heard. And I know most of what goes on around here."

"I don't necessarily mean your particular branch. What I mean is, they're a front for some federal agency. I'm positive about that. I'd like to know who, and just what they're up to."

"If what you're saying is true, there's no way you're going to find out."

"I figure you've got some pretty good connections after all these years. Call in some IOU's."

"Why?" Strickland asked. "What's the interest?"

"Annie Kendall and Harry Gondolian, for starters."

"What's that supposed to mean?"

"Gondolian kept his files in one of those mini-storage places. Phoenix grabbed them the other day. They said they had a tax lien, even showed the proper documents to back it up, and hauled them away. The way I see it, if they grabbed those files, they're the ones who took Annie Kendall's place apart and walked off with what she had. It had to be somebody who could get in and out of the proverbial sealed room and not leave a trace of the coming and going. To me, that spells feds, it spells secret feds. I want to know why, what's behind it, what the hell is going on."

"What you're suggesting," Strickland said, "is very serious business. You could be getting in over your head.

My head, too, if I start to nose around. Maybe you ought to just forget it."

"No can do," Rogers said. "There was something in those files somebody wanted real bad. Bad enough, maybe, to kill Annie Kendall."

"That's crazy."

"Not so crazy. She's dead. So is Gondolian. And maybe we have to throw Morrison into the pot, too."

"Ben, just what the hell are you saying? People I know don't do things like that."

"No? If I had time, I could give you a list. Look, George, I went up to that place. It's down in Chelsea. Some guy, I mean, federal right out of the manual, says his name is John Doe, if you want to believe it, or Richard Roe, or John Smith or Sam Jones, take your choice. He answers no questions. In essence, he tells me if I want to stay healthy I should take a walk. I got a look through the door behind him. They had computers coming out your ass. Why? What the hell are they doing?"

"Your neck. And mine," Strickland said.

"You don't have to show yourself," Rogers said. "You know how. Nice and quiet, a little line here, a little line there, and see what kind of fish you pull in."

"A fucking shark is what I'll pull in."

"I thought you were in this thing with me."

"I am." Strickland fell silent. Rogers could hear the sigh of resignation. "Okay. I'll see what I can find out. Probably nothing. But my head's going to be on the chopping block if it gets to the wrong people."

"That's where my head is now," Rogers said.

25

There were about a half dozen guys standing around outside the small building on Mulberry Street. They looked like they were auditioning for *The Godfather*, *Part 19*. Only Francis Ford Coppola wasn't upstairs. They saw Rogers approaching and their eyes tried to take him apart. He smiled broadly at them, motioned them to part as he turned toward the entrance. They didn't move.

"Come on," he said, "be nice."

They kept staring. One of them muttered, "Fuckin' cop." Reluctantly, they separated just enough for him to move between them. He pushed the button under the plaque. A voice came through the speaker grill. "Yeah?"

"I want to see Mr. Ruggieri."

"Who wants to see Mr. Ruggieri?"

"Tell him Ben Rogers."

The speaker switched off. Rogers waited. The door clicked and he pushed it open, climbed the stairs to the second floor, pressed the button beside that door, there was more clicking and he was inside.

A twin brother of the guys downstairs was waiting

beside the entrance. "Just a second," the guy said as
Rogers started past him. Rogers halted. The guy's hands
went over him, took the gun from the belt holster. "I'll
take this for safekeeping," he said. "You can have it back
when you leave."

"Be my guest," Rogers said and stepped toward the
dyed blonde at the reception desk.

"He'll see you," she said, and motioned him through
a swinging gate in the slatted wooden partition. He went
through. The door to Ruggieri's office clicked and moved
a little off the latch. He went through it.

Ruggieri was just rising from behind his desk. "I am
glad to see you," he said.

"I got your message," Rogers said. "Thanks for the
concern."

Ruggieri lifted both hands in a deprecating gesture.
"You are solving your troubles?"

"I hope so. I think so."

"Good. Now, you want something?"

"Help," Rogers said.

"If I can."

"A long time ago there was a cop named Joe Montefiore. He was on your payroll."

Ruggieri did not react. He waited.

"I want to know about him," Rogers said.

"That was before your time," Ruggieri said finally.
"Long before."

"Right," Rogers said. "I'd still like to know."

"This has something to do with your troubles?"

"It might, and it might not. That's what I'm trying to
find out. Now, about Montefiore . . ."

"In those days," Ruggieri said, "one did what one
had to do to survive."

"That's still true," Rogers said. "Times haven't changed all that much."

Ruggieri smiled and nodded. "Joey," he said, "was a good boy."

"From your point of view, maybe."

"We had confidence in him and he earned our confidence."

"I'm sure he did. How about respect?"

Ruggieri shrugged. "He did what he had to do. He was an honorable man. We provided for his widow and his children."

"They're still around?"

"Mrs. Montefiore died three years ago," Ruggieri said, "and his children are grown."

"Do you know where they are?"

"The son is a doctor on Long Island, the daughter is married and lives in New Jersey."

"You've kept track?"

"Most naturally."

"If I asked, would you give me their addresses?"

Ruggieri shook his head. "That I cannot do. They knew nothing of their father's activities, and they have earned their privacy. Why would you wish to see them? How could they help you?"

"In those days," Rogers said, "Morrison was an assistant DA. Do you know if he was involved in the Montefiore investigation?"

"He was not," Ruggieri said.

"How can you be sure?"

"I am certain," Ruggieri said.

Okay, Rogers thought, strike Montefiore. Rodriguez might dig up some details, but Rogers didn't think it would change anything.

"Now," Ruggieri said, "you will share some coffee with me?"

"Why not?" Rogers said. "If I remember, you serve the best coffee around."

Ruggieri went to a sideboard and poured small cups from a tureen. He carried them to a marble coffee table, set them down and motioned Rogers onto the sofa.

After a sip of the strong coffee, strong enough to corrode the stomach lining, Rogers looked up. "I thought you told me you were retired."

"What I told you is true."

"I saw a bunch of guys downstairs. And another one up here."

"Some young people do not believe me. They have no respect," Ruggieri said.

"So you got yourself a little protection."

Ruggieri shrugged.

26

About eight, the buzzer in the apartment sounded. Sol Melman was downstairs. Rogers buzzed him in, went to the door and opened it. Melman struggled up the stairs carrying a large cardboard carton.

"You owe me a five," Melman said, "for the cab. I couldn't lug this stuff across town on foot."

"Come on in," Rogers said. "I'll take it." He took the carton from Melman. It was heavy enough to bend the knees.

"Two thousand pages," Melman said. "Are you going to read all this stuff?"

"Yeah," Rogers said. "Starting as soon as you leave. You have any trouble?"

"Just getting it here. I thought my back would break."

"You want a drink?" Rogers asked.

"No. My wife's waiting. I'm late as it is, but I wanted to finish this for you." Melman turned and started out. "See you. And happy reading."

When Melman was gone, Rogers opened the carton and stared down at the contents. Thank God, he thought,

Gondolian typed his stuff. He remembered that Gondolian's handwriting was nearly illegible. Gondolian used to say that even he had trouble reading his notes if he let more than a couple of days go by.

By three in the morning, his eyes wouldn't focus anymore. He'd gone through less than a quarter of the stack. Annie Kendall had written that she'd only scanned what she thought, or hoped, were the pertinent files. He wasn't unhappy that she hadn't copied everything. A lot of what he read didn't make much sense yet. It probably wouldn't until he'd gone through everything. Gondolian's notes often tended to be cryptic, and things only came together when juxtaposed with other notes or memos or interviews further along. He'd have to hold off jumping to conclusions until he finished. And maybe even then, the conclusions would be only tentative. If only he had those last files, the ones that had been taken from her apartment. There were just too many damn ifs.

The alarm went off at seven. He reached out groggily and without even realizing what he was doing, he turned it off, rolled over and went back to sleep. The phone woke him an hour later. It was Carlos Rodriguez.

"Damn you," Rodriguez said. "I was up all night."

"So was I. But you got it."

"Yeah. I don't know what I've got, but I've got it."

"Okay. Give."

For the next half hour, Rodriguez recited what he had learned about the five J.M.'s. For once, he said, the papers had a lot of it right. Malone had been, indeed, the bagman in his precinct, spending his duty hours touring the local bookies and horse parlors, the illegal casinos, the after-hour joints, the bars that served underage kids, and walking away with a five here, a ten there, a hundred someplace else. He spread the loot around, and kept a lot, a whole lot for himself. But he had a problem. He was a boozer. In addition to money, he always had a drink or two anyplace that had a bottle on the premises. The lady he was living with was a hooker, and he was not just the precinct's bagman, he pimped for her on the side. The fight wasn't because he came home drunk and started manhandling her. It was because he came home drunk and accused her of holding out on his end of the proceeds she earned at her trade. One thing led to another, and goodbye to thirty-four-year-old John Malone, after twelve years on the force, most of them on the take. His insurance and whatever else he had piled up went to his mother, two sisters and two brothers. His father, who had been a cop, was dead. Malone's mother died fifteen years ago. One of his brothers was a bookie operating in midtown. Another ran a grocery store in Flatbush. Both of his sisters were married. One lived in Cleveland and the other in Atlanta. So much for John Malone.

The papers may not have said that Jason Myles was involved in the narcotics scandal, but, Rodriguez had learned, he was not only involved he was at the center. He was making enough ripping off wholesalers, pushers, and even junkies to afford a fourteen-room house with a swimming pool and tennis courts in an exclusive section of Manhasset on Long Island. Then one fine day, one of the pushers decided he'd had enough of Myles' increasing demands and he sang to the DA's office. Myles went before the grand jury. He took the Fifth Amendment. It did him little good. You may be innocent until proved guilty, but the grand jury decided that at the very least Myles merited an indictment. And, because he wouldn't talk even when offered immunity, he was cited for con-

tempt. The thirty-five-year-old Myles went swimming
and forgot to come up for air. All his benefits went to
his wife, Zelda. She also got the loot he had stashed away,
which must have been enough to last a lifetime or two.
When last heard of, she was living the high life in Palm
Beach. By the way, Rodriguez said, the ADA handling
the case was none other than John Morrison.

Jerome McKenzie's undercover job for the DA's office,
according to Rodriguez's source, and Rodriguez said there
wasn't a better one, was to infiltrate, report on, and maybe
even stir things up a little in the radical underground.
You know, Rodriguez said, what the shysters would call
entrapment. Those were the years when opposition to the
war in Vietnam was reaching its peak. Demonstrations
were one thing, but violence was something else, and
some of the opponents of the government's policies were
using violence as one way to express that opposition.
They were planting bombs, taking over campuses, and
even stealing military secrets when they could. The
authorities wanted to know who they were and what they
were planning. For a while, everybody thought McKenzie
was turning up good stuff, even indictable stuff. But after
a time, what he came up with was pure garbage. Nobody
was sure whether McKenzie had been part of that underground all along or whether he had been co-opted by his
new friends. Whatever, the ADA he'd been working for,
who happened to be John Morrison, and the feds who
were part of the operation, got wise and turned on the
heat. According to Rodriguez's source, they sequestered
McKenzie in a twenty-second-story office, and Morrison
gave him an option. He could either tell everything he
knew, including names, dates and all the rest, in which
case they'd go easy on him, or keep quiet and spend most

of the rest of his life in a bad place with steel bars. They gave him ten minutes to make his choice, and left him alone to think about it. Unfortunately, McKenzie, who was twenty-five, took a third option. One of Morrison's guys went in to check on him, and just as he was a foot inside the room, McKenzie was going out the window. His insurance and a little more went to his widowed mother, Caitlin, and his kid sister, Fiona. Both mother and sister vanished right after the funeral and nobody has the foggiest idea where they went or what happened to them. "They probably changed their names," Rodriguez speculated, "and went someplace where nobody knew them and set up new lives. Lots of people did that from what I hear. The mother was one of those old-time radicals who was always yelling about revolution, so maybe she'd been practicin' what she preached. My guy says Morrison and the feds were very anxious to have a little talk with her. There were a lot of things goin' on back then that are still on the books, so maybe they're still lookin' for her."

Jimmy Macklin was, if the stories were to be believed, a mad bomber. He volunteered for the bomb squad right after joining the force. Apparently he knew everything there was to know about explosives, and he did things disarming them that nobody in his right mind would try. He'd done that while in Vietnam, and it had become second nature. But, like some firebugs, he not only liked to disarm explosives, he liked to make and arm them. And when he discovered there was a ready market for that talent, he went into business for himself. Who bought his little devices? He sold to anybody with the money. Some, rumor had it, found their way into the radical underground, some went to the Mafia, some wound up in the cars of people who had outlived their time, some went to freelancers of all kinds who thought they might have a use for explosives. Unfortunately, he made a mistake one night and that was the end of thirty-two-year-old Jimmy Macklin. Or maybe it wasn't an unfortunate accident after all. The DA and the feds were closing in on his little operation and he was about to face big trouble. The ADA in charge? Who else but John Morrison. About his insurance, pension, and all the rest, he wasn't married so it all went to his mother and father. They're both dead now, resting in a cemetery in Queens, Rodriguez said.

Rodriguez had nothing to add but a few details that didn't amount to much about Joe Montefiore. They only confirmed what Ruggieri had already told Rogers.

"You satisfied now?" Rodriguez said when he was finished.

"You done good, Carlos," Rogers said. "Now go home and get some sleep."

"That's exactly what I intend to do," Rodriguez said. "Only you damn well better let me know what the fuck it all means."

"When I know, I will."

When Rogers went back over Rodriguez's information, he was sure he had the answer. If you believed Gondolian that Justin McCauley was not the right name of the guy he had mentioned, and that "McCauley" had not died in the line of duty, then everything pointed to just one person. Jerome McKenzie. Add to that, the facts in that little story in the Los Angeles paper that Rogers had read that night on the plane and not forgotten. A mother named Constance McCauley and a daughter named Francine McCauley, who just might be, who had to be, Rogers was sure, Caitlin and Fiona McKenzie. It fit.

The thing was, what did it mean, what did it add up to, how did it tie to Gold and Rasmussen and Jessup and Weinstein, and Morrison, and maybe Gondolian and Annie Kendall as well?

The papers that comprised what he had of Gondolian's files covered the dining table, those files from that period twenty to twenty-five years in the past, the time when Jerome McKenzie had infiltrated the radical underground and then jumped out a window. Rogers went to the table, sat down, and picked up the papers and began to read from the beginning again.

For the next three days, he sat at the table reading and re-reading those two thousand pages, sorting and separating, looking for insights, clues, meanings, and links. He didn't sleep much, reading until his eyes filmed over and his brain stopped functioning. Then he went to bed to sleep for a few hours. He didn't eat much, either, lived those days on coffee. He kept the answering machine on and when the phone rang, let the machine take the message.

Harry Gondolian had been planning to write a series on the anti-war movement, focusing particularly on the underground. For two years he roamed the city, and traveled around the country, and interviewed more than two hundred people. He talked to demonstrators, members of a dozen different underground organizations and those who were trying to track them down and stop them, government officials, prominent citizens, liberals and radicals, conservatives and reactionaries. He took meticulous notes and every night typed them up, filling the pages single spaced not only with summaries and verbatim colloquies but with his impressions of people and places.

Gondolian never wrote that series. There was nothing

in the papers spread out on the table in front of Rogers
to indicate why. Gondolian just abandoned it after two
years of research. But he kept his notes, like he kept
everything else, filling file folders, the folders filling file
drawers.

Most of those notes, those interviews, those impressions dealt with people Rogers had never heard of, or
had only a vague and peripheral memory of, and reading
through them a second or a third time he could find
nothing that shed light on the puzzle he was trying to
solve. But there were notes about seven, some of whom
Gondolian had talked with more than once. Those interviews had not taken place one after the other in close
proximity. They had been conducted over a period of a
year or more, Gondolian seeking out one and then, a few
months later, another.

THE GONDOLIAN FILES (Excerpts)

Interview with Melvin Rasmussen

Rasmussen is a big kid, tall, dark, and muscular. He looks like a football player, and he is. He played linebacker for two years on the Columbia varsity, then quit football. "It was just a game," he told me, "and I was interested in real life. Football took up too much time." He's smart, a chemistry major, and he doesn't try to hide his intelligence. It's there in his face, in his eyes, and in the way he holds himself. It seemed to me that if he was your friend, you could depend on him totally. He would not be the kind of enemy you would want. There is an aura of belligerence there. Perhaps it was just in relationship to me, or maybe to any white man. But it's there, along with a watchfulness, and you sense that he is always on the alert, constantly wondering what you're after.

When I first called him, he was reluctant to grant

*an interview. He wanted to know what I wanted. I
told him I was doing research for a series on the
anti-war movement and I was trying to talk to people
on both sides, and in the middle. I had been given
his name as an articulate exponent of the things
he believed in. It took four calls on four different
occasions before he agreed to talk to me.*

*We met late in the afternoon in a booth at the
rear of the West End down Broadway from the
campus. He refused my offer to buy him a beer or
something to eat. He settled for tea, and used the
cup as a prop when he wanted to consider his
answers to my questions. I had been told that he
was a member, one of the leaders, of a small group
of underground radical revolutionaries who had
been planning, and perhaps had carried out, violent
actions to disrupt the war effort. Apparently they
consider this justified in light of American actions
in southeast Asia and both actions against and inac-
tion toward redressing the grievances of America's
minorities.*

*Before I could begin to ask him anything, he
asked why I wanted to talk to him.*

*Gond: I've heard that you're part of the anti-
war movement.*

Ras: Who isn't?

*Gon: But I've heard you're one of the leaders
on the campus.*

*Ras: Look, man, this is a white man's war against
yellow people, only the black man's doing all the
fighting and all the dying. For what? So the white
man can keep things just like they are? Well, I don't
want to keep things like they are. Walk north a*

couple of blocks and you'll see what I mean. You wouldn't live like those people. No white man would. You'd be marching on City Hall, marching on the White House. You'd probably be doing more than marching. So, why shouldn't we? As far as being a leader, that's bullshit. I'm just one of the troops. No black cat is a leader where there are whities involved. They don't want to take orders from guys like me.

Gon: You take the orders somebody else gives?

Ras: I do what I think is right for me, and people like me. If I think what somebody asks me to do will make a difference, fine. If I don't, I tell them to go fuck themselves.

Gon: How far are you willing to go to make your point?

Ras: As far as I have to.

Gon: How far is that?

Ras: What are you trying to get me to say?

Gon: I'm not trying to get you to say anything. I'm just asking you to say what you think and believe.

Ras: What I believe? I believe this country is all fucked up. I believe the fucking war is a total disaster, for everybody, there and here. I believe this country treats black people worse than shit. I believe the politicians talk big, you know, spit out all those dumb platitudes about how America is the land of opportunity and any kid can grow up to be president or a millionaire or whatever he wants. But it doesn't mean a fucking thing, because when you come right down to it, the people who run this country are all a bunch of racists who are out for number one. They want to keep what they've got and screw any-

body who gets in their way. That's not just what I believe, man, that's the fucking truth. Man, I grew up like forty, fifty blocks from here. My mama told me, hell, she didn't just tell me, she preached at me, Melvin, you work hard, you study hard, you make something of yourself. God, my mama, she believed all that crap. She believed if you went to church every Sunday and prayed hard enough, God would provide. She believed if you turned the other cheek, like it says in the Bible, you'd inherit the kingdom of heaven. You know what? When I was a kid, I believed that shit, too. I worked my ass off, I studied, I never missed a day of school, I got into Bronx Science, I got a scholarship here. I went to church every Sunday. You know what I wanted? I wanted up and out. I wanted the fucking American dream. You work hard, you study hard, you can be anything you want. You know what I found out? It doesn't make any difference how hard you work and study. What counts is the color of your skin. And if you've got black skin like me, you end up with the short end of the stick every time, if you even get the short end.

Gon: I gather you don't follow Martin Luther King's idea of a nonviolent revolution.

Ras: Do you want to know what nonviolence gets you? A kick in the ass and a rope from a tree. How many years did Gandhi spend in prison? How many times has King gone to jail, and what do you think happens to him in the white man's lockup? You think they kiss his ass when he turns the other cheek? Like hell. They just smack him a little harder on that other cheek.

Gon: But Gandhi succeeded, didn't he? India eventually won its independence.

Ras: I haven't got that long to wait, and I haven't got that kind of patience. They want to do it that way, that's their business. I have my own preferences and my own priorities.

Gon: You and your friends?

Ras: Who said anything about friends? The only friend I've got is the man you're looking at across this table.

Gon: I've heard that you're very close to four or five people. They say you work together to try to change things.

Ras: They tell you wrong.

Gon: They tell me the people you're especially close to are Steve Gold, Harvey Jessup, Marty Weinstein, Jerry McKenzie, and his mother, Caitlin.

Ras: They tell you wrong.

Gon: Don't you know them?

Ras: I know lots of people.

Gon: Including them?

Ras: I've seen them around. They're all big talkers, especially the old lady. You know, all mouth.

Gon: But you're not close to them? You don't work with them?

Ras: I'm close to nobody but me. I work with nobody but me. You don't look out for yourself, nobody looks out for you.

Gon: You major in chemistry, isn't that right?

Ras: What's that supposed to mean?

Gon: You tell me.

Ras: I'm a chem major, sure. Why not? I was always good at science. I like it. It's pure. It's exact.

You know what you have to do and if you do it, everything comes out right, and if you don't, you screw up. You combine two parts of hydrogen with one part of oxygen and you have water. You combine one part of hydrogen with two parts of oxygen and you don't have water. The color of your skin doesn't mean a thing, it doesn't get in the way. Nobody says because you're black or white or yellow or whatever color the laws of science, the laws of nature don't work for you. The laws of science work for everybody precisely the same.

Gon: Is that what you intend to do with your life, be a scientist?

Ras: Maybe. Maybe not. It depends.

Gon: On what?

Ras: A lot of things. For starters, I'm likely to end up over there and get my balls shot off.

Gon: Don't you have a student deferment?

Ras: You forget one thing. I'm black.

Gon: But right now, chemistry is it?

Ras: Part of it, anyway.

Gon: The rest?

Ras: Man, I'm going to change the fucking world. I'm going to make a difference.

Note: Rasmussen laughed when he said that, but I think he really believed it was possible. There was such an intensity about him at that moment that you almost believed he might even make that difference.

Interview with Harvey Jessup

Jessup is a bright and articulate young man, and very glib. When you talk to him you have a feeling that he has prepared or even rehearsed for the meeting, anticipating your questions and refining his answers. Unlike a lot of the kids I've talked to, he seems to care a great deal about his personal appearance. His dark wavy hair is neatly groomed. He wears a suit, a clean shirt and tie. When I called to ask if he'd talk to me, he seemed almost eager. When did I want to meet him? Did I have a particular place in mind? Could he suggest one? I left it up to him. We met late on Thursday evening at a club in the Village. It was one I had heard of and knew about but had never been in. They knew Jessup there. I gather he is something of a regular. Interesting. The public assumptions being what they are, he would not be readily identified as a homosexual. But then I'd say that's probably true of eighty percent of homosexuals. Sometimes public misperceptions are staggering. About the only recognizable minority in this society are the Negroes, or blacks as Stokely Carmichael and Rap Brown and the rest of SNCC now insist. And women, but then women are probably the majority anyway.

Jessup was waiting for me when I arrived sometime after nine. I asked the man at the door (who, as it happens, was dressed and acted just the way most people envision homosexuals) if Jessup was there. The man escorted me to a table set in an alcove off to the side and when I was seated drew drapes across the front, effectively guaranteeing us privacy.

Jessup started things off before I could ask the first question, and in many ways, he, just like some of his friends, set the tone and the direction of the interview.

Jessup: Mr. Gondolian, the first thing I'd like to do is clear away what are obviously some misconceptions you have about me and my friends.

Gon: I didn't know I had any.

Jessup: Of course you do. Everybody does. You think we're a bunch of wild-eyed, long-haired radicals throwing bombs in Haymarket Square, planning to blow up Congress, selling military secrets to the VietCong, that kind of thing. You think we're latter day incarnations of the 1903 or 1917 Bolsheviks. We're not.

Gon: What are you?

Jessup: We're simply people who think this country is on the wrong road, and we'd like to help get it back on the right one.

Gon: How?

Jessup: By pointing out the errors in the present course and offering logical alternatives.

Gon: Some people claim you do more than that.

Jessup: Well, some people claimed that Jesus was a troublemaker fomenting revolution. Anyone who goes against the current, anyone who tries to make changes is automatically labeled a radical and a revolutionary, and a lot worse.

Gon: An interesting parallel.

Jessup: It's nothing new. Other people have said it, all through history.

Gon: That's your field, isn't it, history?

Jessup: Absolutely. If we don't know where we've been, we can't know where we are or where we're going. You know the old cliché, those who don't remember the past are bound to repeat it.

Gon: And you don't want to repeat the mistakes of the past.

Jessup: Of course not. Your generation had its chance, and you didn't do any better than the preceding one. That seems to be true all through history. People don't learn from past mistakes. Well, now it's my generation's turn, and maybe we'll turn out better.

Gon: Do you really think so?

Jessup: I sincerely hope so. If enough of us try, we can. That's the problem, though, isn't it? Are there really enough of us? If you want my honest opinion, I'd say, no. I'd say we'll probably screw things up just as bad, or maybe even worse than you people did.

Gon: But you and your friends intend to try.

Jessup: Of course.

Gon: How?

Jessup: By unceasingly pointing out the errors of the past and the present and offering alternatives.

Gon: That's all?

Jessup: What else?

Gon: Demonstrations, campus sit-ins, and take-overs.

Jessup: There's nothing wrong with that. We make our point and that way the world has to sit up and pay attention.

Gon: Any other ways?

Jessup: If you have any suggestions, I'm all ears.

Gon: I'd like to hear some from you.

Jessup: I'm afraid you might have to wait a long time.

Gon: Tell me about your friends, the people you work with to make a better world.

Jessup: Do you have anybody in particular in mind?

Gon: A few. Melvin Rasmussen. Martin Weinstein. Steven Gold. Caitlin McKenzie and her son, Jerome.

Jessup: You've missed a few, but they'll do for openers. What can I tell you about them? We're good friends. We believe a lot of the same things. We get together once in a while and talk. That's about it.

Gon: You just talk?

Jessup (he smiled broadly at this): What else? You know, college kids, what else could we do but talk and perhaps dream a little. Maybe we demonstrate now and then. Everybody does these days.

Gon: Including Caitlin McKenzie? In the old days, she was forever preaching revolution.

Jessup: Caitlin's okay. She talks a lot. I guess sometimes she thinks she's still living back in the thirties.

Gon: What does she talk about?

Jessup: Anything, everything. You name it, she's got an opinion. She wants to fix the world.

Gon: And she has a plan?

Jessup: Everybody's got a plan. Why should she be any different?

Gon: Does she talk about her plans?

Jessup: Ask her.

Gon: What about her son? Does he echo her?

Jessup: Jerry? I can't read him. Sometimes you think he's following his mother's script and sometimes he's just off in never-never land. Nobody

*really pays much attention to him. He's just there.
She does the talking for both of them.*

*Gon: How about Rasmussen, Weinstein, and
Gold?*

*Jessup: I guess they've got their own scenarios.
We all do, don't we? In a way we're all minorities,
which means we get the short end all the time.
That's one of the things that brings us together. We
want to fix things, we want to make things better.
I mean, there's the war, and we want to stop that
and bring the kids home and let the Vietnamese
solve their own problems. There's the way blacks
are treated, and that's Mel's big thing. Can you
blame him? Marty's thing is Israel, you know, never
forget the Holocaust and don't let anybody forget
it. I don't think he gives a damn about religion as
such, but I guess if you're Jewish you're paranoid
about gas chambers and concentration camps and
anybody looking at you the wrong way. Steve? For
him the world revolves around the arts and artists.
They make the world a livable place but nobody
understands them. Without writers and painters and
musicians, we'd all be back living in caves. But the
powers-that-be think all artists are parasites. So,
they're all one minority or another, and they don't
like it, who does?, and they want to change it.*

Gon: What about you?

*Jessup: Mr. Gondolian, take a look around. Look
at the people in this place. You don't think we're a
minority? You think we don't end up holding the
proverbial bag? Hell, the bag's empty where we're
concerned.*

Interview with Martin Weinstein

Weinstein is flamboyant. Perhaps it's merely his appearance that makes him appear so. The wiry, curling red hair stands straight up from a pudgy pale face; it looks as though even a curry comb couldn't make its way through that mop. He is round, baby fat still clinging to him, and he doesn't seem at all concerned about the way he dresses. He uses his hands extensively in wild gestures during conversation, stabbing the air, thrusting forward, banging a fist down to make a point.

We met on Sunday morning in his off-campus room in a run-down brownstone a block south and west of the campus. The room was hardly big enough to contain him, let alone the two of us. It had a bed, unmade, a desk and chair, a dresser and books piled haphazardly against every available wall. He was wearing a terry cloth bathrobe that looked as though it had never seen the inside of a washing machine, under it a pair of ragged pajamas, and no slippers. I had some trouble tracking him down because he had moved from his dormitory without telling anyone there where he was going. Fortunately, he had given the university a new address, and a friend in the office passed it on to me. He has no phone, so the only way to reach him was either to write and hope he'd answer, or simply to go to his place and knock at the door. That's what I did. It took a few minutes before he opened it, time probably spent finding and putting on the bathrobe. When he saw me, he demanded to know who I was. I told him, and he said some people he knew had mentioned that I had been around asking questions. I asked if we could talk, and he said that as long as I was there, we might as well, only I should make it short. And he immediately went on the attack.

Wein: Just who the hell are you? Are you a fed?

Gon: I'm a reporter.

Wein: A running dog of the establishment.

Gon: Mao Tse-tung?

Wein: Him and a lot of others, in various forms. True, nevertheless.

Gon: You don't like reporters?

Wein: Not particularly. They rarely write the truth. They write what their bosses tell them.

Gon: In China or Russia, maybe, but not here.

Wein: Oh, sure. America the beautiful, America the wonderful, America of realized dreams, America where everybody's free, including the press. What a laugh.

Gon: What makes you so cynical?

Wein: Look around. Do you see anything to make you stand up and cheer?

Gon: Do you really believe things are so bad?

Wein: Worse.

Gon: Is there anything you believe in?

Wein: Give me a couple of days and I might come up with something.

Gon: How about your friends?

Wein: Score one for you.

Gon: Some of them said they had hope for the future.

Wein: Not the way the world's going. Not without one big shake-up.

Gon: Are you part of the attempt to do the shaking up?

Wein: In my small way, I try.

Gon: How?

Wein: What do you want me to say? That I'm a bomb thrower or something like that? I think and I talk. That's what I am, a big talker. All mouth.

Gon: What would you like to do?

Wein: Take all the goddamn anti-Semites and send them to Auschwitz. Let them get a taste of their own medicine.

Gon: Anything else?

Wein: Sure. Take everybody who thinks the war is some fight to save the world from godless Communism and then sends black kids and dropouts to do the fighting for them, take them, put them on a boat, give them a rifle and tell them to fight their own battle. Then we'd see how great they think it is.

Gon: Anything else?

Wein: Plenty. But I'm not going to get into that now.

Gon: Do your friends think the same way?

Wein: Probably.

Gon: But they're just talk, too?

Wein: Most of the time.

Gon: But not all the time?

Wein: Don't put words in my mouth, mister.

Gon: I'm just trying to understand.

Wein: Well, understand this. I've got people coming in and I have to get dressed. So why don't you run along.

Gon: I suppose we can continue this another time, then?

Wein: I doubt it.

Interview with Steven Gold

Gold seems like a nice young man. He's tall and slim, with dark blond hair and what some people would call a handsome face. The black horn-rimmed glasses don't detract. They make him look scholarly, and serious. If there is a prototypical radical or revolutionary, he certainly isn't it.

We met in a restaurant in the theatre district. When I reached him and asked if he would meet me, he wanted to know, of course, why I wanted to talk to him. I explained what I was doing and that his name had been mentioned to me as someone who was committed to the anti-war movement. He said that while he was committed, as were most college kids, he really wasn't very active. His main interest was the theatre, and he had gotten a part-time job in a producer's office. That, he said, took up most of his time. Still, if I really wanted to see him, we could meet for lunch. He suggested a small restaurant near his office, and I agreed. I bought him lunch. He ate as though it had been a long time since he'd had a decent meal.

On the whole, this was one of the more unsatisfactory of the more than a hundred interviews I've had to date.

Gold: I've heard what you're doing. It must be fascinating to go around the country and talk to all kinds of people about the war. I mean, you must get a million different slants, a million insights.

Gon: It's interesting, yes. But right now, I'd rather talk about you.

Gold: About me? There's nothing interesting about me. I mean, where my head is is in the theatre.

Gon: So you told me on the phone.

Gold: I mean, I saw a Brecht the other night. God, what I wouldn't give to get over there and see his Berliner Ensemble. That and the Habima. What I mean is, repertory, rehearsing until you get it right. Not like here, where everything closes Saturday night unless you've got a year's advance at the box office. God, the commercial theatre. What a drag.

Gon: Aren't you still in school?

Gold: Sure. I just have morning classes this year. You know, I graduate in June and I'm only lacking a few credits. So when I got a chance to take this job part-time, there was nothing in the way.

Gon: Do you still see your friends?

Gold: Now and then. When I'm free.

Gon: Where do you meet most of the time?

Gold: God, everywhere. I mean, sometimes at the West End, sometimes in the Chinese place up on a hundred twentieth, sometimes at Caitlin's. It could be anyplace.

Gon: What do you talk about?

Gold (he laughed when he answered): Changing the world. What else do people talk about these days?

Gon: And how are you going to change the world?

Gold: Me, in particular? I'm going to work in the theatre and put on the best damn plays I can find. Hey, I don't necessarily mean plays that drown you with a message. I mean plays that not only stand for something, that have a point of view, but plays that entertain. I mean, people go to the theatre to be entertained, don't they? They don't go to have somebody preach at them for two and a half hours. I mean, Brecht has a message, but it's there inside damn good drama that entertains. Same with Shaw. Same with Shakespeare. Same with every good playwright.

Gon: What else?

Gold: Nothing else. Why? Did you expect something else?

Gon: Well, some of the people you hang around with seem to have different ideas.

Gold: Everybody does his own thing. I mean, Mel's out to free the blacks, Marty's out to free the Jews, Harvey's out to free the, well, you know, Caitlin's out to free the world.

Gon: And you're out to free the theatre?

Gold: That's it.

The interview lasted another ten to fifteen minutes, but we made little more progress. Gold wanted to talk only about the theatre, not about his friends or anything else. Every time I tried to turn the conversation, he replied that if I wanted to know what they thought, I should ask them.

Interview with Caitlin and Jerome McKenzie

I would have preferred to talk to them separately. That wasn't possible. I don't know whether it was his idea or hers—my feeling is hers—but when I arrived at Caitlin's apartment, he was there and he ensconced himself in the same room. When I suggested that perhaps it would be better if I talked first with Caitlin and then with him, neither one of them thought that was a good idea. Caitlin's daughter, Fiona, was in and out. She's a pretty little kid, about ten I'd guess, and when she was in the room, she stood there and listened, then seemed to get bored and wandered away.

I've known Caitlin for a long time, since the 1930s, when I was in college. Those were the days when she and Jerome, Sr., spent their time on the soap box peddling the message of Trotsky. She's older now, of course, and Jerome has long since gone to his final rest, but she's still a handsome woman, a dominating woman, and still a fire brand; she makes no bones about her dedication to the old message, workers of the world unite, rise and revolt and all the rest. While she has little use for the Soviet Union—as much disdain now as she had in the days of Stalin—or its satellites, she continues to preach the pure gospel of Karl Marx and Leon Trotsky. That's what she's always done. She preaches. When one listens to her, one can picture her with a bomb in her hand or with a rifle leading the troops at the barricades. I think that's the image she likes to project. But if anyone actually put a bomb or a rifle in her hands, that image would vanish like the mist. Back then, she was all talk, and I can't see anything about her to change that picture.

Young Jerry is, to me, an enigma. I can't read him. He's a few years older than the other kids in this group, but he seems and acts younger. There's

*something veiled about him, as though he has
secrets, very deep and perhaps dark secrets that he
can't reveal. If he did, they would cost him dearly.
That is the feeling he left with me. Or maybe it's
just that he's a mama's boy. Certainly when she's
around, he doesn't seem to have any ideas of his
own.*

*It's not necessary to set down most of what we
talked about. All I have to do is go back to the old
Trotskyite broadsheets of the thirties and by just
changing a word or two here and there, that would
be Caitlin today. She still rails against the United
States, though now the country's not just the villain
because of the treatment of the poor, the blacks,
the Jews, the workers, minorities of all kinds, but
also because of the war. She compares this country's
actions in the war in Vietnam to Hitler's, and Stalin's, during the second world war. As for Jerry, he
just sits there and listens and doesn't say much.
Even when I asked him a question, he turned to her
and let her answer.*

Gon: *From what you've been saying, Caitlin, I
gather you'd do just about anything to stop the war.*

Caitlin: *Not just about. I'd do anything. Name it
and I'd do it.*

Gon: *And I suppose you'd bring along those kids
who sit at your feet?*

Caitlin: *That would be their choice. I certainly
wouldn't discourage them.*

Gon: *You'd encourage them?*

Caitlin: *I wouldn't discourage them.*

Gon: *Aren't you at all worried about the authori-*

ties watching you, waiting for you to make a mistake?

Caitlin: Why should I worry? If I worried, you'd never have caught me dead out there in Union Square back when. I'll say one thing for today. When you make a speech, you don't have scabs with blackjacks trying to beat your head in. You only have the cops, but they're worried about going too far because the TV cameras are always pointing at them. Why do you think the black people even got a little crumb down in Mississippi? Because the whole world was watching, that's why, so the people up there, they had to do something to get the heat off themselves. If it wasn't for the TV, things would be just like they've always been.

Gon: That's the only reason you don't worry?

Caitlin: Harry, you ask the dumbest questions. Do you think I don't know what goes on? They think they've got a pipeline right into my bedroom, for chrissake. Well, let me tell you, I've got my own little pipeline right into their secret chambers. So, if they want to make a move, I know about it an hour before, and I'm ready.

Interview with John Morrison, Assistant District Attorney

Morrison was willing to give me ten minutes, no more (less if possible is the way he put it when I called him). He is a true patrician. He looks the part, he acts the part, he is the part. It fits him like a glove.

We met in his office on Leonard Street. One of

his assistants, who never gave his name, sat off to one side and never said a word. He just listened.

Gon: Mr. Morrison, I've been told you are heading a task force investigating the anti-war movement.

Mor: Not the entire movement, Mr. Gondolian. Just the radical underground section that's breaking the law.

Gon: You're working in cooperation with the FBI?

Mor: Correct.

Gon: Could you tell me something about how you're going about your investigations?

Mor: Surveillance. Research. Normal good police work.

Gon: How about undercover?

Mor: That's normal good police work.

Gon: Infiltration?

Mor: That's normal good police work.

Gon: I've been told that some of your people who've infiltrated the movement are actually agents provocateurs. Is that right?

Mor: Wrong. One, that would be aiding and abetting the commission of crimes. Two, such actions would compromise our investigations and our cases. Three, a good attorney would claim entrapment, and he might succeed in having the cases dismissed. We do not have what you call agents provocateurs.

Gon: Are you now targeting specific underground groups?

Mor: We're interested in any group that breaks the law.

Gon: How about the Weathermen?

Mor: If they break the law, we're interested in them.

Gon: How about Caitlin McKenzie's group?

Mor: If they break the law, we're interested in them.

Gon: I've talked with a great many people in the anti-war movement, some above ground and some underground. One thing I've discovered is that the vast majority believe that what they're doing is right and justified. How do you feel about that?

Mor: If they're breaking the law and hurting other people, then what they're doing is neither right nor justified. As long as they demonstrate peacefully, they have a perfect right to be free from interference and to express their views, just as those who support the war and our government have a right to express their views. But once these people descend to violence, they have abdicated that right and we will track them down with everything in our power. There's just no excuse for bombings and invasion of private property and other things of that nature.

Somebody planted a bomb at a chemical weapons plant out on Long Island last night. Classified documents I've seen over the last several months say the plant was making something called Agent Orange. I suppose it wasn't much of a secret. Perhaps whoever planted that bomb thought nobody would be hurt, only the weapons manufacturing facility badly enough damaged to halt production. They set the bomb to go off at three in the morning. Unfortu-

nately, a night watchman was in the area and one of the lab technicians had been working late and was just checking out. They were both killed. Nobody's saying how badly the plant was damaged.

As of this morning, nobody's claiming responsibility. I imagine it could be any one of the groups I've talked to over the last year. Or it could be none of them. I suppose we'll never know unless someone comes forward and claims responsibility. Even then we won't be completely sure. People come out of the woodwork whenever there's a tragedy.

Jerry McKenzie jumped out a window last weekend. I'm told he was a double agent and the authorities learned about it and had him in for questioning. I wonder if the other side suspected him as well. I imagine he took that way out rather than talk about his mother and friends. So that was the secret I sensed in him. It was a dark one, indeed, and it ended up costing him his life.

I'm not exactly sure why, perhaps because I've been so peripherally involved with all these people, but I went to his funeral. Caitlin was stoic, not a tear, which is not unusual for her. Except when it comes to causes, she rarely shows emotion. She saw me and came up to me when the service, if you can call it that, was over. I hadn't seen her since that afternoon a couple of months ago in her apartment. I expressed my sympathy, and she dismissed that.

She said, "You know, they're saying Jerry was a double agent."

"I've heard that," I said.

"He wasn't, you know. He was always on our side. They just thought he was working for them."

What can one say to that? I said nothing.

Then she said, "But there is a double agent. Of that I'm positive."

I asked if she knew who.

She said, "No. But I know there is one."

28

When he finished reading the Gondolian files, those that dealt with Gold and the people around him, and those few last pieces of paper that Gondolian had slipped into a separate folder and which Annie had scanned along with everything else, he went to bed. He slept for twelve hours without stirring.

It was early in the afternoon when he woke. There were, he thought, only a couple of missing pieces and he was sure he knew where to find them. To get them, he would have to take some risks, play some long odds, put himself in what might turn out to be an untenable position. But if he didn't do that, there was not a chance in the world of coming out the other end whole.

In the living room, the red light on the answering machine was glowing. It was time to listen to the messages he had ignored over the last three days. There were two from Rodriguez, wondering if what he'd supplied had been worth the effort. There were two from Strickland. There were three from Melissa wondering why he hadn't called and where he was and what he'd been doing. There was one from Harris Abelman.

He considered the calls, considered what to say. If he said the wrong things, the nearly finished cloth would come unraveled. The easiest to answer was Abelman's. He called the lawyer.

"I told you to check in with me regularly," Abelman said.

"I've been busy," Rogers said.

"Working on getting yourself out of the corner, I trust," Abelman said.

"Exactly."

"And how are you doing?"

"Nearly out," Rogers said. "Anything new on your end?"

"I've managed to get the grand jury postponed for two weeks. Is that enough time for you?"

"It should be."

"Keep me informed."

"I will. But I may be out of touch for a couple of days."

"Why?"

"I have to fly to the coast."

"Call me from there."

"I will if I can. But don't hold your breath. When I do call, I could have news."

He called Rodriguez next.

"Well," Rodriguez demanded, "what gives?"

"A lot," Rogers said. "We're almost there."

"No shit!"

"I tell you true. I need one thing from you."

"Ask and it'll be yours, if possible."

"Back when those five guys were around, about when they bought it. Somebody blew up a chemical plant out on Long Island. Get me the details."

"How soon do you need them?"

"Yesterday."

"Give me a couple of hours," Rodriguez said.

"I'll be here."

"Where have you been?" Strickland asked when Rogers reached him.

"Reading," Rogers said.

"What? What's that supposed to mean?"

"I've spent the last three days reading Gondolian's legacy. And Annie Kendall's."

"I don't get you."

"Those files. The ones that got ripped off from Gondolian's mini-storage."

"I thought you said they were gone."

"They are. The originals. But Annie put them all on her computer before she got killed. She sent me the disks. I had a friend print them out. For the last three days I've been reading, organizing, collating, and thinking."

"My God," Strickland said. "You came up with something?"

"Ancient history. And some not so ancient."

"What the hell are you, an enigma wrapped in a mystery inside a riddle?"

"That's not quite the way Churchill put it, but it'll do. When I get my head screwed back on right, I'll lay it all out for you. Right now I've got fuzz on the eyeballs and cotton on the brain. Now, have you got anything on Phoenix?"

"Not a damn thing. I mention it casually, everybody freezes up. Everybody says they've never heard of it."

"Keep working on it," Rogers said. "If you work hard enough, you could turn over the right rock."

"I doubt it, but I'll try."

"Do. And stay in touch. Oh, one thing. I'm going to be away for a few days."

"Where are you going?"

"California. You know, to see my lady."

"You got a number where I can reach you if I have to?"

Rogers gave him Melissa's number.

"Have a good trip," Strickland said. "I'll talk to you when you get back, if not sooner."

"Where have you been?" Melissa demanded as soon as she heard his voice.

"Everybody asks me that," he said. "I've been right here."

"Then why didn't you answer the phone?"

"I've been reading. I set the machine so it wouldn't bother me."

"For three days?"

"For three days. And nights."

"Just what was so absorbing?"

"History," he said. "Past, present, and into the future."

"I won't ask what that means," she said. "You'll tell me when you're ready. Now, when are you coming out here?"

"Day after tomorrow," he said.

"You mean that?"

"I mean that. Absolutely. I'm waiting for a call back from Carlos, and then I have to talk to three people tomorrow. After that, I'll be on my way."

* * *

Rodriguez was as good as his word. An hour later, he was back on the phone. "Here's what you wanted," he said. "It's not much. You could probably have gotten most of it from the papers."

"But not all?"

"A few things were held back. The bomb went off at three in the morning. It had a timing device, so whoever planted it was long gone. When it went, the night watchman was making his rounds and a lab technician was just checking out. They were both right close to it and there wasn't much left of either one. It had all the earmarks of somebody who was against the war and was willing to do anything to make his point. There were a lot of groups like that back then. Most of the time somebody stepped out and bragged about it. This time, nobody ever claimed responsibility. And there was nothing pointing to any group in particular."

"Any suspects?"

"A thousand. But they couldn't pin it on anybody. Except maybe the guy who made the bomb."

"Who?"

"One of the guys on your list. Jimmy Macklin, the mad bomber. The only thing is, the guy had been dead about two weeks at the time. So somebody else must have stockpiled some of his devices."

"Any ideas?"

"None at all."

29

The same girl was behind the desk in the GALEA's outer office when Rogers walked in. She gave him the same look.

"He's in conference," she said flatly.

"He's always in conference," Rogers said. "Tell him this is more important than his conference."

She glared and took her time before rising from the desk and going through the door behind her. She was back in a couple of minutes. She went behind the desk again, stared at her computer screen, then looked over at him. "He said he's just finishing up. If you can wait, he'll see you in about five minutes."

"I can wait." He sat down in one of the chairs, thumbed through a weekly news magazine that was on the table next to it, and waited. Five minutes later, the inner door opened and Jessup appeared.

"You wanted to see me again?" he said.

"I do."

Jessup stood there for a moment, then nodded and motioned for Rogers to follow. In his office, he went behind his desk. Rogers sat in the same chair he had the last time.

"What's it all about this time?" Harvey Jessup asked.

"I want you to pick up that phone and call your two friends and tell them to get here as soon as they can."

Jessup stared at him, startled. "Just what are you talking about? What friends?"

"Rasmussen and Weinstein."

"I know them, but they're not my friends. Besides, why would they listen to me?"

"You know them," Rogers said, "and they are your friends. Your old friends. Your very close friends. And they'll listen to you and come, because you're going to tell them that if they don't, then the feds and the DA are going to want to talk to all three of you about an old, unsolved crime."

"What are you talking about?"

"The bombing of a chemical plant out on Long Island where two guys were killed."

"I vaguely remember that," Jessup said. "But what's that got to do with me, or with them?"

"I've been reading history," Rogers said. "It made for an interesting couple of days. All about some college kids who used to sit at the feet of a lady named Caitlin McKenzie and plot revolution."

"That," Jessup said, "was a long time ago. It's ancient history."

"Not so ancient," Rogers said. "It's still having repercussions. And they're going to blow up right in your face if you don't make that call. Now, I'm going to walk out of here. But I'll be back in an hour and a half, which will give them plenty of time to get here. If they're not here, I'm going to make that call on my own, and the three of you can talk to somebody else."

He rose, walked out of Jessup's office, not looking at the secretary as he went by her and out of the building and onto the street. For the next ninety minutes, he roamed. He stopped in a bookstore and browsed through the shelves. He stopped in a music store and thumbed through the new releases, and listened to the music that played too loud over the store's speakers. He called the airlines and made a reservation for Los Angeles for the next morning.

When the ninety minutes were up, he was back at GALEA. The girl at the desk looked at him, and this time there was a little awe, and a little fear, and not so much scorn, in that look. "He's expecting you," she said. "You can go right in."

"Is anybody with him?"

She nodded.

He went by her and through the door. The door to Jessup's office was open. He walked in. Jessup was behind his desk. Rasmussen was in a chair to one side, Weinstein in a chair across from him. Rogers stopped and studied all three, one after the other. They were all trying to look calm, perhaps a little puzzled. But they were all there, which said a lot.

Rogers went to a vacant chair and sat. He looked up at the ceiling. "You all remember Harry Gondolian," he said. "Harry spent two years going around the country talking to people. He talked to you, among others. Every night, he went home and typed up those interviews and put them in files. They were supposed to be the research for a series he was going to write. He never wrote it. God knows why he didn't. But he saved those files. Gondolian saved everything, and he never forgot any of it. All through the years, he's been keeping track of some of the people he talked to. The people who were around a lady named Caitlin McKenzie. You. You were all at Columbia then, all about to graduate. In fact, before he finished, you did graduate. You used to sit around and talk. That's what you told Gondolian back then. Over the last couple of months, maybe longer, he's been updating those files. Somebody stole them. They also stole his old files. But not before a friend of his and mine copied them and turned the copies over to me. Because of what was happening back then, one of your friends jumped out a window. Because of what Gondolian came up with, the mayor of this city got killed, and so did Harry Gondolian, and so did a girl named Annie Kendall. And so did a friend of yours named Steven Gold.''

''That's ridiculous.'' One of them said it, but Rogers wasn't sure which one. None of them looked as though they really thought it was ridiculous.

''You don't really think that,'' Rogers said. ''Because it ties to something else that happened back then that's hung over your heads all these years like a sword. You've never been sure it wouldn't drop.''

He waited. They didn't say anything.

''You people weren't just sitting around and talking about how to change the world. You were doing things to make that change happen. And one of the things you did was make a bomb and plant it. I don't think you expected anybody to get hurt. It was timed to go off in the middle of the night and just disrupt the factory. But a night watchman happened to be there and so did a guy who worked in the lab. They both got killed.''

''We never planted a bomb,'' Jessup said. ''We used

to talk, yes. Who didn't in those days? But that's all we
ever did."

"No, you did more than talk. You acted. And after-
wards, you all panicked. You and Gold ran to California.
I didn't think the reason he ran was because he got picked
up in a bathhouse doing what he shouldn't have been
doing. I think you both ran because you were scared to
stay around, scared that if you stayed somebody might
find something to implicate you. So you and Gold ran
west, and you," he looked at Rasmussen, "ran south, and
you," turning to Weinstein, "ran to Israel, and Caitlin
McKenzie took her daughter, Fiona, and disappeared.
You three came back when you thought it was safe. You
know what tipped me? The fact that all of you took off
like you were wearing track shoes at the same time, and
that was right after the bomb went off."

"That's just your theory," Rasmussen said. "A theory
that doesn't happen to be true."

"It's true enough," Rogers said. "I'll bet you guys
thought you'd be safe when Jerry McKenzie took his
dive rather than give you all up. With him gone, you
were sure there was nobody and nothing to implicate you.
What you didn't count on was that there was somebody
else who knew exactly what was going on."

"Still only a theory," Rasmussen said.

"I know where Caitlin McKenzie is," Rogers said.
"And I know where you got the bomb." He waited.
Nobody said anything. "You've got a choice," he said.
"You can talk to me now, or I turn over everything I
know to the right people. They'll run with it. You can
bet your lives on that, and that's just what you'll be
betting. Because they'll take that stuff and it'll point them

in the right direction, and the right direction is sitting in this room at this moment. Which is it going to be?"

The three exchanged glances. Weinstein nodded. "Will you excuse us for a few minutes?" he said.

"Take all the time you need," Rogers said. "Talk it over, weigh everything and see which way the balance tips." He rose, walked out and went back to the waiting room. The girl behind the desk stared at him. He ignored her. He sat and picked up one of the magazines and thumbed through it without seeing the words. About fifteen minutes later, Jessup appeared in the doorway. He looked a little sick. He motioned to Rogers and without waiting, turned and moved away.

Rogers didn't hurry. By the time he was back in the office, Jessup was behind the desk and the other two were in their chairs. He resumed his seat.

"What's it to be?" Rogers said.

"How do you know there was somebody else involved?" Weinstein said.

"Everything points to it," Rogers said. "When you people talked with Gondolian back then, there was one thing you all agreed on. Caitlin McKenzie was a great talker. That's what she did, talk. He knew her from the old days when she was up on the soapbox. She was all talk. So he bought your description. And I think he was probably right. She might have talked about revolution and bombs and things like that, but that's all she would have done. Actual bombing would have been somebody else's thing. So, if the bomb wasn't Caitlin McKenzie's thing, then it sure as hell wasn't Jerry McKenzie's. According to Gondolian, he wouldn't ever have done anything without checking with mama first. If we rule out those two, that leaves us with you three and Gold. I don't read Jessup or Gold as the bomber types. That narrows it down to you two.'' His eyes moved from Weinstein to Rasmussen. He fixed them on Rasmussen. ''You're a possibility,'' he said. ''You were a chemist, which means you knew about explosives. And the way you talk now, and then, you wouldn't hesitate at action.''

''I,'' Rasmussen said flatly, ''have never made a bomb. I have never used a bomb.''

''Now you,'' Rogers turned to Weinstein, ''are a violent man. You preach violence.''

''As self-defense,'' Weinstein said. ''About explosives I know nothing.''

''But the bomb went off, and you all knew about it. You probably went along for the ride. It would have been the thing to do. After all, nobody was going to get hurt, and production of Agent Orange was going to be crippled. A noble endeavor, right? But if I believe you, then there had to be somebody else involved.''

The three exchanged looks. Jessup stared at Rogers. ''There may have been,'' he said slowly.

''Who?''

''We don't know,'' Jessup said. ''I think Jerry knew. I'm not sure about Caitlin. But we were in the dark.''

''How about Gold?''

''I don't know. He never said anything.''

''Tell me what happened?''

The three looked at each other. ''We talked about that just now, while we were waiting for you,'' Jessup said. ''We wondered how much you really knew. We guessed a lot, too much actually. And you're right. This has been hanging over us all these years. We'd been doing a lot of talking about the war, and about what, if anything, we could do to stop it, or at least make a difference. We all knew about that plant out on Long Island. Who didn't? But we didn't really think very much about it. It was guarded and there didn't seem to be any way anybody could get to it. Besides, as you said, we were essentially talk. Oh, we did a few things. I mean, we did some sit-ins and we were part of the campus takeover, things like that. But nothing really violent. Then one night Jerry said he knew where we could get explosives. And he said he knew how we could get in and out of the place and nobody would know. Everybody got excited. I mean, this was really our chance to do something big. I can't remember Caitlin saying anything." He looked at the others.

"She didn't say a word," Rasmussen said.

"She just sat there," Weinstein said. "But there was a look on her face. To me it said she had no objections. To me it said that finally she was going to turn her words into deeds. And without danger."

"We went there and it was just like Jerry predicted," Jessup said.

"He was with you?"

"Of course. He had a map with safe routes in and out. He said if we followed it we wouldn't be detected. He's the one who actually planted the thing. And then we were out and back to the city. The next thing we heard was that the thing went off and those two people were killed. My God, do you have any idea how we felt? We didn't mean for anybody to get hurt. We were just trying to do something good, something that would help bring that damn war to an end. We never thought it would turn out that way."

"I'm sure you didn't. Every time something like that happened, you people were always saying that you never expected anybody to get hurt. But people got hurt," Rogers said. "Do you know where McKenzie got the explosive device?"

"No," Rasmussen said. "I asked. I think everybody asked. Jerry said he had a source. That was all."

"Do you know where he got those directions in and out?"

"No. He had them written down. He said they came from a reliable source. He wouldn't say who. Whoever gave it to him also provided him with a car, so whatever happened nobody could trace it back to us."

"Steven Gold was with you that night?"

"Actually," Rasmussen said, "we went during the day. We were told it was safer then. There were people around and a few more people, especially since we had those ID badges and passes and other things, wouldn't cause any commotion or suspicion. Yes, Steve was with us. We were all there."

"Except Jerry McKenzie's source."

"Except him."

"There's another thing," Rogers said. "Over the last three or four years, Gold has been sending you three a lot of money. A couple of hundred thousand each. Why?"

"It's been more than a few years," Weinstein said. "Actually he's been doing it for about ten years, ever since he started making a lot of money in motion pictures."

"Why?"

"Some of it was to support what we were doing. All of us operate on a shoe string, and most of the time that shoe string is near to breaking. His money helped keep us going."

"You said some of it. What about the rest?"

"It went into trust funds for the families of those two people who were killed. We agreed when it happened that if we ever could, we would help them out. Steve said he knew somebody who could do it secretly, so nobody would ever know who set up the trusts or where the money was coming from. It couldn't all come from one source. That might arouse some suspicion. So we arranged that he would make those donations to my synagogue, to Mel's church and Harvey's organization, and then we would funnel the major portion of those donations into the trusts without arousing suspicion."

"That's why you met Gold when he was in New York, and he called you?"

"Yes."

"What I still can't figure out is your relationship with Morrison."

"That shouldn't be difficult," Rasmussen said. "Of all the candidates, he was the one who was most likely to support the things we wanted. It was just that simple."

"I'll buy part of that," Rogers said. "But I still wonder how you got so close."

"That was Steve's doing," Jessup said. "I'm not sure exactly how or when, but Steve got to know Morrison pretty well at some time over the years. He said they were good friends. He introduced us. Everything just grew from there."

"You knew that Morrison was the guy who ran the task force looking into the anti-war movement?"

"Of course. That was common knowledge."

"It didn't bother you later?"

"It bothered me," Jessup said. "But Steve said we had nothing to worry about. And it never came up with Morrison."

"What happens now?" Weinstein asked. "What are you going to do?"

"About you people?"

"About us."

"If what you've told me is the truth, I'm not going to do anything. At least not for the moment. I'm after the guy who killed Morrison, Gondolian, Annie Kendall, and your friend Steve Gold. You people have lived with what you did for a long time. You'll have to live with it for the rest of your lives. I think you have to do some serious thinking. If I was able to come up with this after all these years, there's nothing to say that somebody else won't. You'll have to decide whether you want to have that happen and face those consequences, or whether the best thing might be to go in and talk to somebody and see what you can work out."

30

The loudspeaker at Kennedy was calling his flight. Rogers started down the ramp toward the gate. He stopped and turned into a phone booth and dialed a number he had called before. A female voice answered.

"George Strickland," he said.

"I'll connect you," the voice said. He waited. After a moment, the voice came back on. "Mr. Strickland is out of the office. Would you like to leave a message?"

"No message," he said and hung up.

Melissa was waiting as he came into the terminal. They held each other, and then he held her off and re-memorized her face. "I didn't expect you to meet me," he said. "I thought you were working."

"We wrapped last night," she said.

"Then you can come home."

"Soon as I can," she said. "God, I'm glad to see you."

In her car moving north along the freeway, she said, "If you're not too jet-lagged, we're going to make a stop on the way."

"I suppose we have to," he said.

"You do," she said. "Abby's been waiting to see you forever."

"Then let's get it over with," he said.

She glanced at him out of the corner of her eye. "Something's wrong," she said.

"A lot of things are wrong."

"He didn't do it," she said.

"No," he said. "But he did something else."

"What?"

He told her.

"Oh, God," she said. "Poor Abby. I suppose it's all going to come out now."

"I don't know," he said. "Probably."

"You won't tell her?"

"I haven't made up my mind about that. I think I may have to."

"She's having a rough time. This is going to make it worse."

"Better from me than from the feds or the newspaper guys."

"Yes," she said. "Now, how are you?"

"I'll tell you when we're alone."

"We're alone now."

"This is not the kind of alone I have in mind."

She glanced over at him and smiled just a little, then her eyes returned to the road.

The guard in the gate house at the entrance to Bel Air saw the car turn in and stop. He leaned out and there was recognition in his eyes when he saw Melissa.

"We're on our way to see Mrs. Gold," she said.

"I'll call ahead and tell her," he said and waved the car through.

"That guard is a blessing," Melissa said as they headed

up the road. "You can't get past him. If he weren't there, Abby would have been besieged by reporters. As it is, she's had the police in and out constantly."

"To be expected," he said.

Gold's house was at the end of a cul-de-sac halfway up the hill. It was a large sprawling house with a lot of meticulously groomed landscape, lawns, gardens, trees. Melissa parked and led Rogers toward the front door, rang and waited. The door was opened by a man with the manners of a good servant. "I'll tell Mrs. Gold you're here," he said. "Would you wait in the library?" He didn't have to escort them. Melissa knew the way.

The library was just what its name said. There were bookshelves from floor to ceiling on three walls, filled with books, not sets but books that looked as though somebody had read them. There were a couple of Impressionist paintings on the other wall, originals, not reproductions. A large desk fronted one of the bookcase walls. A sofa fronted another, and there were comfortable chairs, a coffee table, and some end tables. On the desk were some framed pictures, one of a handsome woman, the others of two teenagers. They were all smiling in those pictures.

A door opened and the woman from the picture walked in. She was wearing light-colored pants and a white silk shirt. She was prettier in person than in the picture, though there were dark bruises under her eyes and some new lines in her face, and she wasn't smiling. She looked like it had been a while since she'd smiled.

"You must be Ben Rogers," she said. "When Melissa told me you were coming out today, I hoped you'd stop here."

"You must be tired of questions," he said.

"Very tired. Always the same questions. Sometimes different people, but always the same questions. And no privacy. They come and they search through Steve's things, his books and his papers, and then somebody else comes and does the same thing. I feel it's never going to end."

"It'll end. It always does," he said.

"God, I hope so. Now, sit down and ask me what you want and I'll try to answer. Would you like something to eat, something to drink?"

"Nothing, thanks," he said. She settled on the sofa. Melissa sat next to her. Rogers took a chair across from them. "If it will make you feel any better," he said, "your husband did not kill John Morrison or Harry Gondolian, and he didn't kill himself."

She took a deep breath and nodded. "At last," she said. "Somebody who knows the truth. If only the rest of the world did."

"It will," he said.

"I hope so. It can't be too soon. Now, you have questions?"

"A few," he said. "Mrs. Gold, did your husband ever tell you why he left New York?"

She hesitated just an instant, then slowly nodded. "Yes," she said.

"It wasn't because he was arrested in a bathhouse, was it?"

"No," she said.

"And it wasn't because the person he was with killed himself that night, was it?"

"No," she said. "And he wasn't with the person who killed himself. He was with somebody else, an older man."

"Did he say who?"

"He said it was the producer he worked for. The man made some promises and Steven was so anxious to get ahead that he was willing to do anything. He said it was the first and only time he ever did anything like that."

"You believed him?"

"Of course. I know him . . . knew him."

"He didn't leave New York because he was afraid the news would get out and that would be the end of his career?"

"Of course not. In New York? In the theatre? In any of the arts? Not many people would have thought much about it, even back then, or held it against him. No, he left for another reason entirely."

"Do you want to tell me?"

She thought for a moment, trying to find the right words, trying to frame her answer. "He was very young then," she said slowly, "just out of college, just at the beginning. He was involved with some people. You must remember, there was a war on then, a war that so many people hated. He was one of those people, and he was willing to do almost anything if it would help end that war. He said they did something that didn't turn out the way they hoped. There was an accident. A person he knew, not quite a friend, he said, but somebody he thought he could trust, told him that if he stayed in New York, he might be suspected. This person told him if he left, nobody would know exactly when and he would be in the clear. This person said he would make sure Steven was protected."

"He had reason to believe this person?"

"He said he did."

"Why?"

"He said this person was in a position where he could do certain things."

"Did he say what kind of position and what things?"

"No."

"Did you ask?"

"Yes. But he said the less I knew the better."

"Did he tell you what he and his people did?"

"No. He just said it was something that turned out badly, and he's regretted it and been sorry about it ever since and tried to make amends."

"How?"

"He never told me. I asked, but he said the less I knew the better."

"Did he ever mention Harvey Jessup or Marty Weinstein or Mel Rasmussen?"

"Yes. They were his friends then."

"Were they still his friends?"

"I imagine so. He saw them when he was back east. And I know he gave them money to help in the work they were doing."

"A lot of money?"

"I don't think so. I wouldn't really know. He never told me much about our finances. But I know he gave money to a lot of people to help in their work. I don't know how much."

"Did you ever meet them?"

"No," she said. "They were never out here. If they'd come here, I would have met them. But they didn't."

"Did he ever mention Caitlin McKenzie?"

"She was older. He said she was sort of like the den mother for the people he was close to. He liked her a lot."

"Did he tell you she was a radical?"

"He said she'd been a Trotskyite during the thirties and that she was still very dedicated to all those causes, but particularly to ending the war."

"Do you know if he's seen her or heard from her since he left New York?"

"I don't think so. If he had, I'm sure he would have said something."

"How did he feel about John Morrison?"

"He admired him very much."

"He'd been in touch with Morrison?"

"Yes. I told the authorities that. Over the last year, perhaps a little longer, he called Mr. Morrison several times and he saw him when he was back east. That was the reason he made that last trip. He was planning to offer whatever help he could in the campaign. I told the authorities that. Do you know what they said? They said it was all pretense. They said he just wanted to get close to Mr. Morrison so he could kill him."

"Do you believe that?"

"Of course not. It's nonsense. Besides, Steven could never have killed anybody. He was not a violent man."

"Did he ever say how he came to know Morrison?"

"He said somebody he knew introduced them."

"Did he say who?"

"No. Just an old acquaintance. I remember that. He didn't say friend, he said acquaintance."

"You asked?"

"Naturally."

"And that's all he said?"

"All. He said I wouldn't know the person, so the name wouldn't mean anything to me."

"Did you think there was something strange about that?"

She considered that, then nodded slowly. "Yes. But when Steven made up his mind about something, wild horses couldn't get him to change it. And I suppose he'd made up his mind that he wasn't going to tell me that person's name."

"Not even whether the person was a man or woman?"

She sat up. "Now that you mention it, he didn't. I always assumed it was a man. But he never said one way or the other. Could it have been a woman?"

Rogers let that pass. "But he's been in contact with that person?" he said.

"Oh, yes. Of course."

"Often?"

"I don't know. I assume so. But I don't know for certain."

"Did he ever mention a company called Phoenix Trans-World Shipping?"

"Not that I can recall. Why?"

"No particular reason. Just a name that's come up. Did he ever mention Harry Gondolian?"

"Isn't that the reporter who was killed with Mr. Morrison?"

"Yes."

"I don't think Steven ever mentioned him. I can't be certain. I know I recognized the name when I saw it. But that may be because I've read the things he wrote. Steven got all the New York newspapers."

"When your husband was in New York, he usually stayed at a small hotel on the east side. This last trip, he stayed there one night and then moved to the hotel where Morrison had his campaign headquarters. Do you know why he moved?"

"No," she said. "I didn't even know he had until the police told me. I can't understand it."

"Did your husband take sleeping pills, barbiturates?"

"No. He hated drugs. The only medication he ever took was when his doctor prescribed it. He never took sleeping pills. He said they could be dangerous."

He looked at Melissa. She was watching him carefully, waiting. He debated whether to tell Abby Gold what he knew. The way she looked, he wasn't sure just how she would take it. It would certainly not be welcome. He decided to pass it up. It was always possible that nothing linking Gold to the bombing would ever come out, that if those three musketeers back in New York decided to wash their consciences, they might leave Gold out. Let it stand as it was. It wouldn't help now to tell her. Melissa saw the decision in his face. She took a deep breath and smiled a little.

He rose. "I want to thank you, Mrs. Gold."

She looked startled. "You don't have any more questions?"

"Not now," he said. "Perhaps later."

31

"That was nice," Melissa said as they drove back down the hill, through the gate and onto Sunset. "You were kind."

"Not so kind," he said. "There just wasn't any reason to tell her, not then."

"Even so, you could have. She's been through so much I'm not sure she could have taken another blow."

"I saw that," he said.

"Did you get what you wanted from her?"

"I think so," he said.

Melissa was renting a small house built into a hillside on one of the small streets off Beverly Glen. Surrounded by trees and shrubs and a garden with tall plants, it seemed isolated, the closest houses invisible once you drove into her driveway.

He carried his suitcase through the door and into the bedroom beyond the living room. She followed and watched as he started to unpack the few things he had brought with him and put them in an empty drawer. She came up and put her arms around his neck.

"Now," she said, "it's just the two of us."

"Just the two of us," he echoed. "No interruptions?"

"No interruptions."

"Fine," he said. "Then let's go to bed."

"It's early," she grinned.

"Not by my time. It's never too early."

Later, much later, she rolled onto her elbow and looked down at him. "I haven't asked you. I've been waiting for you to tell me. How are things in New York?"

"Working out," he said.

"You told me the truth about you and that girl?"

"I told you the truth."

"Now what? They still think you killed her, don't they? And they're going to try you."

"They think so, at the moment," he said. "But they won't."

She looked down at him. "You're so sure?"

"That's why I'm out here."

"Not for me?"

"For you, too. I would have come anyway. But out here is where it has to end." She was staring down at him, and he felt she could read his thoughts. He looked away. "I have to go away for a while tomorrow."

"You just got here."

"I know. I won't be gone long."

"Where?"

"Up north."

"Where up north?"

"Around Monterey."

"What in Monterey?"

"A lady."

"A young lady? Somebody I know? Somebody you know?"

"Nobody you know. Nobody I know, either. And she's not young. I'd guess she must be going on seventy now. She calls herself Constance McCauley. Her real name is Caitlin McKenzie."

"You asked Abby about her."

"I did."

"Would you like company?"

"I don't think so," he said, still not looking at her.

"Because it's going to be dangerous? Isn't that it?"

"Maybe," he said.

"I still want to go. I can take care of myself, you know that."

"You could be in the way."

"You always say I'm never in the way."

"You never are. But it's possible there could be trouble. I don't want to have to worry about you if it comes."

"I could help."

"Sure, the perfect backup. Let's not argue about it. You're not coming with me."

"That's what you say now," she said. "We'll see in the morning."

"There's nothing to see," he said. "I'll rent a car and then I'll see you when I get back."

He was up early, though it didn't feel all that early. It was seven California time, which meant ten in New York. Melissa was still asleep. He got out of bed as quietly as he could, did all the early morning things and then went into the kitchen, picked up the phone and called New York. Out of the corner of his eye, he thought he saw

Melissa come out of the bedroom and pass by. He wasn't sure.

Rodriguez answered right away. "Where are you?" Rodriguez said when he heard Rogers' voice.

"California," Rogers said. "I told you I was coming out here. Carlos, I want you to do something for me."

"Name it."

"If you don't hear from me in the next twenty-four hours, go to my apartment, pick the damn lock if you have to. On the dining room table, you'll find a lot of papers. You'll also find something I wrote out. It'll explain the papers, and a lot more. Take everything. Read everything. Then you'll know what you have to do."

"I don't like the sound of this," Rodriguez said.

"It's just an insurance policy," Rogers said. "I don't think we'll need to cash it in."

"I sure as hell hope not. Now, where are you off to?"

"Monterey. I'll call you from there, tonight or about this time tomorrow." He hung up before Rodriguez could ask anything more.

He picked up the phone again and started to dial an auto rental place.

"Don't bother," Melissa said from the doorway, as he inquired about a rental.

He held the phone and turned toward her. "I thought you were asleep."

"I heard you get up," she said. "I wanted to be ready when you were."

"I told you, I'm doing this alone."

"No way," she said. ".I'm going along. I'm better with ladies than you are, anyway, so I can help there. I drive a hell of lot better than you do, and I know this part of the country better. So stop arguing and just accept the inevitable."

He started to object again, shook his head and accepted.

North of Malibu, the traffic eased along Route 1, the Pacific Coast Highway, and the smog receded behind them. Off to the west, the ocean danced a clear blue-green in the brilliant sunshine. They didn't hurry. There was plenty of time.

For the most part, Melissa left Rogers alone with his thoughts. Once she asked, "What do you expect when we get there?"

"I'm not sure," he said. "Some answers. The rest of the answers."

"From her?"

"Maybe."

"Is somebody else going to be there?"

"Maybe. I'm not sure."

"How dangerous is it going to be?"

"At first, not very. Later? I can't tell."

About halfway up the coast, they stopped for lunch in a small restaurant she knew, a restaurant she said Abby and Steven Gold had taken her to a couple of times. The food was good, and they didn't hurry.

They reached the small town about three. It ran in a semi-circle around a cove. The houses were mainly Mexican adobe style with rust-colored tile roofs. In the center of town, along the main street, were a dozen or more small and well-kept stores, and down at the end a supermarket. It looked out of place. Back from the street and down along the shores of the cove the private homes had enough space between them to offer some sense of privacy. From a small rise just before reaching the town it was possible to see a wide golden sand beach, with people sun bathing and swimming.

They parked along the main street. The afternoon was hot, feeling hotter after the hours in the air conditioned car. The store they were looking for was near the end of the block. The sign said, "Nature's Own."

Rogers opened the door and he and Melissa walked in. It was cool inside, not from air conditioning but from the way it was built. The shelves were lined with herbs and spices, vitamins and jars of condiments, and around the floor there were baskets of fruit and vegetables, all raised without benefit of herbicides and pesticides, all organically grown. They were smaller than what you'd expect to find in a supermarket, but they looked as though they probably tasted better.

Sitting behind the counter thumbing through a catalog was a large woman. She was about seventy, with white hair looking as though about all she ever did was run a comb or a brush through it in the morning. She was wearing an apron over a pair of old jeans and a faded blouse that must once, long ago, have been bright with color. There was a stoic sense about her, a sense that she had seen and experienced all there was, that she had accepted her gains and her losses, and the world held little more. She was just going through the paces for what time remained.

She looked up from the catalog. "Can I help you with something?" Her eyes fixed on him, then moved to Melissa. She smiled at Melissa. It changed her face, made it warmer and more human. When she looked back at Rogers, the smile vanished.

"I hope so," Rogers said.

"I haven't seen you here before," she said. "Are you

just passing through? You don't look like the usual tourist crowd."

"What do they look like?"

"Oh, you know. You can always tell." Her eyes fixed on him then, studying. She closed the catalog and waited, not moving.

"Mrs. McKenzie," he said.

She didn't look or act surprised. "You're who you are, aren't you? I was always able to spot a cop. I guess I haven't lost that."

"You never do," he said.

"He said you might be coming. He said I should expect you."

"I thought he might."

"I always thought you'd turn up one of these days. I don't think there's been a single day when I didn't expect you to come walking in that door. You, or someone like you."

"It had to happen, didn't it?"

"I suppose so," she said. "He said no one would ever find us. I tried to believe him. In here," and she tapped herself on the chest, "I knew it wasn't so. It just took longer than I imagined. He said when you showed up, I shouldn't talk to you. But what the hell, why not? After all these years, why not? Besides, I'm tired of pretending. Who am I going to protect now? Francie's gone, Jerry's gone, there's just me, and I'm too old to care. He can take care of himself. Tell me, how did you find me?"

"Purely by accident," he said. "I was reading the L.A. paper on a flight back from here and I stumbled on an item about you."

"Not about me," she said. "About Francie."

"About you and your daughter and granddaughter. You

gave yourself away when you said your son had been a New York cop killed in the line of duty. I couldn't remember a Justin McCauley. I asked other people and nobody ever heard of him, and neither did the PBA. That was the start. Why did you ever say that?''

She sighed, looked at him, then at Melissa. ''Francie kept talking about her brother to everybody,'' she said. ''I had to come up with some explanation, and that was the first one that came into my head.'' She looked toward Melissa. ''You understand, don't you?''

Melissa nodded. ''I imagine,'' she said, ''you felt you had no other choice.''

''I suppose I could have kept my mouth shut,'' the older woman said. ''But not me. That's always been my trouble. Me and my big mouth. I talk too much.''

''You do,'' he said. ''Harry Gondolian said that.''

''Harry,'' she said. ''My God, Harry. He said Harry knew it all. Poor Harry. He always had a big nose. I told him a long time ago that his nose would land him in a heap of trouble one day. I told him the same thing when he came out here to see me.''

''He was out here? I didn't know that.''

''Oh yes, about a month ago. I'll tell you, he looked like he had one foot in the grave. Somebody told him about that piece, about Francie and Jerry. I guess it was you. He just put two and two together. That was Harry. He could never leave well enough alone.''

''Why the initials, the same initials?'' Rogers asked. ''That was probably what gave you away to Harry.''

''It was his suggestion.'' Rogers knew the *he* this time was not Harry Gondolian. ''He said when you change your name, at least keep the same initials. You never know what you have around with those initials on it. If

you don't, somebody's liable to find something and begin
to wonder what's up, and that could start a whole train
of things. And he said if you use the same initials, they're
easier to remember. He even suggested the names for us,
Fiona and me. I made up Jerry's myself, on the spur on
the moment. It took a while to get used to the new names,
let me tell you. But for the first four or five years, he had
us moving around every couple of months, first here, then
there, then someplace else, never anyplace long. He said
we had to throw people off our tracks. Finally, when he
thought it was safe, he brought us here, and here is where
we stayed."

"He was your double agent, wasn't he, the one you
told Gondolian you had on the inside?"

"Sure," she said. "Some of those kids, they were
positive it had to be Jerry, especially when they found
out he was a cop. Hell, Jerry was a cop because I told
him to be a cop. He got the job he got because I told
him to go for it. Poor Jerry. He never had an idea of his
own, not in his whole life."

"That's what Gondolian said. He said Jerry did whatever you told him."

"Not always. At the end, he did what he told him. He
looked on him like, well not exactly a father but an older
brother. He idolized him."

"You want to put a name to him?"

"No," she said. "I'll bet you know his name anyway.
He said he was sure you did."

"He killed Gondolian, didn't he?"

She shrugged.

"Why?"

"I told you. Harry was getting too close. He said Harry

knew about him, maybe even who he was. He said he couldn't take the chance."

"Why did he kill Morrison?"

"You'll have to ask him that. I don't know the answer."

"How about Steven Gold?"

"Poor Steven. Such a sad case. He was a real innocent, that boy. Steven was another one who thought he was God's gift or something. I remember when we were all getting ready to light out, Steven said if it wasn't for him, we'd all be brought in for questioning and we'd probably all get charged. Steven said if it wasn't for him, we'd all probably land in prison. I guess he was right. Still and all, from what *he* says, he had Steven jumping through hoops all these years."

"And Rasmussen and Jessup and Weinstein?"

"Sure. All of us. Francie, too. She was in love with him. From the time she was old enough to have ideas, they were all about him. It's kind of strange. I keep thinking about her as Francie, not Fiona. I guess I just got used to it. First ten years, she was Fiona. The rest of the time, she was Francie. What's in a name, anyway?"

Melissa's eyes had been watching Caitlin McKenzie carefully. Now she said, and it wasn't a question, "The child was his."

The woman nodded. "Who else? She didn't run around with the boys from here. She didn't know any other men. Just him. He used to drop in on us every couple of months. When Francie got a little older, they'd go off together."

"Didn't that bother you?" Melissa asked.

"At first, sure," she said. "He was a lot older and she was just a kid. But try telling your kids that and you'll know just how much they listen to you. The only way I could have put a stop to it was to lock her up, and even if I'd done that, she'd have found a way out. I tried to talk to him, but that was like talking to a stone wall. He and Francie, they had something that nobody was going to break. And he was good to her. He was good for her. He gave her things, he treated her fine, which is more than I can say for a lot of people. What I mean is, Francie was never quite right in the head, not from the time she was little. She used to do strange things you wouldn't do if you were in your right mind, which she wasn't. And it got worse after Jerry died, she was so close to him. People used to make fun of her. He never did. He was always kind and loving with her, always treated her like she was just as good as anybody else, he always treated her like what she did was just the right thing. So I gave up and accepted it. What else was I going to do? Besides, we owed him a lot. Jesus, I guess we owed him everything. Where would we have been if it hadn't been for him?"

"But she had his body," Melissa said.

Caitlin McKenzie nodded. "I talked to her about protection. I guess it must have been an accident."

"How old was she then?"

"Twenty. Same age I was when I had Jerry."

"That was when she went to the hospital?" Rogers said.

"Pretty soon after," Caitlin McKenzie said. "She had postpartum depression, a very bad case. Only she didn't come around. It kept getting worse and there wasn't anything anybody could do with her. We had to send her someplace. He agreed with me. He found the place up near San Francisco, and he paid all the bills. He paid for Francie and he sent me money every month to pay Jennie's way, all through the years. Gave her everything she wanted, and more. Spoiled her. I guess that's what fathers do when they only see their kid every once in a while. It must have set him back a fortune. God knows where he got the money."

Rogers was pretty sure he knew.

"Your daughter was in the hospital from then on?" Melissa asked.

"Most of the time," Caitlin McKenzie said. "They'd let her out now and then, but she'd be home a couple of days and she'd start to act crazy, and we'd have to send her back. I think every time she saw him, she'd go off the deep end. Something must have happened between them around the time Jennie was born. He never said and you could never get sense out of her. But just seeing him would be enough. There wasn't any way to handle her then."

"You raised your granddaughter yourself?" Melissa asked.

"There wasn't anybody else," she said. "I didn't have a choice. Oh, he'd come around and bring her presents and things, and take her off for a day or two. He loved her. That was obvious. After all, she was his daughter. But then he'd be gone. She was a nice kid, Jennie, a little wild maybe, but smart. I was getting too old to be raising a teenager, but what can you do? I tried. I did my best. But there was her mother in the hospital and there was her father who wasn't really around when she needed him most. I think everything would have come out right, though. And then they let Francie out that last time." Her face turned inward and was suddenly filled with ineffable sadness and loss.

"Was he here then?" Rogers asked.

She nodded slowly. "He brought her home from the hospital. He was trying to be kind and gentle, and everything seemed all right until she saw him with Jennie. Then she just blew up, fell apart. We locked her up in her room and called the hospital. They couldn't come for her until morning. God knows where she got that gun or how she got out of her room and into Jennie's. But she did."

"What did he do?"

"When he saw there wasn't anything he could do for either one of them, he left before the police came."

"He's here now, isn't he?" Rogers said.

"He was here," she said. "He's gone now."

"When was he here?"

"A little while ago."

"Do you know where he went?"

She shook her head. "No. He didn't say."

"Will he be back?"

"He didn't say. He only said I'd probably get a visitor before long—you. He said I shouldn't tell you anything, I shouldn't admit anything." She gave a deep sigh. "Well, it's up to me, isn't it? I'm just tired of running and hiding. I'm tired of being somebody I'm not."

"One thing puzzles me," Rogers said. "I keep wondering why you ran in the first place. According to the files, there wasn't anything to tie you to the bombing, at least no more than any other group."

"He said the suspicion would come around to us if we stayed there. And if anyone knew, he did. Besides, once Jerry died, there wasn't anything to keep us there. All the kids were leaving and Jerry was gone, and we had that terrible thing hanging over us. I think even if he hadn't told us we had to leave, we might have anyway."

"Did you know he killed Jerry?"

She froze. She stared at him. And then her head started

to move back and forth in denial. "No," she said. "They told Jerry he had to tell everything he knew or go to prison. He wasn't going to tell. If you knew Jerry, you'd know he'd never do that. And he didn't want to go to prison. He knew what happened to cops in there. So he . . . he jumped out that window."

"I think he was pushed," Rogers said.

"No," she said.

"Yes," Rogers said. "They left him alone in that room. Then somebody went in to check on him. You know who that was, and so do I. When he went in to check, that's when your son went out the window. Think about it."

"No," she said.

"Yes," Rogers said. "He couldn't be sure that your son might not decide to talk. If he talked, he'd implicate everybody, and your friend couldn't afford to take that chance. Think about it."

"No. I can't believe it," she said. "He told me the way it was."

"I'm sure he did."

"Oh my God," she said, and crumpled. Melissa went to her, put her arms around a woman who had suddenly grown very old, who had lost the last of the things that had sustained her, and tried to comfort her. There was no comfort. She broke free from Melissa, turned and stumbled across the store into a back room. She closed the door behind her.

"That," Melissa said, "was cruel, and terrible."

"It had to be done," he said.

32

When they came out of the store, it had grown darker. The sun was beginning to set in a brilliant orange flame out over the ocean. It was still hot, though the air outdoors had a freshness that had gone from the interior of the store. There was relief in being away from there.

They didn't talk then, just strolled slowly along the street, past the shops that were beginning to close, down toward the sea wall that protected the town from the ravages of ocean tides. They went down a flight of steps and were on the beach. It was empty, the last sun bathers and swimmers on their way home. They moved toward some large boulders abutting the sea wall.

Melissa looked at Rogers. "What happens now?" she said.

"I want to think for a few minutes," he said. "Let's just sit here for awhile."

"You think he's somewhere around here, don't you?"

"Yes," he said.

"You have to find him."

"I think he'll find us," Rogers said. "I want you to do something for me."

"That depends on what."

"I want you to go back to the car and wait."

"No," she said. "I've come this far. I want to be with you until it's over."

"Then at least go over there," he said, pointing to a niche in the sea wall about a hundred feet down the beach. "I don't want to have to worry about you when he shows up."

She studied him, then nodded slowly, rose and moved along the sand. His eyes followed her. She reached the niche, moved into it and he could see her no longer. He took a deep breath and stared out over the Pacific, watching the sun dip lower into the sea. It be would dark soon.

He waited. Then he heard scuffling sounds on the sand. He didn't turn to look toward them. He waited until they were closer. He said into the air, "Hello, George."

"Ben, I'm sorry about this," Strickland said.

Rogers turned and looked at him. Strickland was about ten feet away. He was holding a gun in his right hand. There was a silencer on the end of the barrel. "Are you?"

"Believe me, I am. I kept trying to steer you away. You wouldn't be steered."

"It kept coming back to you," Rogers said.

"It didn't have to."

"I'm afraid it did. You threw me Gold. It wouldn't wash. Carlos had his doubts from the beginning, and then Melissa knocked that down. You tossed Santangello. He was a bad guy and he had a reason. But he was killing other people for better reasons. When you killed him, you must have thought maybe I'd buy that. I didn't. Why the hell didn't you just kill me then? You could have laid that at Santangello's feet. What's one more or less where he's concerned?"

"Believe me, I thought about it that night, Ben. I discarded it. I wasn't sure how close you were, and you were talking to Rodriguez about Santangello. It stood to reason that you'd told him what we were up to. If he knew you were with me, it would have raised a lot of questions. Sure, I could have fixed it so it looked like you and Santangello wasted each other. I could have done that. But there'd always be questions, and I didn't want that."

"I didn't tell Carlos that night."

"My mistake then," Strickland said.

"Everywhere I looked," Rogers said, "you were somewhere near. I told you that Annie Kendall had Gondolian's files. I didn't mention it to anyone else. And her place was broken into without a trace and the files hauled away. I told you she'd read those files and she'd come up with something and was going to tell me when we got together. I don't think I told anyone else. And right after that, she was killed just as I was coming through the door, and the whole thing wrapped around my head. I told you about the old files in the mini-storage place, and somebody with all the right official papers got to them before I could. I did something else. I asked you to check on that Phoenix outfit. You told me nobody'd heard of it. Yesterday, before I got on the plane, I called there and asked for you. They told me you were out of the office."

"I figured you were the one who called," Strickland said. "They beeped me and said I had a call from somebody who wouldn't leave his name or a message. That could be only one person."

"How many notches have you got in that gun now,

George? Can I even count them all? Morrison, Gondolian, Gold, Annie, and how many others? Tell me, why Morrison? You said you loved the guy. I believed you." Rogers' eyes kept flicking toward the western horizon. Keep him talking, he thought. As long as he's talking, nothing's going to happen. It'll be dark soon, and then I'll have a chance.

"I did love that man. I would have done anything for him. He protected me all down the years. He believed in me. And I believed in him. And all the years we used each other, we were good for each other. But there wasn't any other way, Ben. It had to be done. Gondolian worked the whole thing out and he was going to Morrison with it. And he was going to turn everything over to the FBI. You know what that would have meant?"

"You didn't even know Gondolian?"

"As it happens, I did. Back in the old days, when he was around asking questions, I met him. I was there in the room when he interviewed Jack about the underground. When Caitlin told me he'd been out here asking her questions about that old thing, it was obvious. And then I had lunch with Jack that last week and he told me this old reporter had been trying to see him about something important, something from the old days. Jack was putting him off until after the convention. Gondolian must have dropped a hint at least, because Jack was kind of cold that day and he looked worried. He said Gondolian had told him he ought to take another look at some of his old cases. It's obvious, isn't it, that I couldn't let that happen, and I sure as hell couldn't let the two of them get together."

"So you set up Gold to take the fall."

"That wasn't hard. He believed he owed me everything, he was sure if it hadn't been for me, he'd have spent his life in some joint. All I had to do was ask him for something and he never even asked why, he just did it."

"That's where you got the money for Fiona, or Francie, or whatever you called her, and for your daughter."

"Most of it. I was blessed with a rich friend who was generous."

"You told him you had a room for him where he could be close to Morrison during the convention."

"It was that simple. I even arranged for the two of them to get together that week. Gold was going to be the big money raiser. And Jack figured he needed every penny he could raise to run the right kind of race."

Keep him talking, Rogers' mind repeated. "I can imagine the rest of the scenario," Rogers said. "You had a drink with Gold and slipped him a Mickey, and when he was out, there was Morrison coming out of the hotel on his way to the Garden. And what luck. Gondolian comes out of the crowd and the two of them start talking. You got two for the price of one, and then threw Gold into the pot for the bargain. From the beginning, way back then, you were behind everything."

"You've got it."

"You got the explosives, something that mad bomber Macklin made. You were working for Morrison then and that was one of his cases. You got the plans for the chemical plant. That couldn't have been too hard for a guy in your position. You planned the whole thing, and then you let those poor jerks who thought they were part of a noble cause doing the right thing, you fed it to them and you backed away and stood on the sidelines and cheered them on while they did it."

''Pretty much that way.''

''You were what they call a mole.''

''Don't be such a romantic, Ben. *Mole* is such a romantic notion.''

''You used everybody.''

''Why not? They wanted to be used. If it wasn't me, it would have been somebody else.''

''Who were you really working for?''

''It depended on when,'' Strickland said. ''I began one place, moved on to another. Change is the essence of life.''

''And, of course, there was the money.''

''You're a cynic, Ben. It was always more than the money. Which is why I succeeded. Nobody ever doubted me. Not on any side. I always gave, more than they expected. It was the only way to play the game.''

Rogers kept moving his eyes toward the horizon. There was only the top of the sun now above the sea, dipping, exploding in brilliant oranges and reds, dazzling the west. In a moment it would disappear, and when it was gone, there would be darkness.

''Now, don't do anything foolish, Ben,'' Strickland said. ''I can kill you before you get your gun out.''

''You could. But it wouldn't do you any good.''

''It all dies with you.''

''Not any more,'' Rogers said. ''Too many people know.''

''Not that many. And I'm not worried about them.''

''No? I think Rasmussen, Jessup, and Weinstein are about to give themselves up.''

''If they do, it's their loss. They never knew me.''

''I wouldn't be too sure about that.''

''I am sure.''

"There's always Caitlin McKenzie."

"She's an old lady. She's run the course. She reached the finish line a little while ago."

"You think of everything."

"That's why I'm where I am. Now, call your young lady out from wherever she went and let's get this over with."

"I don't think I'll do that."

"Then I'll just have to find her. It'll take a little longer, that's all."

"Carlos knows," Rogers said.

"I sincerely doubt that."

"Maybe not this minute, but if I don't call him by tomorrow, he'll have Gondolian's files and a letter I wrote laying it all out."

"Your mistake, Ben. He'll have nothing. Ten minutes after you left yesterday, my people went in and took those files."

"Ah, Phoenix."

"Yes, Phoenix. My operation. I set it up. I run it. Anti-terrorist group. We do good work. We get results."

"Obviously."

"Now, Ben, be good and call the lady out."

"I don't think so," Rogers said. He called back down the beach, "Melissa, stay where you are. Don't move."

And then the sun was gone in a last brilliant display, and in an instant, it was dark. Rogers moved, diving to the side, into the shelter behind the boulders.

The shot, hardly more than a ping muffled by the silencer, sparked off the boulders. Rogers pulled his gun and held it, searching through the darkness. There was the sea, off to his left, iridescent. There were the stars flickering in the sky. Everywhere else there was only blackness. He waited.

"That was stupid, Ben," Strickland's voice, moving to the side, toward the sea wall.

He didn't answer. He was not about to let Strickland target his voice. He waited, listening. There were no sounds now. He prayed that Melissa was staying where she was, not moving. The darkness and the niche in the wall where she was hidden were an impenetrable shield. He hoped so.

"Come on, Ben. Give it up. You know I'll find you. You don't have a chance." He thought Strickland's voice had moved closer, but that might have been only an illusion. It echoed off the stones of the wall, distorting it and disguising distance.

He reached down, untied his shoes and slipped them off. As silently as he could, he started to slide away, keeping low, hugging the wall. He must have made a sound. Another muffled ping and the wall just behind him sparked. He felt rock splinters cutting into his back. He ignored that.

He had to wait it out. He didn't have a silencer to hide the gun flash, so he couldn't use his gun right now. The flash would light him and Strickland would know where he was. There was a rattling on the sand off to his right. He tried to cut through the blackness to see what it was. There was only the shimmering of the ocean. Another rattling, a soft pattering sound. The rattling repeated itself again and again, coming a little closer off to his right every time. He knew what it was. Melissa was moving from the niche, moving toward him, hiding her movements across the sand by throwing pebbles. Damn it, he thought, I told her to stay where she was.

Strickland's voice came then, a hollow sound. He must be standing near the sea wall, echoing his voice off it so it was impossible to know precisely where he was. "An old trick, Ben. Forget it. I don't bite that easy."

Something touched his shoulder. He turned his head fast, his gun coming up. He made out Melissa just behind him. She shook her head and put a finger to her lips. She reached out and held something in front of him. She had a small flashlight in her hand. She motioned with it in the general direction of where Strickland must be. He shook his head and made a gesture that said, wait, not just yet. The odds were evening up.

From a little distance above them, over the sea wall, came the sound of a dog barking. It came closer. Somebody out walking his dog. Up on top of the sea wall, there was a flickering beam of light. Whoever was with the dog had a flashlight.

Rogers raised the gun, held it with both hands to steady it and aimed it down the beach toward where Strickland must be. He looked over his shoulder at Melissa and made a motion that said, be ready. She nodded that she understood. She raised her flashlight, her finger on the switch. They waited.

The barking and that small glint of light kept coming closer, moving toward the stairs to the beach. And then it was at the top of the stairs, the beam playing down onto the sand, the shapes of a man and a large dog looming just behind it.

The light caught Strickland moving down along the shelter of the sea wall. It held him for an instant. He started to turn toward the source of the light, his gun rising.

"Now," Rogers said to Melissa.

Her finger moved. The light beamed out, caught and held Strickland. There was a muted ping from his gun and the man with the dog at the top of the stairs started to tumble, his light dropping and going out. Strickland turned toward the new light.

Rogers' gun held on the figure trapped in the rays from Melissa's flashlight. He fired, once, twice, a third time, the sound loud, shattering the stillness of the night. Strickland recoiled, the hand with the gun dropping toward his side. The gun started to come up again. Rogers fired again and then once more. The gun slipped from Strickland's hand onto the sand. Strickland reeled a little, swayed and then collapsed.

"Stay where you are," Rogers shouted at Melissa, rose and sprinted across the sand toward Strickland, his gun ready. Strickland wasn't moving. Rogers kicked Strickland's gun away and then bent over him. Strickland would never move again.

Over at the bottom of the stairs, the dog was barking shrilly as it stood guard over its fallen owner. Rogers moved that way. Melissa's light came closer and moved with him, catching the man and the dog.

The dog's hackles rose as Rogers neared, a menacing growl coming from its mouth. "Easy, boy," Rogers said softly. "Easy, easy." The man was groaning. At least he's not dead, Rogers thought. The dog wouldn't let him come any closer.

Melissa moved up beside him. She started talking in comforting tones to the dog. It still remained on guard, but began to relax. Rogers, Melissa at his side, moved slowly toward the man and dog. Melissa reached out and began to rub her hand across the dog's head. Rogers bent over. The dog walker was bleeding from the shoulder. He'd be all right.

There were shouts, a lot of movement and the beams of several flashlights on top of the sea wall, approaching the stairs. The lights started down. A couple of cops were holding them. The rays of the light fixed on the scene, on Rogers and Melissa, on the man and the dog. One of the lights played along the beach, caught and held on Strickland.

"What the hell is going on here?" one of the cops shouted. His gun was out and he stepped quickly toward Rogers and Melissa.

"You'd better get help for this guy," Rogers said, nodding toward the dog walker.

The cop looked down and then shouted toward the top of the stairs, "We need help, we need an ambulance here right away." He turned back to Rogers. "You'd better have a good explanation, Mac," he said.

"I do," Rogers said. "It's a long story."

The Dollmaker was a serial killer who stalked Los Angeles and left a grisly calling card on the faces of his female victims. With a single faultless shot, Detective Harry Bosch thought he had ended the city's nightmare.

Now, the dead man's widow is suing Harry and the LAPD for killing the wrong man—an accusation that rings terrifyingly true when a new victim is discovered with the Dollmaker's macabre signature.

Now, for the second time, Harry must hunt down a death-dealer who is very much alive, before he strikes again. It's a blood-tracked quest that will take Harry from the hard edges of the L.A. night to the last place he ever wanted to go—the darkness of his own heart.

THE
CONCRETE
BLONDE

"Exceptional...A stylish blend of grit and elegance."
—Nelson DeMille

THE CONCRETE BLONDE
Michael Connelly
_____ 95500-6 $5.99 U.S./$6.99 Can.